THREE

COLORS OF

COURAGE

THREE COLORS OF COURAGE

BOOK THREE OF A COLD WAR TRILOGY

TARYN R. HUTCHISON

Library of Congress Cataloging-in-Publication Data
Hutchison, Taryn R.
Three Colors of Courage / Taryn R. Hutchison 1st ed.

Printed in the United States of America

Print ISBN: 979-8-218-51278-1

OTHER BOOKS BY TARYN R. HUTCHISON

FICTION

One Degree of Freedom
(Book One of A Cold War Trilogy)

Two Lights of Hope
(Book Two of A Cold War Trilogy)

NONFICTION

We Wait You: Waiting on God in Eastern Europe

Sentenced to Life:
The Path to Redemption and Freedom for Prisoner E-25212

PRAISE FOR *THREE COLORS OF COURAGE*

In Hutchison's novel, a young Romanian woman finds renewed strength as her country's regime unravels. How is it possible to reclaim one's humanity in a country with hidden microphones, informers, and secret police everywhere? This is the problem that Adriana Nicu and her best friend, Gabriela Martinescu, face in the final installment of the author's Cold War trilogy, set during the final unwinding of Romanian president Nicolae Ceaușescu's iron-fisted rule. … Over the course of this novel, Hutchison delivers a skillfully crafted narrative that is by turns comic and caustic; its main characters' fortunes effectively zigzag between triumph to terror, which captures the arbitrary nature of authoritarian regimes everywhere. Also, as antidemocratic extremism gains ground in various places in the real world, this novel will remind readers of the power of resilience, and its ability to flip even the bleakest of political scripts … An unsettling evocation of Cold War–era repression, whose legacy seems timelier than ever.

~Kirkus Reviews

In *Three Colors of Courage*, author Taryn Hutchison paints an unforgettable picture of the terror of life lived under Romania's watchful Communist government and its leader, Nicolae Ceaușescu. Suspense and tension appear on nearly every page as we watch brave characters wrestle with who to trust in a land of spies, hidden microphones, and risky church services. This gripping historical novel honors the unimaginable courage of ordinary citizens willing to fight their oppressive government. Writing with the vivid authenticity of someone who once lived in Eastern Europe, the author introduces a painful period in history and the people who risked and sacrificed so much to gain basic freedoms others take for granted. A must read!

~ **Linda MacKillop**, award-winning author of
The Forgotten Life of Eva Gordon

With the nimble prose and deft characterization only an author of her skill can achieve, Hutchison plunged me into the harrowing heart of Cold War Romania's underground resistance and her teen protagonist's quest for freedom. One can't read this well-drawn work of immersive historical fiction without extracting insight about one's own liberty and drawing courage to guard it. An excellent, highly relevant work.

~**Cheryl Grey Bostrom**, award-winning author of
Sugar Birds and *Leaning on Air*

It takes more than courage; it takes hope to change the course of history. Taryn R. Hutchison deftly explores these life-changing, albeit world-changing values in this grand finale to her Cold War Trilogy. These novels remind us why "freedom is not free" in an era when so many have forgotten the cost. The revolutionary journey of Adriana and her classmates is deeply personal, relatable and heart-wrenching. Readers will share their fears, their cries of injustice, and their dreams. Hutchison delivers a powerful tribute to those who chose not to run, but to serve the greater good, even to the point of death. This series should be required reading for every high school student; it's that powerful, inspiring, and true.

~**Margaret Ann Philbrick**, award-winning author of
House of Honor: The Heist of Caravaggio's Nativity

Taryn Hutchison's *Three Colors of Courage* is a stirring story that puts faces on a pivotal moment in Romania's history—the 1989 revolution. I found myself drawn in by the young characters and how they navigated the dynamics of friendship, grief, and love against the harrowing backdrop of war. Hutchison's research is impeccable, the setting palpable, and its heroes' search for hope despite their circumstances inspiring. Readers are sure to be gripped by this powerful finale to A Cold War Trilogy, and left pondering what it truly means to be free.

~ **Kendra Broekhuis**, author of *Between You and Us*

Taryn Hutchison does it again as she continues the story of Romania and its people in this much-anticipated book three of her trilogy. She writes with an intimate knowledge of the country that brings you right to the time and place with accurate descriptions and colorful characters. Continue the journey with Adriana as her courage and faith are tested by the horrors of war. A well-crafted, inspiring, and beautiful story.

~**Terri Kraus**, author of *The Project Restoration Series: The Renovation, The Renewal, The Transformation*

Three Colors of Courage is a beautiful story set in 1989 Romania, with Eastern Europe on the brink of revolution. Heartfelt and fast-paced, the story takes readers into the intertwined lives of a group of students living in Bucharest as they face the many hardships forced on them by the Communist leaders. It's a story of family, friendship, and courage triumphing over fear during one of the most pivotal times in recent history. If you're too young to remember or you weren't paying enough attention when it happened, you'll want to read the series!

~**Peggy Wirgau**, award-winning author of *The Stars in April*

Three Colors of Courage, as the third in the series of beautiful works of historical fiction, picks up the story of well-beloved characters whose lives readers have read through a future-knowing lens of anticipation—recognizing that these teenagers we've grown to know and love would live through one of Romania's most important political, national, and ultimately personal events. Hutchison masterfully weaves the lives and stories of characters living through these events so that a teenager today can easily relate; wondering at the bravery, faith, and courage of the characters while identifying with the age-appropriate struggles of coming of age and love. Readers who love Ruta Sepetys' *I Must Betray You* or Jennifer A. Nielsen's *A Night Divided* will love Adriana's story, and the degrees of freedom she and the other characters work to recover.

~**Rebecca Detrick**, Writer and Educator

Taryn Hutchison's novels *One Degree of Freedom* and *Two Lights of Hope* opened my eyes to events in history that I knew little about. The story of Adriana and her friends informed me of a dark period in Romania during Communist rule. However, the tale told also felt like an important warning for our current culture in America where God is often ignored, or worse, rejected. *Three Colors of Courage* brings the trilogy to a fitting end. You will be captivated by the brave Romanians who fight to overthrow their communist leaders and regain their liberties. You will eagerly turn the pages as Adriana and her friends fight with courage for the freedom of their country.

    ~**Sharla Fritz**, author of *Measured by Grace and Waiting*

I was alive during the whole of the events described in *Three Colors of Courage* but I was safe in my little corner of the USA. Taryn Hutchison's story brought what was happening in Eastern Europe to life. From the previous books in the series, *One Degree of Freedom* and *Two Lights of Hope*, we get a heaping helping of what it felt like to live in Communist Romania. *Three Colors of Courage* will give you a deep empathy for people around the world who are still living under the iron thumb of dictators. To find faith and freedom in such a place is really a miracle. Taryn Hutchison immerses you in the story through believable characters whom you grow to love starting with the first page.

    ~**Stephanie Reeves**, devotional writer and editor of *Peace with the Psalms* and *Cast Your Cares*

Dedicated to Lucia and Emi,
my favorite YA girls:
May you become women of courage.

ADRIANA NICU'S FAMILY AND FRIENDS

» Gabriela Martinescu, her best friend

» Alexandru Oprea, her friend and classmate

» Corina Lupu, her classmate

» Liviu Negrescu, her classmate

» Elisabeta Filip, her new professor

» Ramona Nicu, her mother

» Violeta Zaharia, her aunt

» Mihai Zaharia, her uncle

» Margareta Dumitrescu (Bunica), her grandmother

» Uri Goldmann, mentor to Adriana and Gabi

» Timotei Grigorescu, her cousin from Timişoara

» Timotei's friends at the university: Marcu Andrei, Simona Vucescu, Beni Barbu, and Serghei Ursu

Adriana Nicu's Reading List

» *To Kill a Mockingbird,* by Harper Lee
» *Animal Farm,* by George Orwell
» *Sense and Sensibility,* by Jane Austen
» *Les Misérables,* by Victor Hugo (abridged version)
» *A Christmas Carol,* by Charles Dickens

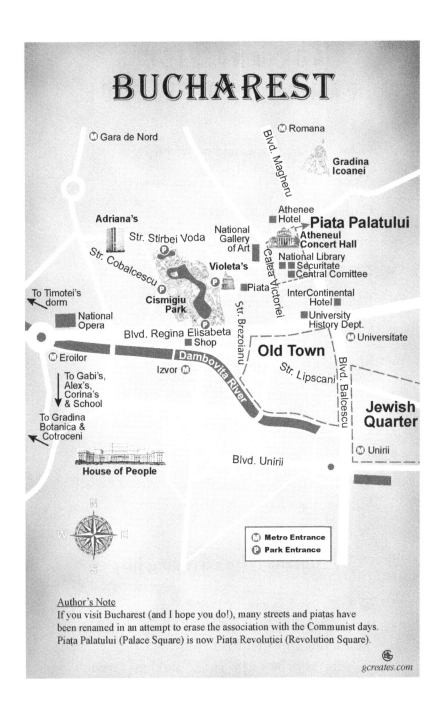

BUCHAREST

Gara de Nord

Romana

Blvd. Magheru

Gradina Icoanei

Adriana's

Str. Stirbei Voda

Str. Cobalcescu

National Gallery of Art

Athenee Hotel

Piata Palatului

Atheneul Concert Hall

Calea Victoriei

National Library

Securitate

Central Comittee

Violeta's

Piata

InterContinental Hotel

Cismigiu Park

University History Dept.

To Timotei's dorm

National Opera

Str. Brezoianu

Universitate

Blvd. Regina Elisabeta

Shop

Old Town

Eroilor

Izvor

Dambovita River

Str. Lipscani

Blvd. Balcescu

Jewish Quarter

To Gabi's, Alex's, Corina's & School

To Gradina Botanica & Cotroceni

Unirii

House of People

Blvd. Unirii

N
W E
S

| Metro Entrance
| Park Entrance

Author's Note
If you visit Bucharest (and I hope you do!), many streets and piaţas have
been renamed in an attempt to erase the association with the Communist days.
Piaţa Palatului (Palace Square) is now Piaţa Revoluţiei (Revolution Square).

gcreates.com

THREE COLORS

Romanians have sung about their flag's *trei culori*—red, yellow, and blue—for centuries. The lyrics changed when the Socialist Republic of Romania came to power. However, the earlier language of the old patriotic song more accurately represents the people who stood strong in 1989.

Red as the fire that burns
in my heart, longing
for its freedom,
loving my homeland.

Gold as the proud sun
shall be our future,
purer than an eternal flower
shining bright forever.

And blue as the faith
for the nation we cherish,
unwaveringly loyal
until death, so are we.

CHAPTER ONE

ADRIANA: THE PROMISE

Late August 1989
Armonia, Romania

ADRIANA NICU SAT ON the bench across from her father's hilltop grave, with a freshly-picked bunch of multi-colored wildflowers beside her.

"I'm going back to Bucharest tomorrow, Tati," she said. "It'll be my last year of high school, if you can believe that."

She stood and placed the flowers in the concrete vase at the base of the headstone, then she stroked his name inscribed in the stone: *Daniel Adrian Nicu.*

In some ways, time had slowed; it felt like she'd been trudging through thick mud for the last year and four months since he died. But when she remembered the trauma of his death, it hurt like it happened yesterday.

Adriana looked all around her, the way she always did, before she whispered, "That man that killed you, his son is after me. But he doesn't scare me." *Who am I kidding?* "Okay, well, he *does* scare me.

But I refuse to let him see it. Besides, what's new about that? I've had to watch out for spies my whole life. I'll be good and quiet, and I won't do anything to draw attention to myself."

Adriana planned to spend much of her free time doing her favorite thing—reading—in her favorite place—the room hidden in the wall of her aunt's apartment and filled with stacks of banned books.

"I promise you, Tati, I'll be brave. I'm not going to let that man or anyone spoil this year for me."

CHAPTER TWO

TIMOTEI: NEWS

Early September 1989
Timişoara, Romania

TIMOTEI GRIGORESCU FOLDED HIS last shirt and placed it in his duffel bag while his mother hovered. She kept turning her head away as though she heard something in the kitchen, but she didn't fool Timotei. He knew she was crying. If he wasn't so excited about embarking on this new adventure at university, he'd cry too.

He fastened the clasp on his bag and bent to kiss his mother on both cheeks.

"I'll write you every day, Mama."

"I'm counting on it," she said. She sniffed and mustered her brightest smile. "Study hard, son, and make us proud. Don't forget the sandwiches I packed. It's a long ride, and you'll get hungry." Mama cupped his face in her strong hands. "You sure you don't want me to walk you to the train?"

"It's better this way." Timotei turned for one final look at his mother. "Tell Tati goodbye." His voice caught as he walked out the door.

He hurried down his street, Strada Sibiu, toward Timişoara's train station on Strada Garii, stopping a few blocks short to duck into an apartment building, tall and plain and made of concrete like all the others.

Timotei sprinted up the stairs to apartment 425 and knocked on the door before opening it with his key. He strode into the tiny kitchen and tinier pantry, where his friend sat with headphones on, facing a short-wave radio.

Timotei put his hand on his friend's shoulder and watched him visibly jump.

"Sorry, Vasile," Timotei mouthed.

"I wasn't sure you'd make it." Vasile slipped off his headphones and held them out for Timotei. He spoke in a low voice. "Here. You have to listen to this." Vasile practically bounced out of his seat. "It happened a couple weeks ago. Crazy how long it takes for us to get the news, but at least we have it now."

Timotei had received a directive to bring the latest word from Hungary. Even though Hungary's Communist government controlled their airwaves too, Hungarians still had more access to what was happening in the world—and even within Romania—than Romanians did. The state censors in Romania worked quickly to bury the news, always trying to keep their citizens in the dark.

"Can you hear?" Vasile asked.

Timotei sat and adjusted the headphones. He strained to listen, raising his hand toward Vasile.

Being situated right at the border, any intel from Hungary reached their city first. From there, it moved along an intricate underground network. Information came at a steep cost. Short-wave radios were banned and listening to Radio Free Europe or Voice of America was considered an act of treason, punishable by imprisonment, or sometimes even execution.

Over the static, Timotei could barely believe the words he heard.

"On 24 August, after forty-five years of rule, the Communist regime in Poland has collapsed," the voice on Radio Free Europe proclaimed. "I repeat: the rule of Communism has ended in Poland."

Timotei sat back in the chair and whistled. "This can't be true," he said, more to himself than to Vasile.

"Oh, it's true." Vasile pumped his right fist in the air. "Poland is free!"

Timotei clicked the radio off and closed his eyes a moment. He had to take in what was happening. A country in the Soviet Bloc was free.

Timotei opened his eyes and looked intently at Vasile. "Can it be starting? What we've hoped for, worked for." He rose from his chair. "I can't … I don't think I really believed this was possible."

"Oh, it's happening," Vasile said. "Our time is coming." His whole face lit up with his smile.

"I need to go." Timotei lifted his duffel bag. "You know how to reach me."

"You be safe in the big city." Vasile hugged him. "Stand strong, brother."

Timotei walked toward the door. With his hand on the latch, he turned to whisper, "You be safe too. I don't think our government will let this happen without a fight."

Then Timotei bolted out of the flat and ran to catch his train bound for Bucharest. He was headed to the capital to start his first year as a university student. He planned to study history.

As far as history went, this year—1989—looked like it could be one for the books.

CHAPTER THREE

ADRIANA: A WARNING

Bucharest, Romania

I T WAS STILL MORNING, early enough that the September sun hadn't scorched the ground. Adriana Nicu and her best friend, Gabi Martinescu, had agreed to meet in the park near Adriana's flat for their last official day of summer, the last day before the new school year commenced. Adriana had only been back in Bucharest one week after spending all of summer break in the Transylvanian mountains with her grandmother. While she was away, she kept thinking of things to tell Gabi, but after seeing each other a couple times, they had already covered all the important topics.

Today, they sat silently side-by-side on the old stone bridge that arched over the lake—Gabi's favorite spot in Cişmigiu Park—and tossed smooth stones into the water. Adriana realized she'd be content to stay like this all day, but Gabi had already let her know—a few times—how boring this was. Adriana smiled.

They couldn't be more different. Gabi thrived on action and drama, but Adriana preferred calm, quiet, contemplative activities. Gabi's hair and eyes were dark brown, but Adriana had distinctive green eyes and blonde streaks in her hair thanks to the summer sun.

Even now, Gabi kicked her long legs while Adriana sat with hers lazily dangling over the edge. The other people in the park didn't seem to be in a hurry either. They slowly strolled about or rested on benches on their free Sunday.

"Can you believe another year of school starts tomorrow?" Adriana said.

"Not really." Gabi tossed another stone, her eyes trailing its progress as it skipped over the glassy surface of the water. "I can't wait for us to be finished with school."

"I think this year will be uneventful," Adriana said. "At least I hope so."

Adriana thought about the last two years at the Science and Mathematics High School. It felt like she kept climbing up a steep mountain, stumbling and rolling back down toward the valley, then clawing her way back up only to slide down again. Such highs and lows. This school year could never live up to that level of excitement.

"I'm looking forward to seeing Alex and Corina. I have a hard time picturing them as a couple," Adriana said. "You see them much this summer?"

"Not much." Gabi twisted the end of her long ponytail on her finger. "I've been so busy with family, especially taking care of my brother."

"Family!" Adriana looked at her watch and jumped up. "We're having a big family dinner for my cousin today and I'm late!"

"Good thing you live so close," Gabi said.

Adriana quickly kissed Gabi on both cheeks. "See you tomorrow!"

With that, she took off sprinting toward the park exit on the east side. She sped past people ambling along the path and did what Romanians were taught to never do: she drew attention to herself.

Most Romanians were afraid to even make noise in public. That's what the packs of wild dogs did, the ones who prowled the city streets at night. People wanted to keep as low a profile as possible, always hoping to blend in.

When she reached her aunt's grand old building, she raced up the three flights of stairs and arrived at the door, doubled over and panting.

Her aunt's resident informer, Mrs. Stoica, had cracked open her door across the hallway. Mrs. Stoica was elderly, but there was nothing wrong with her ears. She never missed a thing.

"Hello, Mrs. Stoica," Adriana said.

Before she could knock on Aunt Violeta's door, it opened, seemingly by magic. Whoever opened it stood hidden behind the door.

Adriana peered around the door frame. "Timo? You're here!"

Her cousin jumped out from his hiding place and tripped over the basket of slippers, landing on the hallway bench with a thud.

She laughed. "That was graceful."

"I've been practicing." Timo took a bow. "So, how've you been, Green Eyes?"

Adriana adored her cousin, just one grade ahead of her in school. Timotei was fearless. He had thick curls and a tall, lanky frame, one that had been stretched taller since she last saw him. In earlier summers, at her grandmother's mountain village, she and Timo had a knack for making adventures happen whenever they were together. But he'd been too busy to visit Bunica's the past two summers, and she'd missed him.

She put her hands on her hips. "You would know if you had come to see Bunica and me in Armonia. But no, the big college guy had better things—"

Aunt Violeta appeared from the kitchen. "There you are, Adriana." She kissed Adriana on each cheek. "Your mother's helping in the kitchen."

"Where's Uncle Mihai?" Adriana asked.

"He'll be here shortly," Violeta said. "They're practicing for tomorrow's concert."

Mihai Zaharia, a perfectionist when it came to his art, often worked long hours at the Atheneum. As the concertmaster and first violinist, he always walked onto the stage first to tune the orchestra, then he'd take his seat in the violin section and signal for the conductor to enter.

"What can *we* do to help?" Adriana asked, glaring at her cousin as he made his way into Violeta's spacious tall-ceilinged living room and flopped onto the sofa. Typical. From her vantage point in the hallway, Adriana could see into both the kitchen and living room.

She watched her mother, Ramona Nicu, lean over the pan on the stove, an apron tied around her waist, and flip the meat. She pushed her thick hair off her forehead with the back of her hand. "We could use some cucumber, draga. Can you run over to the *piaţa* to see if they have any? If they do, get two."

"Yes, Mama," Adriana said. She grabbed her aunt's canvas *punga* from the hook by the door, spun on her heel and left, running down the stairs and across the street to the tiny outdoor market.

She scanned the tables. Some vegetables were still available since it was technically summer. Tomatoes, parsnips, carrots, potatoes. Finally, she spotted cucumbers. The peasant lady sitting behind the table watched Adriana as she picked up one cucumber after another, thumping each in turn to check if they were good. She could feel others crowd behind her at the table. When she settled on two good ones, the peasant lady held out her wrinkled palm for the five lei piece that Adriana produced.

"*Mulţumesc*," Adriana said.

The lady grinned, a toothless smile.

Adriana stuffed the cucumbers into the *punga* hanging on her shoulder and turned to leave. The person behind her pushed in closer, making it hard for her to move. "Pardon," Adriana said without making eye contact.

Whoever it was didn't acknowledge her or budge.

"Pardon!" she repeated, this time looking at the person to emphasize her point.

Suddenly, the blood in her body ran cold.

It was *him*. Comrade Zugravescu. The man who had terrorized her last year. The one who'd interrogated her for an entire night at the Securitate headquarters. Before he'd released her, he promised that if she slipped up, he'd be there. Since visiting Armonia, she'd almost forgotten about him.

Zugravescu took her elbow and steered her to the edge of the *piața*, away from the crowd.

"How was your summer at your grandmother's? What's the name of that village … Armonia, is it?" he said, a glint of humor in his cold eyes.

"Fine," Adriana said, trying to wriggle her arm free from his grasp.

"Don't be in such a hurry to leave," he said, tightening his grip. "Maybe I've missed you. Let's see. What's new with you? I know your cousin from Timișoara is here to attend the university."

Her eyes grew wide. How did he know that?

Zugravescu laughed. "I see you're surprised. You shouldn't be. Didn't I make a promise to you? I remember saying that wherever you go, whatever you do, I'll be watching. Listening."

Zugravescu hated her. Adriana's father had killed his father, Comrade Groza, in self-defense after Groza poisoned him with polonium, but Zugravescu didn't see it that way. Zugravescu wanted nothing more than to avenge his father's death and to keep a debt alive that Groza had held over Adriana's grandfather since World War II. He'd use whatever means necessary to see that happen, even threatening a schoolgirl.

Adriana hated him too. The man was evil, just like his father.

She didn't know what to say. She was afraid her voice would betray her if she tried to speak. But she stared her iciest stare straight into his eyes.

"Tell your family I said hello," Zugravescu said.

With that, he released his hold on her arm and walked away.

Adriana stood still for a moment. She bent forward, sliding her hands down to her knees, and tried to slow her breathing. The *punga* on her shoulder slid down to her elbow, causing the cucumbers to bump against her thigh.

After a relaxing summer in the mountains and a nice morning with her best friend, Adriana came thudding back to reality. She'd always have to look over her shoulder. As long as she could feel the invisible eyes and ears bearing down on her wherever she went in Romania, she wouldn't be free.

Adriana longed for things to be different. Was change even possible?

CHAPTER FOUR

FAMILY

WHEN ADRIANA CAUGHT HER breath, she spotted her uncle approaching his building on the other side of the street. Not only was Uncle Mihai tall, but with his larger-than-life personality, he did not blend in easily.

She sprinted toward him. They met at the foot of the stairs.

"Is something wrong, *Scumpita*?" His little precious one.

Adriana nodded. Her chin quivered.

Uncle Mihai opened his arms wide for her.

She let him envelop her. He was her safe place. Her father had chosen Uncle Mihai to watch over her. There was no one better for the job.

"Did I see a man—"

"Not just any man," she whispered, her heart rate returning to normal. "It was him. Zugravescu."

Mihai clenched his jaw. "What did he want?"

"He wanted to scare me," she said. "And he did."

Mihai scanned the surroundings. "That's all he can do. Believe me, if he had a reason to take any of us in, he would have."

"He had a message for my whole family," she whispered. "He said he'd be watching."

"Look, your mother and aunt know that someone's always watching and listening. All Romanians know that. But Ramona and Violeta, they've lived it. We don't need to give them more to worry about."

Adriana bit her lower lip, the way she always did when she was thinking.

"You've told me that you don't like the way your mother tries to control your every move," Mihai said. "Just imagine what she'd do if she had more reasons to worry."

A laugh spurted out of Adriana. "She has been getting better. It's been over a year since Tati died, but still … she's still Mama." She sighed. "You're right. I won't worry her."

"You alright to go up now?" Mihai asked.

"Yes. I just want to forget about that man. I don't want him to mess up my fun with Timo and everybody."

Mihai kissed the top of her head as they entered his building.

When Adriana opened the apartment door, the first person she saw was her mother. Mama stood in the hallway, her arms crossed over her chest. She looked relieved when she saw Adriana.

"Where have you been?" Mama paced the floor. "Did you have to go to another *piața* for those cucumbers?"

"Just ran into Uncle Mihai." Adriana bent to remove her shoes.

Her mother whispered into Adriana's ear. "We'll talk later. Now go slice these."

Aunt Violeta was already spooning *sarmale* and *mititei* onto plates in the kitchen. Adriana washed and cut the cucumbers, adding a few slices to each plate. She helped her mother and aunt carry the dishes, filled with everyone's favorite stuffed cabbage and tiny sausages, into the living room, placing them on the wobbly coffee table. Mihai and Timo stood chatting by the tall windows.

"Everyone, take a seat." Violeta gestured to the sofa and stools encircling the coffee table.

Mama and Aunt Violeta sat on the sofa. Timo and Adriana took the stools across from them, and Uncle Mihai sat in the armchair at the head of the table.

When everyone was seated, Violeta wished them a good appetite. "*Pofta buna!*"

Over their midday meal, they discussed only safe topics. Nothing that the Securitate, probably listening in on hidden microphones, could question. Mama asked about Timotei's parents, whom Adriana called Uncle Pavel and Aunt Sofia, even though they were her mother's first cousins.

"They're fine. They send everyone their love," Timo said. "I'm supposed to tell you they'll come visit."

"Tell us about where you'll live," Violeta said.

"When my train got in late last night—and I mean after midnight late, I took a taxi straight to my dorm," Timo said. "It took all of ten minutes to unpack everything." He shrugged. "I didn't bring much."

"Were your roommates there?" Mihai asked.

"Some. I have seven of them." Timo took a bite. "Classes start tomorrow, so I imagine they'll all be there when I get back."

Adriana groaned. "Don't remind me. Mine do too."

"Your parents told me you'll study history. What do you intend to do with that degree?" Violeta asked.

"I've got four years to decide that," Timo said. "Political history is what I like. I want to understand how different countries work, learn from past mistakes—"

Mama cleared her throat when he said *mistakes*. She glanced up at the chandelier where Mihai had found a microphone planted last year, and raised the volume of her voice. "Naturally, you mean mistakes from other countries, because we all know President Ceaușescu doesn't make mistakes. Our country runs better than any other country in the world."

"Of course, Aunt Ramona." Timo looked subdued. "That's exactly what I meant."

Adriana watched her mother level her famous stink eye on Timo. She thought that look was reserved only for her. But there was something else. Her mother seemed nervous, almost scared, the way she used to act around Tati's high-ranking colleagues.

Could she possibly know Zugravescu had talked to Adriana?

"And another thing. You can use your education to help Romania. We owe so much to our Supreme Leader, and it's a privilege to work to show our gratitude." Mama put her napkin to her mouth, lowered her voice, and continued. "You said you're studying history because *you* like it. There's no place in Romania for citizens whose interest is what makes *them* happy. Individualism. Independence. That's America's weakness. People in the West are out for themselves, but we—*we*, not I—work together for the good of the state."

After some moments, Timo wiped his mouth with his napkin. "I apologize. Aunt Ramona, everyone, I'm sorry. I didn't phrase my words well—I guess I'm more tired than I thought." He leveled his unblinking gaze at Mama. "I'm sorry if I implied something that's just not true."

Mama cleared her throat. "Thank you for that. My husband spent his whole life dedicated to the Communist Party, to our country, and to our Supreme Commander. No one ever has any reason to question how loyal our family is."

Adriana eyes roved around the table. What was that all about? Even Mama didn't normally justify the family's standing in the Party, especially at a family dinner, unless she felt she had to.

Timo scooted his stool back from the coffee table. "I hate to leave so early, but tomorrow is the first day …"

Violeta stood. "No, it's alright. You go, Timotei. We understand."

"I need to stretch my legs," Mihai said. "Why don't I walk with you to your dorm? I'd like to see where you live."

"I'll go too," Adriana said, jumping to her feet.

Timo nodded and smiled. "Sure. I'd love the company." He turned to Aunt Violeta, then to Mama. "Thank you both for an excellent meal."

Adriana grabbed her plate and Timo's to take to the kitchen. "*Mulțumesc*," she said and kissed her aunt on both cheeks.

Mama rose from the sofa to follow her into the kitchen. She cut her eyes toward the front door and mouthed the words, "I saw you."

"What?" Adriana said.

Mama clicked on the transistor radio. "You and that man."

For the second time that day, Adriana felt her blood go cold. She could only stare at her mother.

"I've seen him before," Mama said. "Lurking nearby." She lowered her voice. "Is he the one … from the jail?"

Adriana nodded. "How'd you know?"

"A mother's intuition. Ever since you were released, I've been on the lookout." She pursed her lips and spoke so softly Adriana had to strain to hear. "All those years with your father, I know how interrogations work. They want you to think they're setting you free, that they couldn't find any reason to hold you, but they don't let anyone go without following them."

"He just wanted to frighten me," Adriana whispered. "He has nothing on us. And I promise, I won't let him find anything."

"Just be careful, draga." Mama pulled Adriana close and squeezed her. "You're all I have. Please. Be careful."

Adriana kissed her mother's cheeks. "I will."

CHAPTER FIVE

COURAGE

Adriana, Timo, and Uncle Mihai decided to take the tram to Timo's dorm. They weren't in a hurry, and Timo said it would help him learn his way around if he could see where he was going rather than ride a metro train underground.

The tram rolled down Boulevard Regina Elisabeta, past the main entrance to Cişmigiu Park, past the state-run grocery store where Aunt Violeta worked. Soon after the street name turned into Boulevard Mihail Kogalniceanu, the Romanian National Opera appeared on the right and the Dâmbovița River on the left.

The three got off the tram to walk the rest of the way, following the curves of the narrow river. The afternoon sun shone as brightly as it had a few weeks ago, but the intense heat had lessened in anticipation of autumn. Soon they arrived at a stretch of sidewalk that was clear of people and buildings.

Timo took advantage of this spot to turn to his uncle.

"I need to tell you what I heard from Radio Free Europe," he said in a low voice. "I didn't feel right repeating this inside—"

"Very wise," Uncle Mihai said. He stopped walking.

19

"It's good news." Timo's eyes shifted from Mihai to Adriana. "You can't tell—"

"Please," Adriana said. "I know how things are."

"It's about Poland," Timo said. "The Communist regime. It's out."

"Out?" Mihai asked.

"Out," Timo said. His whole face smiled.

"You mean …"

"Poland is free!"

Adriana stared at her cousin. She watched Uncle Mihai's eyes widen and his mouth open, but no sound emerged. His expression changed from incredulity to astonishment, but he still didn't speak.

Adriana broke the silence. "What do you mean, free?"

"Have you heard of the Solidarity movement in Poland?" Timo asked.

Adriana shook her head.

Mihai found his voice. "They're a trade union. A big one. So big the government has been afraid of them for years."

"On 24 August, the Communists finally gave in to them and ended decades of one-party rule. The government appointed one of the Solidarity men as the new Prime Minister. The first non-Communist leader in more than forty years."

"They just … gave in?" Mihai asked.

"Yes. It was a peaceful transfer of power." Timo smiled. "No fighting."

Mihai let a low whistle escape from his lips. "The first domino."

"Why do you say that?" Adriana asked.

"If you have dominoes stacked up on end in a line and one is moved …" Mihai whistled again. "Someone needed to be the first. One country falls, maybe it'll cause a chain reaction. Another country will fall, then another, and another—"

"Even Romania?" Adriana asked.

Timo shrugged, but he grinned. "Hard to imagine, isn't it?"

"It's coming. But I doubt it'll be peaceful," Mihai said. "Not here."

This couldn't be real. Adriana knew she had a vivid imagination—was she dreaming? She looked around. Everything looked the same, but she knew nothing was. She didn't want to move from that spot, or do anything that might bring reality crashing back.

Finally, Timo spoke again. "If more people know this, it may give us all courage to take a stand for change. And who knows what might happen then?"

"Agreed," Mihai said. "We need to pass the news on, but we need to be careful—very careful—who we tell." He raised his eyebrows at Adriana as he said that. "And now, if you'll excuse me, I need to go. I can think of several people who need to hear this." He patted Adriana's shoulder. "Can you escort Timo to his dorm by yourself?"

"Of course," she said.

"You don't mind, do you?" he asked Timo, offering his hand.

"Go. News like this needs to be spread," Timo said.

They shook hands, and Mihai jogged away.

Adriana and Timo continued walking along the river until they saw the Grozavești metro station sign.

"This is where you would normally get off the metro," Adriana said. "This street is called Splaiul Independenței."

"I recognize this from the taxi last night," Timo said.

"I've never been to a boys' dorm before." Adriana said to her cousin as they continued walking along the riverbank. She laughed. "I've never even been to a girls' dorm."

Rows upon rows of concrete block buildings, dormitories rather than apartment blocks, lined up like sentinels facing the river. The first set of buildings consisted of six tall ones. Timo said those were the foreign student dorms.

"How do you know this already?" Adriana asked.

"My taxi driver. He knew everything."

Beyond those dorms, the ones for Romanian students were shorter: they had three floors each and stood in two rows. Timo said he'd counted twenty-four of these dormitories when he explored this morning, twelve in the front row facing the river and twelve in the back. Some students he met told him that each dorm was filled with people majoring in the same field, whether mathematics, chemistry, engineering, or whatever.

"My building is over there." He pointed to the front column. "P-12. We're all history students. It'd be so easy to get to class on time if I studied there." Timotei pointed across the Dâmbovița, where a footbridge connected to the Polytechnic, enclosed with a guardhouse and armed soldiers. "I'll need to take the metro every morning to the Universitate stop in the center of the city."

"Lucky you," Adriana said. "I love those old university buildings. They have so much character, not like these plain ones. I'll have to take classes here at Polytechnic next year." She screwed up her face. "And live at home with Mama."

Timo took her arm and guided her to the concrete bank containing the river, fenced in by black wrought iron. They sat down, slid their legs between the fence slats, and dangled their feet over the edge, far above the shallow water. "Can't you go to university in Cluj or Brașov or someplace else? Just to get away and get some independence?"

"Mama needs me too much. Ever since Tati died—"

"I know. But what about you? What do you want?"

"Not science." Adriana sighed. "I want to be bold enough to do what makes me happy and stand up to anyone who tries to get in my way. No matter what my mother says, I want to be an 'I', not a 'we'. Like you."

"Sometimes I need to keep quiet. For my own sake, and especially so that my so-called boldness doesn't get my parents—or my cousins—in trouble. I couldn't bear that." Timo raked his fingers through his thick hair. "What would you study, if you had the freedom to choose?"

"Literature. I've come to tolerate engineering, but I'll never love it like I love stories and words."

"I can see that. You've always been a sensitive soul."

"No use thinking about my pretend life. In my real life, I have to make the best of what I have. And that's the Science and Mathematics High School."

"You can still dream."

Adriana smiled. "Can I tell you a secret?"

Timo nodded.

"I've been reading novels." She lowered her voice even more. "Forbidden ones. Novels by British and American authors."

He raised his eyebrows. "Where do you find these books?"

She thought a moment. "I'll show you. Next time you come to dinner at Aunt Violeta's."

His eyes twinkled. "What's the last book you read?"

"I just finished one. And I loved it! It's called *To Kill a Mockingbird*, and it's written by an American woman named Harper Lee. Have you heard of it?"

"No, tell me."

"It's about a girl in the American South in the 1930s, Scout Finch. Her father, Atticus, is a lawyer, and he proves a black man couldn't have done what he's accused of doing. But at that time and in that place, the truth doesn't matter. The white people still claim the man's guilty, and they put him in jail, but he tries to escape and they kill him. So there's no justice after all, but Scout is still proud of her father. When she's at the courthouse, the black people stand when her father passes by because they respect him. He may have lost, but he lost doing what was right."

"That stuff really happens in America?"

"Yes. It's fiction, but it was totally believable."

"Sounds like here. A land without justice. Where only certain people have the power to decide the fate of all the rest." Timo looked her straight in the eye. "We need courageous people who will stand up to injustice. Like the lawyer in that book. Like the Solidarity people in Poland."

"Atticus Finch says that real courage doesn't have anything to do with guns or physical force. He says courage is when you know you can't win, but you try anyway, and you never give up trying."

"Sounds like a really good book." Timotei looked around, then whispered. "I have another good one, a skinny one, for you to read. It's up in my room. Come on up and I'll get it."

"Me ... in a boys' dorm?"

"It'll be okay. You'll be with me."

Timo took her hand and led her into the lobby of his dorm, up the stairs to the third floor, and down the hall to Room 308. "Wait here," he said.

He opened the door and looked in. She heard him speak to someone, and then he motioned to her to join him.

Adriana walked to the door and stood there like a statue. Timo pulled her the rest of way inside. "I'd like to present my cousin."

He spoke to a boy whose straight dark hair hung in his eyes. The boy sat on a top bunk in front of the window, reading. He looked up from his book and smiled.

"Adriana Nicu, my roommate, Marcu Andrei."

As Adriana nodded to Marcu, her eyes roamed around the crowded room. Four bunk beds filled every meter of the small space. Timo fumbled in a drawer beside the bed he'd claimed for himself, the bottom one below Marcu. With his back to Marcu, he pulled out a thin volume and, in one quick motion, slid it inside his shirt. Marcu could not possibly have noticed the transfer.

"Come on outside," he said to Adriana. As they walked down the hall, he pointed out the bathroom shared by half the rooms on the floor. "Eight guys to a room, and four rooms to a shower. That's thirty-two guys."

Adriana tried to imagine how that many people could get in and out of the shower in the one hour per evening the government turned the water on. Maybe it wouldn't be so bad to live at home with her mother next year after all.

Once outside, she and Timo walked beyond the line of dorms. Timo pulled the book out from his shirt.

Adriana read the cover. *Animal Farm: A Fairy Story.* A pig was on the cover. She noticed the author's name was George Orwell.

"It looks fun," she said.

"Oh, it's not fun at all. It's a tragedy."

"A fairy story?"

"It's really a story of rebellion. The animals drive out the farmer, Mr. Jones, a really mean man. At first, it seems good, but then everything goes horribly wrong." Timo smiled. "You read it, then we'll talk. I want you to tell me what you think."

"Thanks for the book." Adriana made sure nobody could see and slid the book inside the secret pocket she'd sewn in her jacket.

"Don't let anyone find that book," he warned.

"I promise." She stood on her tiptoes and kissed his cheek. "I should go. My first class is tomorrow too."

As she walked away toward the metro, Timo's words, "Be courageous, cousin!" wafted after her.

CHAPTER SIX

BACK TO SCHOOL

ADRIANA SHIMMIED INTO HER seat beside Gabi, minutes to spare before class started. Her super punctual friend Alex hadn't taken his seat yet. Instead, he leaned over Corina's desk and beamed at her with a smile that reached to the crinkles around his eyes. Adriana hadn't seen a smile that broad on his face since ... actually, she couldn't remember ever seeing that.

Their row had reverted to how she liked it: a row of four desks, not five, arranged alphabetically with her sitting between Gabi Martinescu and Alex Oprea, and with Corina Lupu on Gabi's other side. Last year, the addition of Liviu Negrescu had upset her world. Today, she smiled to notice his desk was missing. With Liviu gone, her last year of high school might not be so bad after all.

Her happiness over this thought didn't last long. Before she could ask if Gabi knew anything about Liviu, their new professor walked in. Adriana and Gabi exchanged looks of raised eyebrows when they saw that, for the first time at the Science and Mathematics High School, they had a female professor. And a young one at that.

Following behind the instructor, Liviu himself strode into the room, wearing his long, black leather coat and red necktie, as usual.

He must be the teacher's assistant. He was still the citywide leader of the UTC, the Union of Communist Teens, even though he'd been humiliated in front of their class last year.

When she'd first seen him, Liviu's striking good looks had Adriana head over heels for him. However, discovering his total lack of character had destroyed her infatuation. Now everything about him disgusted her. In fact, the coldness in his eyes gave her a chill, even on a warm September day.

With a smug expression on his face, Liviu took his seat in the back of the room. His teacher-sized desk didn't look like the other students' desks. A solid red tablecloth covered it, and two small flags sat on either end—the Romanian one in red, yellow, and blue stripes, and the red Communist Party one. Adriana noticed a projector on his desk, with celluloid film threaded through the reels.

From this desk, Liviu would have the perfect vantage point to do what he seemed to love: spy on the class and report anyone who talked to a neighbor or did anything out of line. This set Liviu up in good standing with professors, but it didn't make him very popular with his classmates. They had to deal with enough spies in their everyday life; they didn't want to be looking over their shoulders for someone their own age.

But Liviu wasn't their age. He'd admitted he was a year older. His parents had sent him to that special training school for boys—a boarding school in Pitești—and then he'd been reassigned to Bucharest. With his broad shoulders, he certainly looked older than the rest of the boys, but whenever he opened his mouth to speak, it was obvious he wasn't very bright. The fact that he didn't open his mouth very often saved him from everyone figuring that out. It was good for him that he was all action and little talk.

Just thinking about Liviu made Adriana's body tense up. It had been so nice to get away from him for the summer. She had to try to put him out of her mind, something that would be easier since he no longer sat beside her.

Adriana decided to turn her focus to their new professor, who was stacking books on her desk, below the critical gaze coming from President Ceaușescu's massive photograph on the wall. The professor was pretty in a way that seemed effortless, as though she didn't give her appearance any attention. Her dark hair was pinned back in a messy bun that didn't quite catch all the strands. She wore a charcoal gray suit in need of patches on the elbows and had a run up the back of her right stocking. Her eyeglasses hung around her neck, attached to a cord, the same way a much older lady would wear them. The professor picked up a piece of chalk and wrote *Prof. Elisabeta Filip* on the blackboard, then wiped her chalk-smeared hands on her pencil skirt, streaking the dark fabric with white.

"Good morning, class. You will call me Professor Filip. I look forward to a good year of instruction with each of you." She cleared her throat. "For our first order of business, all students in every classroom in Bucharest are required to watch a film. You already know my assistant. He will start the film." She nodded to Liviu.

Liviu turned off the light switch and clicked on the motor. A smiling image of Nicolae and Elena Ceaușescu, surrounded by happy schoolchildren wearing their red kerchiefs flickered on the screen. In the corner, a scowling and emaciated Uncle Sam cowered in fear.

Adriana's last year of high school had begun with a propaganda film.

When school let out, Gabi and Adriana rushed out of the building. Without a word exchanged between them, they both knew to put some distance between themselves and the other students so they could talk. They were headed to Gabi's flat.

"What a crazy first day," Adriana said when they'd gotten far enough away.

"I'm *dying* to know what you think, Adri." Gabi stopped walking. She drew out certain words and punctuated them by spreading her arms far apart. Gabi liked to add a dramatic flair. "What do you think of our professor? A *woman* scientist?"

"She can't be any worse than the men we've had," Adriana said. "I'm hoping she might stand up for us girls."

"And what about that film? So boring," Gabi said. "When they try to convince us how evil Americans are by showing us pictures of their huge houses, don't they know we see mansions every Friday night when we watch *Dallas* on TV?"

"That part doesn't make sense. Shouldn't the big houses make us want to defect? But I get why they show us people living on the street," Adriana said. "We've never see that on *Dallas*."

"How's your English coming?" Gabi asked. "Can you understand what the characters say on the show?"

"Some," Adriana smiled. "But I'm glad I have the subtitles. That helps."

Corina came running up and put her hands on both girls' shoulders, squeezing her way between them. Corina took up her spot, fitting perfectly in the middle. The girls were like stair steps, from Gabi being the tallest to Adriana being shortest.

"Corina!" Adriana gave her friend a hug. Her friendship with Corina had endured a few rough patches, mostly due to Adriana forming some wrong assumptions.

"Didn't you hear me yelling to wait up?" she said, out of breath.

"Where's Alex?" Gabi asked.

"He said he had to stop someplace. He's so mysterious sometimes."

Adriana smiled to herself. She knew why he had to be secretive.

"So, what'd you do all summer?" Adriana asked Corina.

"She spent all her free time with Alex," Gabi said. "Didn't you, Corina?"

A small smile played on Corina's lips. She blushed and changed the subject. "I'm excited about our study group this year."

"We're supposed to choose a place to meet," Adriana said. "We can meet at my flat. I mean, isn't it the only logical place?" She didn't want to hurt her friends' feelings, but Gabi had to keep her parents' underground church under the radar, and both Corina and Alex had the problem of a single parent who was always unreliable: drunk, in Alex's mother's case, or distracted by his girlfriend, in Corina's father's case.

"Sounds good," Gabi said. "My little brother would totally monopolize if we met at my place."

"I'm just happy it's all four of us, together," Corina said.

"And without Liviu," Adriana said. She linked arms with Corina who in turn linked arms with Gabi. "When Professor Filip divided the groups between herself and Liviu, I just knew we'd be stuck with him monitoring us."

"We totally lucked out by getting her," Corina said.

"I'll reserve judgment on her until later," Gabi said. "I mean, she's making us have our first meeting *this week*."

"But there's no homework tonight. When's that ever happened?" Adriana said. "I'd rather have study group than homework."

"Isn't she gorgeous?" Corina said. Of course Corina would say that. She was gorgeous herself. All the boys noticed Corina, with her glossy black hair. "We've never had a teacher so young. And a woman! Do you think she's married?"

"All I know is she's making us take that military class: Youth's Preparation for Defense of the Motherland. And we still have to be part of the Union of Communist Teens," Gabi said. "I don't think that's so lucky."

"True, but I doubt she's the one behind that," Adriana said. "And at least it doesn't start until October."

"Imagine!" Corina said. "Basic army techniques for all of us—girls too."

"Gabi, why are you so negative about Professor Filip?" Adriana asked.

"I just … until we know her, we can't be sure what she's really like. She might be the same as all of them."

"Maybe she's worse," Corina said. "Maybe she's a spy, trying to get us feeling comfortable so we let our guard down and trust her and then she—"

Gabi laughed. "Okay, I get it. I'm probably overreacting." She turned to Corina. "Adri's coming over to my place to see my little brother. You want to come?"

"Love to," Corina answered.

The girls arrived at Gabi's building to find her mother on her knees in the lobby, scrubbing the floor with a wet rag. Mrs. Martinescu was dressed in a white apron that covered her simple dress. Her chubby baby was trying his best to wriggle out of the stroller he was strapped into. When he saw his big sister, he clapped his hands together and squealed.

"Teodor!" Gabi said, holding out her hands to the squirming infant. She unhooked his straps and lifted him in her arms.

Her mother greeted Adriana and Corina, but she raised her eyebrows at Gabi.

"Gabriela, what's going on?"

"Mama, I invited my friends over to see Teodor."

Adriana watched Mrs. Martinescu inhale and square her shoulders. She thought she knew why. Gabi couldn't have friends over for fear they'd see something of their secret church meetings.

"I have another building yet to clean. We'll talk later. Be good now." She kissed Teodor and resumed her scrubbing. "Goodbye, girls."

Adriana headed for the stairs, but Gabi stopped her. "Not with this heavy sack of potatoes." She pushed the button for the lift. "Let's just see if this is working first."

Usually, the tall apartment buildings' lifts were defective. Adriana seldom even checked the one in her building. She'd become so accustomed to taking the stairs all the way up to her flat on the eighth floor, sometimes sprinting and sometimes trudging, it seemed lazy to ride up to Gabi's on the fifth floor. But after Gabi pushed the button, they could hear the creaky lift starting its descent downstairs. Another minute and the lift stopped, about one foot higher than the floor.

Corina opened the outer door and Adriana pulled the accordion-style latticework gate apart. They stepped up into the lift. Gabi handed Teodor up to Adriana first, and then his stroller, before climbing in herself. They started their slow, squawky climb up five flights.

Once inside her flat, Gabi set Teodor down on the living room rug.

"He is adorable!" Corina said, plopping down next to him and rubbing his soft chubby arm. She proceeded to talk baby-talk to him. "How old is he?"

"Just turned five months," Gabi said.

"When's he supposed to start crawling?" Adriana asked.

"Not for a few more months." Gabi bent down to look the baby in his eyes and wag her finger at him while he laughed at her. "Teodor Ştefan, you need to be a good boy today, okay?" To her friends, she said, "I'll warm up his bottle and make us some tea. He'll be content with that for a while."

While she busied herself in the kitchen, the doorbell rang. "Adri, can you get that?"

Adriana hopped up to answer the door. A man she didn't know stood on the threshold. He seemed surprised to see her. "I'm sorry," he said. "Maybe I have the wrong address."

"Wait right here," Adriana said. She turned and called, "Gabi!"

Gabi walked out into the hallway. Adriana watched the man bend down to whisper to her, but she couldn't hear what he said.

Gabi stepped back inside, twirling the end of her dark ponytail. "I'm so sorry, but I forgot … that man needs to wait here for Papa. Maybe you should …"

"We need to go anyway," Adriana said. "First week of school and all. See you tomorrow, Gabi."

"It was so nice to see Teodor," Corina said. "*Mulţumesc.*"

The two girls kissed Gabi goodbye and walked out into the hallway. The man had disappeared.

Corina raised her eyebrows at Adriana, but Adriana said nothing. Gabi's parents' secret life was just one of the many secrets she kept.

CHAPTER SEVEN

GABI: PROMISES

GABI AND ADRI HAD a promise to keep to an old man they'd grown to love. On the first Sunday after classes started, they met early in the morning so they could fulfill their responsibility and make it back in time for study group. They picked their way carefully along the curvy, cobblestoned streets of the Old Town section of Bucharest to the Jewish Quarter. Between them, they carried two bunches of yellow mums, a trowel, a short-handled broom, a rag, and a bucket of water—much of which had already sloshed out onto Gabi's brown leather shoes.

They arrived at the old cemetery, opened the black iron gate, and headed straight to the double grave of Uri Goldmann's parents. Most of the people buried here were long forgotten and their resting places neglected, with no family left to tend them. Uri's gnarled fingers didn't work so well anymore, so they had pledged to take over this labor of love.

"Does Uri know we're coming today?" Adri asked as they set down their supplies.

Gabi studied the ground as she spoke. "I told him, and he said he'd stop by later, but I don't think his memory's all that great anymore." She bent down and scooped up some big leaves that had settled on the top of the Goldmanns' graves, stuffing them inside her pockets. "Papa says they've found him wandering lately."

"Well, I've missed him. I hope he'll stop by." Adri followed Gabi with the broom. She brushed the tops of the tombstones, where dirt had gathered on the Stars of David, and the fronts of the stones, around the outline of the Hebrew letters.

"Gabi, thanks again for getting that address from him. It meant so much to Bunica."

As the girls swept every stone in the fenced-in cemetery, Gabi thought about the story Uri had told them of a young boy he knew who'd survived the Holocaust and settled in Israel. At the time, Adri was trying to discover what happened to Bunica's childhood friend, a Jewish girl named Ester. Unbelievable as it seemed, the details in Uri's story were the clues Adri needed to realize the boy was Ester's little brother.

"Did you ever think that if we hadn't gotten to know Uri, we never would've heard his story, and your grandmother never would've found out about her friend's brother?" Gabi lifted her hands to either side of her head, her fingers spread out. "It blows my mind!"

The girls continued sweeping, gathering leaves, and wiping the headstones. With tired backs, they finally arrived back where they began, at Uri's parents' graves. Adri squatted once more on the ground and wiped his parents' twin headstones clean with the rag.

Gabi picked up the trowel and started turning up the earth at the base of the stone. She sat back on her heels and observed her handiwork. "Do you think this hole is big enough for the mums?"

Neither of the girls knew very much about gardening. They'd always lived in the city, in concrete apartment buildings with no yards. Adri's grandmother tended a garden hidden in the woods outside her mountain cottage; Bunica had taught Adri the basics.

"Looks good to me. Let's try it." Adri took the mums and broke up the dirt clinging to their roots. She put a few pebbles in the hole they'd dug. "Bunica said that helps the water drain." Then she stuffed the mums in the hole.

While Gabi sprinkled water on the flowers, Adri finished tidying up the grave and collecting the things they'd brought.

"That looks pretty," Adri said. She wiped her hair out of her eyes with the back of her muddy hand.

"Ready?" Gabi said.

As the girls walked out through the gate of the Jewish cemetery, they nearly collided with their friend. With his long white beard and black fedora, he was impossible to miss.

"Uri!" Gabi cried.

The old gentleman looked confused. He stared at them blankly for several seconds. "Who—"

"Uri, don't you remember us? We're your friends," Gabi said.

He rubbed his temples. He appeared almost frightened.

"I'm Gabriela, and this is Adriana." Gabi touched Adri's shoulder.

"You showed us around and told us all about the history of the Jews here," Adri said.

Uri's cloudy eyes began to clear. "Of course! My two angels!" He'd never been able to keep their names straight, but as long as he remembered their faces, that's all that mattered to Gabi.

Adri grabbed his hand and gave it a squeeze. "I've missed you! How have you been?"

Uri nodded. "Good … good …"

"We came to tend the graves," Gabi said. "We're keeping our word to you."

"Ah! The graves." He continued rubbing his forehead. "I'm honored. It's a good thing to keep your promises."

"Are you still making stained glass?" Gabi asked. She had learned that when Uri seemed confused, if she directed the conversation to his craft, he usually had a lot to say.

Uri started to perk up. He nodded.

"How are your windows coming?"

"Slowly." Uri stretched his fingers apart, huge misshapen knobs on each knuckle. "These fingers … they don't move like they used to."

"When will you be finished?" Adri asked.

"A long time," Uri said. "But some windows are finished now."

"Really?" Adri said.

"Yes, some have been installed by now. The showiest windows in the front, the ones in the most important rooms." Uri seemed himself now. "But don't forget there are over a thousand rooms in the whole building. I think it'll be a while."

"I walked by the other day. The palace is impressive," Gabi said, adding in a whisper, "and sickening."

"As long as it impresses the big man, that's all I care about. President … I wish I could forget the man, but how can I forget his name?" Uri rubbed his temples again.

"Ceaușescu," Adri offered.

"Of course. Our Supreme Leader Ceaușescu expects us to pick up the pace. How we'll do that, nobody knows. Nobody but the Almighty."

Uri, long past mandatory pension age, had been called back into service for the state because of his skill. He and thousands of others shared three shifts a day so that the work on the House of the People could continue around the clock, never ceasing.

Once Gabi had asked how he could remember all the intricacies involved in his work after retiring and then picking it back up again. He'd told her that some things he'll never forget.

"Thinking about work makes me tired. I need to go home to rest," Uri said. "I'm turned around. Which way is my house?"

Gabi took Uri's arm, and the three of them plodded to the corner.

He lowered his voice. "Many of the laborers who work on the underground floors go missing."

Gabi shivered, despite the heat. "You told us about some of them last time—"

"It's happening more and more as we near completion. I assemble my windows in those secret tunnels. The ones built to shuttle the President in case of an emergency." Uri put an arthritic hand on each girl's shoulder. "They can't let us have that knowledge. Look, if you don't hear from me—"

"What are you saying?" Adri asked.

"I've lived a long life. A full life. I've defied death so many times."

A lump formed in Gabi's throat. She couldn't speak.

"I'm saying I'm ready." He smiled at his young friends. "If anything happens to me, don't be sad. Death is just part of life. We all face it at some time, and at my age, it can't be too far away."

With that, he kissed the girls. "I need to go home. I'm an old man, and my bed is calling to me." His eyes appeared cloudy again. He rubbed his brow and looked as if he didn't recognize the girls. "Where am I? Can you take me home?"

Gabi caught Adri's eyes. Adri looked concerned too.

The girls each took one of Uri's arms and guided him into his apartment building. At the front door, Uri became agitated.

"Where's my hat? I've lost my hat!"

Gabi pushed his black fedora down lower on his head. "I found it."

"Be careful!" he cried. "The Iron Guard. They're everywhere. Don't let them see you."

Adri looked at Gabi and mouthed, "*Iron Guard.*" It had dissolved in 1941, almost fifty years ago.

"We'll be careful," Gabi said.

"Promise me. You can't let them catch you."

"We promise," Adri said, patting his hand.

They led Uri up the stairs in his building, helped him unlock his door, and got him settled. He laid down on his cot.

When Adri and Gabi were certain Uri was safely asleep, they crept out. They remained on the street outside his building for several moments, looking at the window that was his. Neither one spoke.

Then they walked back to the cemetery, gathered up their trowel and broom and bucket, and walked home.

"I've never seen him like this," Gabi said. "I'm worried about him."

"He knows the location of those secret tunnels," Adri said. "What'll we do if he goes missing?"

Gabi closed her eyes to block out the thought. "Or will he forget where he is and lose his way first?"

Adri sighed. "We can't worry about any of that now." She looked at her watch. "We need to get back to my flat for study group."

CHAPTER EIGHT

ADRIANA: ELISABETA FILIP

October 1989

S TUDY GROUP SOON BECAME Adriana's favorite time of the
week. Not only did she get to be in a group with her three
best friends, but at the second meeting in her flat, Professor
Filip joined them. She said she'd be splitting her time between the
study groups she was responsible for, and Liviu would take the rest.
Adriana had to bite her cheeks to keep from smiling at her good
luck. Professor Filip had reiterated the purpose of the group: to take
notes from the one textbook each group shared and help each other
process what they'd learned.

Alex had been Adriana's tutor for a couple years now. He helped
her understand engineering. Now that they had study group, there
was no need to continue meeting with Alex. The only downside
to this new arrangement was that Adriana missed the one-on-one
time with her friend.

Mama often had to work extra shifts at the factory on Sundays,
but she made sure to be home the day Professor Filip came. Mama
sat in the kitchen and gave them free rein of the living room. It
bothered Adriana to watch her mother act so deferential to her
professor, just like she used to do with Tati's colleagues at all his

Communist Party events. Even though every Romanian suppos- edly received the same pay and was considered equal, there was a definite pecking order in society. Party members ranked far above everyone else, and the average person revered professors more than factory workers. When Mama peppered Adriana with questions about Professor Filip, Adriana wondered if she may be a tad jealous.

At the least, Mama seemed curious, and for good reason. Young female science teachers, especially those that taught engineering, were a rarity in Romania. But it bothered Adriana when Mama said that young women should think of their work for the state more as a job than a career, because their priority was taking care of their husbands and raising children. Mama said that, in the end, family was *all* that mattered for a woman. How could she say that? Adriana didn't deny that she hoped for marriage and motherhood … someday. But wasn't there more to life than that? She hoped so.

After getting to know strong heroines like Jo March, Anne Shirley, and Elizabeth Bennet from the novels she'd read, Adriana decided a couple years ago that she wanted to draw on their exam- ples. She was willing to wait for marriage, even to never marry if that meant being able to pursue the things that interested her. Now she had a real-life role model in Elisabeta Filip, a kindred spirit to add to the growing list of her fictional ones. Why did her mother have to criticize her new hero?

Now with three study groups complete, this Sunday promised to be the best one of all. Professor Filip had invited them to meet at her flat this morning. Adriana promised her mother she'd describe everything about it in detail.

She felt happy as she walked along the city streets, marveling at the beauty of the trees. They'd just begun their annual ritual of trad- ing their green leaves for golds and rusts. The four friends planned to meet outside the Izvor metro station so they could arrive to- gether. When Adriana got there, Alex was the only one present. Of course. Alex was never late.

He didn't see her at first, and Adriana was tempted to turn around. She hated to admit it, but she still felt awkward around Alex, her friend from first grade on, who'd been like a brother to her most of her life. That all changed when he and Corina started dating. That's what it took for Adriana to finally come to her senses and realize she wanted more than a friendship with Alex, but it was too late. She knew she needed to just get over her feelings for him. Nothing had changed from Alex's perspective; they were still friends, and that's all they'd ever be.

She put an extra bounce in her last few steps to try to appear nonchalant and tapped Alex lightly on the arm when she reached him. "So how are you doing?"

Alex seemed lost in his thoughts. He pushed his glasses up his nose and blinked. "Adriana! I was think—"

"Thinking about something good, I hope," she said. She noted Alex's complexion had cleared up over the summer. He was looking pretty good in his brown wool jacket.

"Just something Professor Filip said."

"What's that?"

"Remember last week when she said that no degree—including an engineering degree—is complete without giving some thought to philosophy? That we must know our personal philosophy."

"Yes ..."

"She said whether we admit it or not, we each have a philosophy of life. Hers is that we're here for a reason. She said we may feel strongly about lots of things and some things we don't care about at all. But then something comes along and it catches our attention, and that's when we know that it's *our* thing. Our purpose for life. And it's important enough that we're willing to take a risk—a big risk—for it." Alex cleared his throat. "I guess I was thinking about what my purpose is."

"And I thought you were wondering when the metro will arrive." Adriana laughed. "But no, nothing light for my friend Alex. No sir!"

She punched his arm playfully. "No wonder it's hard for you to see the reason you're here. Not at this metro but on earth, I mean."

"What do you mean?"

"Your reason used to be to tutor me in engineering. But then you taught me so much that I became smarter than you, and now I don't need you anymore. You need a new purpose." Adriana laughed again.

Alex smiled, but he looked somehow wounded at the same time.

While Adriana was still laughing, Corina arrived. Adriana noticed Corina's eyes shift between Alex and herself, but of course Corina didn't say anything. Her words and her actions always conveyed that she felt secure with Alex and she trusted Adriana, but her eyes gave her away.

Before Adriana could speculate further, Gabi appeared.

"It's too nice to ride the metro," Gabi said. "It's only one stop. We'll get there faster by foot."

The other three agreed.

The group walked along the river to the Eroilor metro station, Gabi and Adriana in the lead, with Alex and Corina lagging behind. A couple times when Adriana turned to say something to them, she noticed they were holding hands and talking softly to each other, oblivious to anyone else.

The foursome passed the University's Law Department and the Opera House across the river before they arrived at a small grassy area in front of the station. True to her word, Professor Filip waited for them at the metro entrance. She seemed surprised when they didn't come up the stairs from inside.

"Good for you," she said after she greeted them. "Getting some exercise on such a fine October day. You never know how long this nice snap of weather will last."

She looked different today. Her hair, wavy and dark, hung down to her shoulders. Rather than a workday suit, she wore a navy-blue pullover and something Adriana rarely saw; Professor Filip had on blue jeans!

All three of the girls gawked.

Professor Filip laughed, and leaned in. "Haven't you seen *bluj* before?"

"Only in pictures," Gabi said.

"Where did you get them?" Corina asked.

"A gift. From an old friend," she said, then straightened. "Follow me. Have you ever been inside a home in Cotroceni before?"

The students murmured "no" as they followed their teacher down short curvy roads with actual houses, one of only a couple old historic districts that Ceaușescu hadn't demolished to build the rows of ugly sky-high apartment blocks. They passed the University's stately Medical Department on Strada Doctor Carol Davila and turned onto Strada Ana Davila.

Professor Filip gestured to the impressive white building that came into view as they rounded the corner. "This building, Cotroceni Palace, is the reason my district escaped the wrecking balls," she said. "Do you remember the Vrancea earthquake in 1977? That was twelve years ago, so you all would have been, what—five?"

"I remember," Alex said. "At least I remember my father talking about it. All the structural damage to buildings." He looked down. "He was a civil engineer."

"Well, Cotroceni Palace was damaged in the earthquake, and they've been repairing it ever since." Professor Filip cleared her throat and lowered her voice. "About the same time as the Vrancea earthquake, our Supreme Leader returned from North Korea and started building another palace, his House of the People. In his speeches, he said he planned to model Bucharest after North Korea's capital, Pyongyang. And not just the city layout, but the army's discipline, the adoration of the people, their efficiency. He admired everything about North Korean society."

Adriana looked at Gabi and raised her eyebrows.

The houses around them were lovely and reminded Adriana of the ones where Aunt Violeta lived, close to the city center. Most of them had three stories and a variety of rooflines, all with orange tiles. Some of the houses looked like miniature castles with towers and turrets.

The house that Professor Filip led them to was one of the ones with a turret that jutted out from the third floor.

The students followed her up the outside steps to the thick wooden front door, which she unlocked with a skeleton key. They entered a hallway with two doors facing each other and a stairway in the back. They walked past the doors and up two flights of steps to another hallway with a small door beside the stairs. Professor Filip opened this door and ushered them inside a narrow cylindrical tower. They climbed the curved concrete steps to the top, where she unlocked the final door.

"*Bine ați venit!*" she said, welcoming them to her home.

Adriana had never seen anything like it before. The circular flat was just one cozy room. The front part contained a sofa and wing-back chair, and across from it sat a stove and sink and small table. In the back, a bed was visible. A door stood opposite the bed, which Adriana assumed housed the bathroom. The size of the flat reminded Adriana of her grandmother's cottage in the mountains, with the addition of indoor plumbing.

"Everything is in one room!" Corina said.

"Haven't you seen a *garsoniera* before?" Professor Filip asked.

"Never," Gabi said.

"It's just perfect for one person," she said as she slipped out of her shoes. "I moved here from Suceava to teach and had to find something."

Adriana and Gabi exchanged glances when she said "one person."

"You have heard of Suceava, right? Way up at the northern end of Moldova." Professor Filip walked into the kitchen area and poured water into a tea kettle. "And by that, I mean Moldova the region of Romania, not Moldova the republic of the U.S.S.R." She pulled out five cups and saucers. "You know, Moldova's where the prettiest monasteries are. One of them, Sucevița, is right near my town. And then Voroneț—where the color Voroneț blue comes from—isn't too far."

Adriana hardly heard any of that.

"You mean you're not married?" Adriana asked, then blushed when she realized that she'd asked something much too personal.

"No, I'm not. I'm satisfied with my career," the professor said, then winked. "Besides, I haven't found anyone I want to marry. And I'm not about to settle. I'd rather never marry than do that."

This was radical. Adriana couldn't wait to report back to her mother. If Mama thought female engineering teachers were scarce, what would she think of a *single* career woman who taught engineering? Especially one who was willing to postpone marriage? It was unheard of.

The professor motioned toward the sofa. "You all find a seat. I'll bring the tea."

The four of them squeezed onto the sofa together. They left the best seat, the wingback chair, for the teacher. Professor Filip carried a tray filled with cups of tea and a saucer of sweet crackers and placed it on the coffee table.

"First, let's get to know each other, more on a personal level," she said taking a sip of her tea. "Tell me. What's your favorite season?"

"Autumn," Alex blurted out.

"And why is that?" Professor Filip asked. Even though she'd asked a simple question, she studied each of their faces as though she could read what went on inside their minds.

"I guess I like school."

The girls laughed and Alex blushed.

"What about the rest of you?"

"I like spring," Gabi said. "After the long gray winter, I love seeing the colors pop out."

"Summer," Adriana said. "I love going to the mountains to see my bunica."

Corina thought a minute. "Probably autumn for the colors and the crisp air, but I like them all. Well, maybe not winter so much."

"Good answers," Professor Filip said. "Very thoughtful answers. Here's another question: do any of you have siblings?"

"Just me," Gabi said. "I have a baby brother."

"None for the rest of you?"

They shook their heads.

"What about you?" Adriana asked, and then felt her face flush again. "Siblings, I mean."

"I have a brother," the professor said. "We had a sister, Cristiana, but she died before we were born. My brother Cristian was named after her."

The students nodded and politely diverted their eyes. They looked down into their teacups.

"I'm sorry," Corina said.

"I'm probably not the only one in this group who's experienced loss," Professor Filip said. "Adriana, I know you have one parent. Perhaps that's true for others of you."

Alex nodded, and Corina said, "My mother died when I was young."

Adriana noticed Alex rubbing Corina's forearm tenderly. At least he didn't try to hold her hand in front of their professor.

"I'm different again," Gabi said. "I have two parents, but I did lose someone. Another baby brother."

"I'm sorry. Sorry for all of it." Professor Filip sighed. "I hate it that loss seems to be one of the common denominators among us. And I'm sorry. I meant to ask you light questions, and here I go with something heavy and sad." She took a sip of her tea. "Maybe I should be the one to tell you who I am. You're probably curious about me."

Gabi shrugged and Corina nodded.

Professor Filip laughed. "It's okay. I'm twenty-eight years old. This is my second teaching job. I graduated from the university nearest my home, in Iași, and taught for five years before being transferred here."

More information for Mama. Never before had a teacher been so open and informal with them.

"And now that you know more about me, let's get to our study group. I want someone to explain to me, without opening your notebook, what we talked about this week," Professor Filip said. "Degrees of freedom."

Alex cleared his throat. "There are six degrees of freedom—three translation and three rotation. For example, a ship at sea is a rigid body, but it has all six degrees of freedom. It can move up and down, left and right, forward and backward. Those are the translation ones." He ticked them off his fingers. "Then it swivels and tilts and ... something else—"

"I know," Adriana said. "It pivots."

"Very good. But what's that mean? It feels like you're reciting from a textbook," Professor Filip said. "Dig deeper."

"A degree of freedom is a physics term," Gabi said. "It's a principal for all types of engineering. Mechanical, aeronautical, civil—"

"Yes, but what affects this freedom?"

"The number of parameters," Alex said. "Independent parameters."

"And what are those?"

"They're the six things Alex said at the beginning," Adriana said. "Well, actually I think he only named *five* of them." She looked at Alex and pointed to herself, mouthing *I said one of them.*

Alex smiled and shook his head at her. Then he nudged her with his elbow.

Adriana noticed Corina watching their exchange.

"You're all correct, and I'm proud of you," Professor Filip said.

"But I still don't think anyone's explained it simply enough. Imagine I'm not a scientist. How would you describe it to me?"

"Isn't it how easily something can move?" Corina said. She seemed unsure of her answer.

"That's it!" Professor Filip said. "Bravo! So, what about a rail car? How easily can it move?"

"It has one degree of freedom because it's constrained by the track," Corina said.

"Excellent. Let's think of this in a non-scientific way," Professor Filip said. "To help with that, we're going to take a short field trip outside."

Gabi looked at Adriana and raised her eyebrows.

"As we walk, I want you to observe and think. Think about whether plants can have degrees of freedom. What about animals and people? Are people free, or are they constrained? If you think any living things have degrees of freedom, what are the parameters that affect how much freedom they have?"

Adriana studied her young professor. Freedom? And people? Those were dangerous topics. No wonder she wanted them to discuss them outside. Away from microphones and listening ears.

The students quickly drained their teacups, stepped into their shoes, and followed their professor down the circular stairs and onto her little road. They crossed over a bigger road to Gradina Botanica, the botanical garden not far from Timotei's dorm.

Professor Filip led them past trees and bushes tinged with the reds and golds of autumn, past vibrant beds of chrysanthemums and dormant rose gardens, each plant labeled with a sign announcing its Latin name. Adriana noticed an orange leaf pirouetting to the ground. Birds flitted from one tree to the next, while squirrels raced each other up the trunks before jumping down and scurrying off into the brush.

"Are you observing?" Professor Filip frequently stopped to ask. "Are you thinking?"

They continued down a wide path past a large glass greenhouse until they reached a pond with water lilies floating on the surface. Adriana noticed a frog hopping onto a round floating leaf. One thing marred the beauty of this garden. Directly behind the garden, and towering above it, stood two gigantic cooling towers for the central electric facility.

Professor Filip turned at the pond and meandered along a side path until they reached an even smaller path, with a couple of benches hidden by the trees. They sat on the benches.

"Let's talk," Professor Filip said. "Tell me what you observed on our walk. What are your thoughts about freedom?"

"Plants can't move on their own, but the wind makes them sway a little," Adriana said.

"What constrains them?"

"The earth. Their roots," Adriana said.

"Plants are limited, but animals have all six degrees of freedom," Alex said.

"Unless it's a bird in a cage or a dog chained up, animals can move and roam the streets whenever they want," Corina added.

"Just like the packs of wild dogs that roam the streets at night," Gabi said.

The others grimaced.

"How do animals compare with people?" Professor Filip asked.

The students were silent.

Adriana bit her lip. "Animals have more freedom than we do."

Professor Filip looked into Adriana's eyes. "Are you in a cage?"

"Not a physical one, but—"

"Do you have chains?"

Adriana thought about her response a moment. "I'm not chained up, but I can't do whatever I feel like doing or go wherever I want." Adriana spoke softly. She liked thinking about freedom, but her stomach felt tied in knots when she said these words out loud.

"We all have constraints," Alex added. "Every day." He looked over his shoulders. "Even what we say is controlled."

"Class, freedom is a state of mind," Professor Filip said, and lowered her voice. She fixed her penetrating gaze on each of them, one at a time. "I understand your feelings, and you're correct in what you said. But I need you all to understand something. Even if someone locks you in a prison, they can't truly imprison you. Not your spirit. Never your mind. The most important thing I can teach you is to think for yourselves. Don't accept what others tell you. It may be right; it may be wrong. You must learn the difference."

"But what can you do if you're in prison—" Gabi said.

"Be like the birds. Soar above your circumstances." Professor Filip tapped her temple. "In here."

"But does that really help?" Adriana said. "I mean, you can think all you want, but your thoughts don't get you out of your cage."

"There may come a time—and you'll know when it's right—when you need to stand up to those who try to keep you imprisoned in your cage. And be willing to risk everything."

Alex spoke softly, as though he only spoke to their professor. "Like you're doing now? Talking this way to us?"

"Yes," Professor Filip said. "I sensed this group would be open. I'm good at reading people. But if I'm wrong, if any of the four of you are informers, I decided this was a risk I'm willing to take." Again, she looked each student in the eyes, ending with Adriana. "I think I made the right choice."

As Professor Filip spoke, Adriana didn't stop observing, her eyes constantly scanning the area. Suddenly she noticed two people dart into a shed. One was Timo. The other was his roommate, Marcu.

When the others parted to make their way home, Adriana begged off, saying she wanted to look at more of the foliage. Really, she wanted answers.

What is Timotei doing here?

CHAPTER NINE

TIMOTEI: RESISTANCE

TIMOTEI AND MARCU CREPT into the lean-to shed, filled with rakes and shovels and a handful of other university students. They squeezed in beside Beni Barbu, a quiet soft-spoken guy, and Timotei's old friend from Timişoara, Simona Vucescu.

The leader, Serghei Ursu, held his finger to his lips. "We'll wait a few minutes for the others," he said in a low voice. Every time Timotei looked at Serghei, his initial impression was reinforced: Serghei resembled a Bolshevik revolutionary, with his goatee, round wire-rimmed glasses, flat worker's cap, and wild-eyed expression.

Timotei had joined an underground group, Students for a Free Romania. He hoped that his association with this group would allow him to make a real impact for change in his country. He had to admit, however, that for a secret society, it hadn't been hard for him to break in.

When he first arrived in Bucharest, he had looked up Simona. He'd grown up with her, first playing together outside their apartment block, and later in school. Simona was several months and one grade ahead of Timotei, but he always thought of himself as the older brother who needed to protect her. The two friends

53

even resembled each other. Both Timotei and Simona had thick, unruly hair. People often told Timotei that his unkempt look gave the impression of someone gone mad. But Simona's wild curls and the twinkle in her eye showed another quality: her mischievous spirit.

Simona had already been at the university a year before Timotei arrived. Here in Bucharest, she got to play the part of the older sibling showing the younger one the ropes.

Simona knew where Timotei stood in terms of dissatisfaction with the present regime. They'd been whispering about that for years. It hadn't been much of a risk for Simona to invite Timotei to one of these secret meetings, but she showed a lot of nerve asking him in front of Marcu. Timotei didn't know Marcu's views at that time. Now he did.

There was nothing Marcu wouldn't do to see his beloved homeland free.

Simona had led the two guys to the first meeting in Gradina Botanica's tool shed a few weeks ago.

"You are here because Simona vouched for you," Serghei had said when they were introduced. He glared at Simona as he said this. "You are not to tell anyone—not *anyone*—of this group or what we discuss. Do I have your word?" Serghei had stared into Timotei's and Marcu's eyes with ferocity.

"Da," Timotei said. What else could he say?

Marcu echoed him.

The tone of the small group was serious. Everyone there wanted change. They all longed for freedom. But nobody more than Serghei.

Talk about intense. The more Serghei Ursu spoke, the more Timotei felt like a kitten next to him. His last name, which meant bear, fit him. Serghei the Bear. The group had a job to do, and according to Serghei, each person present was merely a partner in the task, not a friend.

Serghei had grilled Timotei and Marcu after that first meeting. Marcu, always the outgoing one, had tried to lighten the mood with his friendly banter, but Serghei didn't seem to appreciate it. Even after Marcu's failed attempts at sociability, they both must have passed, because they were invited to a second meeting. It helped that Timotei had delivered news the group hadn't received yet: the report from Radio Free Europe about Poland. Having access to that kind of information put him in good standing with Serghei.

At the second meeting, Timotei and Marcu were both initiated into the secretive society, Students for a Free Romania. Through his new association, Timotei had become connected to a web of other societies, layer upon layer, that all led back to one source: The Resistance.

Timotei smiled to himself. His friend, Vasile, was part of the Resistance, one link in an invisible chain spreading throughout the country. Vasile regularly intercepted news from Radio Free Europe and Voice of America broadcasts. A network of couriers buried deeply into the normal fabric of everyday Romanian life spread the news from these transmissions. Lately, Timotei had come to suspect his great aunt, Adriana's own bunica, to be one of these couriers.

As he waited for the other students to arrive, Timotei thought about how being part of an official group of dissenters motivated him to take full advantage of the University's vast library in the center of the city. He dug through the old volumes, obsessed with finding answers to questions such as why certain regimes flourished and others didn't; and if they didn't, how the end came about. Did the regimes die peacefully in their sleep, or were they murdered? And if their citizens brought them down, how did they do it?

There was another reason he spent all his time at that particular library. The very location of the grand old building, situated in the heart of Palace Square, near the old royal palace-turned-art museum and next door to Securitate's headquarters, was part of his motivation for being there. He didn't just read; he observed. He listened and watched. And then he reported back to the Students for a Free Romania.

After just a month of college, his life had grown quite lop-sided, with all his free time spent studying, doing research, or meeting with the student resistance group. He had no social life to speak of, but that was his decision, and he thought it was worth the sacrifice. Sometimes there were more important things to life, and this was one of those times.

Suddenly, Timotei heard voices outside. Judging by his expression, Serghei did too. Serghei motioned to Timotei and the others to flatten themselves against the wall.

All at once, Claudia, the last to arrive, walked in, dragging a girl by the arm. Timotei gasped. The girl was Adriana!

"I found this kid with her ear up against the door," Claudia said.

Serghei straightened. "So you brought her inside?" he hissed at Claudia.

Then he turned to face Adriana. "Who are you, and what are you doing here?"

Timotei cleared his throat. He put his hand on Adriana's shoulder. "She's my cousin."

"I don't care whose cousin she is," Serghei said. "Why are you here?" He glared at Adriana.

"I … I was in the garden with my class. I saw some people—"

"Look, I can vouch for her. Her name's Adriana," Timotei said. "She's on our side. She's been interrogated all night by the Securitate, something that hasn't happened to any of you yet. I'd say she can be trusted to keep this a secret."

Claudia whispered something to Serghei. As she spoke, he shook his head adamantly at first, but after they'd conferred a few minutes, he stood tapping his finger against his chin and paused as though he was thinking.

"Claudia thinks it could be beneficial to us to have some eyes and ears of a high school student in our group from time to time." Serghei paced a few steps in the tiny shed, his hands clasped behind his back. His eyes bore into Timotei's. "Against my better judgment, your cousin may stay. I will hold you responsible if anything goes wrong because of this."

"Understood," Timotei said.

"And you," he spoke to Adriana, wagging his finger in her face, "you cannot repeat anything about what we say or who we are."

"I promise," Adriana said.

Serghei shot a fierce expression at the rest of the group. "Let's get started then. We'll discuss any new chatter you've picked up. The growing unrest in Hungary. Anything else that's relevant." He glowered at Adriana. "And we'll need to find a new, more secure, place to meet in the future."

CHAPTER TEN

ADRIANA: ANIMAL FARM

WHEN THE SHORT MEETING ended, Timo took Adriana's hand and, after looking both ways, they crept out of the shed together. "We need to talk," Timo said.

Adriana blew out a big whoosh of air. "What was that? I mean, what kind of group?"

Timo took a moment to answer. "University students who want to see our country change for the better."

"I'm sorry if I caused you problems—"

"It's okay now." Timo waved his hand. "But I'm curious. Why did your class meet outside?"

"My professor brought our study group here. She talked about some things—well, before all this happened, I was planning to ask you about those things."

"Hold that thought until we get to our talking spot. You okay to walk to my dorm with me?"

That was fine with Adriana. She thought best when she walked. Troubling things began to feel less difficult; confusing things got sorted out. Today, she had lots to muddle through. The ideas Professor Filip had broached were so radical, they swirled around in her mind. She didn't know what to make of them. And then there was Timo's secret group she'd stumbled into.

Timo led her back to the place where they had sat before, on the edge of the river beyond the dorms, facing the Polytechnic.

"What do you want to talk about?" he asked.

"Well, that book you gave me, for one. I started reading it right away and I've already finished it. You said we could discuss it."

"Do you have it?"

"Not on me. I didn't expect to see you."

"So, tell me. What'd you think of it?"

"It was good. Confusing though. Today my professor—well, she said some things that made me think of the animals in that book. How they felt like they weren't free. What they did to try to change that, and how it didn't work out in the end." She looked up at him. "Will you explain it to me?"

He looked around them. They were alone. He began in a lowered voice. "I will. But first, tell me about this professor."

"She's young. And she teaches much more than engineering. She teaches us to think. Today she talked about …" Adriana dropped her voice even lower, "freedom, degrees of freedom. She understands we're not free. She said someday we may need to take a stand and risk everything to become free. Like some of the things I heard in your group today."

"Sounds radical. I like her already." Timo smiled. "So, about the book. You know George Orwell was a genius, don't you? He wrote *Animal Farm* back in 1945, right after World War II ended, but what he described was in the future. But also in the past."

"You're not making sense," Adriana said.

"Well, the rebellion against Mr. Jones would be like the Bolsheviks against the Russian aristocrats, the October Revolution of 1917 that Lenin led. Obviously, that happened in the past."

"I thought that's what he meant. But wasn't that revolution good?"

"In theory it was supposed to be. The oppressed people standing up against their oppressors. Some people would say that the pure vision of Marx and Engels was supposed to be all about equality. But here's the thing: people are people, and we're all basically greedy, some more than others. The leaders of the revolution wanted more for themselves than what went to the peasants. The peasants, the proletariat, were the ones who died and did all the work. In the end, the revolutionaries treated the people worse than the original aristocracy did."

"The rebellion against Mr. Jones seemed good. Necessary even." Adriana thought a moment. "So, who is the old pig, Old Major, supposed to be? Karl Marx?"

"Could be. But I tend to think of him as Lenin himself. I do know Mr. Jones represents the last czar, Nicholas II."

"When Old Major dies, that other pig who takes over, Napoleon. He was the scariest."

"He represents Stalin. This is the part that was in the future when Orwell wrote this." Timotei's jaw hardened. "And you're right to be scared of him. We live with the consequences of Stalin every day. The animals have to go through reeducation programs, same as us in Romania, to make everyone conform to one—and only one—correct way of thinking. They're brainwashed with propaganda, same as us. The pig named Squealer has to spread Napoleon's propaganda. And when anyone disagrees, they vanish. Killed, most likely."

"So, you're saying we're the animals."

"We are indeed. Like the horse named Boxer, we go along with it all. We invited it in the first place. We didn't know what we were getting, but we still invited it. We're the ones who say things like, *I will work harder* and *Napoleon is always right*."

"Only we say Ceaușescu," Adriana looked around. Nobody stood within earshot, so she whispered. "*Ceaușescu is always right.* We say it whether we believe it or not."

61

"The best line in the whole book is this: *All animals are equal, but some are more equal than others.*" Timotei slapped his thigh. "Open your eyes, Adriana. This is happening today. Romania is the animal farm."

Adriana nodded. "My eyes *are* open, Timo. But I still have a question. Would the animals have been better off if they never tried to change things? If they just stayed with Mr. Jones?"

Timo shrugged.

"How can anyone know?" Adriana's voice rose. "Is it even possible to know what's right? And if you do take a risk, how do you know things will improve? Or when you should do it?"

Timotei exhaled. "These are the big questions. All I can say is, you have to follow your own mind. Think for yourself. Don't just blindly follow the crowd."

That was the second time today someone told her to think for herself.

CHAPTER ELEVEN

THE MOTHERLAND

T
HE NEXT SUNDAY, ADRIANA'S class started their training for the Youth's Preparation for Defense of the Motherland, to be held every other week, alternating with study group. The training class replaced the Patriotic Workdays her class had to participate in during years past. Adriana never enjoyed the workdays, but she'd give anything to have one today instead of this military training.

She had to get up as early as she did on school days—on her one supposedly free day!—and report at the military training grounds at 7:30 sharp. Adriana didn't want to find out the consequences of being late, so she was one of the first to arrive for their first session.

She looked out over the group of teenagers, representing every high school in the city. How would she find the School of Science and Mathematics?

As she scanned the crowd, she spotted Liviu Negrescu, who was taller than most of the boys. He stood ramrod straight, making himself appear even taller. Rather than wearing his usual long black leather coat, he was dressed in a khaki military uniform. Of course he'd wear that. The Union of Communist Teens was helping with the operations.

A small cluster of students from her class stood beside Liviu. She recognized Alex in that circle. She walked over to join them. Soon Gabi and the others arrived. But not Corina.

Liviu held his clipboard as he took roll call.

"Corina Lupu?" he called.

No answer.

"Does anyone know where Corina Lupu is?" Liviu asked, making a mark on his form.

Nobody answered. Adriana looked at Alex. He shook his head, but he looked worried.

Liviu had them line up in an orderly fashion, in straight rows, facing an empty platform with a microphone stand. After all the parades they'd had to participate in as Young Pioneers, they were accustomed to that. Adriana's small class lined up quickly.

They stood at attention, not looking to the right or to the left. They knew the drill.

A soldier came to microphone and introduced himself.

"Welcome to the first day of boot camp," he barked. "The UTC commanders for each school will help form and supervise the various platoons, but be assured that I, Drill Sergeant Popescu, am the one who will do the drilling. By the end of this year, you will be prepared to defend the Motherland. You will learn basic army techniques. I will break you and rebuild you and make you comport yourselves as trained, combat-ready soldiers. You are no longer just students. You are also soldiers."

Adriana affixed her gaze straight ahead, so she didn't see the next speaker approach the platform until he stood directly behind the microphone.

It was Comrade Zugravescu. It took all Adriana's strength to keep her legs from buckling.

This evil man was going to prepare them? Zugravescu's father, Groza, had "prepared" her father by leaving him alone for days in the mountains when he was just a boy, and even hunting him.

Zugravescu himself had been molding Liviu into his image since Liviu was young, in a gulag turned training school for boys.

Zugravescu introduced himself to the assembled group as *Captain* Zugravescu, Chief Reeducation Officer for the Securitate.

"You are the future of Romania," he said. "You are the soldiers who will defend the beloved Motherland. You are not just being trained for some far-off future; but you are needed now. Now, at this moment, enemies lurk, waiting for an opportunity, hoping the Motherland will stop paying attention so they can strike. But they will be mistaken. The Motherland never sleeps. This group of students before me—you—are to answer those attacks and report all traitors and infiltrators. It is your duty. It is your privilege. It is the price you owe to the Motherland for all she has given you. It is the debt you owe to our Supreme Commander, President Nicolae Ceaușescu."

Zugravescu stepped off the platform, and Drill Sergeant Popescu returned to the microphone.

"You will be trained in physical readiness: jumping, crawling, lifting, and navigating obstacles. We will do road marches and ropes courses. You will learn techniques such as proper marksmanship, hand-to-hand combat, how to maneuver around obstacles, and survival skills. Before the school year is finished, we will make soldiers out of all of you. Every other Sunday at 7:30, you are to report at this same spot for your training to commence. And now the UTC commanders will issue further instructions and organize you into platoons with platoon leaders."

As Popescu stepped away from the microphone and Liviu lifted his clipboard, Adriana noticed Captain Zugravescu, now standing on the sidelines. He looked at her and smirked.

She hadn't forgotten his threat. She could never forget.

CHAPTER TWELVE

CORINA: THE ULTIMATUM

ORINA TRIED TO GET up in time for the military training on Sunday morning, but she couldn't. She pushed back the covers and sat on the side of her bed for several minutes, staring at her wardrobe, not moving. How could she face Alex today? What would she say to him? She knew she wouldn't be able to hide how she was feeling from Gabi and Adriana.

Better for her not to go at all. Sure, she'd be reprimanded, but people did get sick, didn't they? She could explain that to Professor Filip and apologize.

The one who should apologize was her father. He'd upset her world.

Corina laid back down on the bed. She pulled her duvet over her face and cried. She didn't think she had any more tears left.

In her mind, she tried to recap what had happened. She went to school as usual on Saturday. But when her father came home Saturday evening, she knew immediately that something was wrong.

Her father had never been warm and affectionate to her, not like she'd observed in how Gabi's father treated his daughter, but last night his face looked harder than normal.

"Corina," he'd said. "Come sit down here. We have to talk."

Her father sat in his armchair and lit a cigarette. Corina sat on the edge of the sofa. She looked intently at Tata waiting for him to start. Her mind had raced to try to figure out what she'd done wrong. Did she burn his dinner? Had she been unfriendly to his latest girlfriend, Marta? It never took much to set her father off, but still. Judging by his tone, she'd done something terrible.

He took a drag on his cigarette. "I have an ultimatum for you," her father said. He exhaled a ring of smoke. "You must break up with that boy Alex."

"What?" She was stunned. "But why?"

Tata didn't answer her. "If you refuse, I will turn him in to my bosses. Let me be clear: by that I mean the Party bosses."

"But, Tata," Corina pleaded. "I don't understand. What did Alex do?"

He rose from his chair. "What did he do? Do you pretend not to know?"

Corina knew her face must have shown how clueless she felt. "No, I don't know."

"I've spotted Alex slinking along the walls of buildings after curfew. I know he's involved in …" here he lowered his voice, "subversive activity."

She was genuinely surprised by the news. Surely her father could see that.

"Corina!" He raised his voice. "Stop pretending you don't know."

Emotion choked her voice. "I'm not pretending. I don't have any idea what you're talking about." She slapped her thighs. "Hasn't everyone been out after curfew some time or other? And if you do, of course you'll sneak back home so you won't be seen."

"I've spotted him more than once. And sneaking off in the opposite direction from where he lives."

She stared at him in unbelief.

"So, you're telling me you don't know your boyfriend is a spy?"

68

A gasp escaped from Corina's lips. Of course she had no idea. Not that she believed her father, but if it was true, Alex certainly had never hinted at that.

Tata walked to the balcony window and stood with his back to her as he looked out on the city, his cigarette between his fingers.

It gave Corina a few moments to think. True, Alex didn't hide the fact that he was dead set against the present regime. And Professor Filip encouraged him with some radical ideas. But who would know that? Only the students in their study group, and none of them would have passed on information about what they discussed. Could Professor Filip be a plant? Did she just pretend to have those kinds of thoughts so she could trap them? Corina exhaled. No, of course not. Professor Filip was authentic. Corina could tell that. She needed to resist the urge to suspect everyone. That's what the regime wanted, for suspicion and fear to control every citizen.

Her father bent down and snuffed out his half-smoked cigarette in the ashtray on the coffee table. "Alexandru Oprea *is* a courier for the Resistance. I want to believe that you never knew, but I'm having trouble with that." He paused. His eyes bore into Corina's. "But whether you knew or not, you are *not*—and I cannot stress this enough—to ever see him again. Do you understand?"

"But, Tata, he sits in my row in class."

"Don't you sass me, young lady! Naturally, you will still attend class, but you are not to speak to him. Not one word."

"But he'll wonder why. What do I say?" Corina ran her hands through her hair. "You said to break up with him. How do I do that without words?"

"You're a smart girl. You'll think of something." Tata sat down and lit another cigarette. "Just tell him you are breaking up because you've found someone else. Or you just don't care for him. Or whatever reason you want." He puffed on his cigarette. "Just do it quickly, and then stop talking to him."

Corina sat, stunned, staring at her father.

Another pause and another long drag. "Don't test me on this. If you don't do as I say, I will turn him in. I can only guess what the bosses will do to him, but one thing I can say for sure is that the implications will be severe. *Înțelegi?*"

"I understand what you want, Tata." Corina sucked in her breath. "But I think you're wrong."

He slammed his fists onto the arms of his chair. The ash from his cigarette fell onto the rug.

Corina jumped. She'd never seen Tata like this, and it scared her. She glared at him.

He looked into her eyes and then looked down. He placed his cigarette in the ashtray and rubbed his hands down his face.

In a gentler voice, he said, "Corina, I'm doing this for your own good." He exhaled. "Let me start over. You don't know how difficult it can be to go through life saddled with someone who brings trouble to your door, destroys your reputation. Someone who lands on the wrong side of the regime. I'm trying to save you from that."

Corina looked at him, puzzled. She knew better than to speak.

A long silence hung between them.

Finally, Tata spoke again. "You see, Corina, I know what it's like. Your mother was that person for me."

"You never talk about my mother. I don't remember much about her."

Tata got up and switched on the radio.

"First of all, you need to know your mother loved you. That was the best thing about her. She was so happy to be your mama. And she loved me. At least in the beginning. We were too young when we fell in love and got married. The first year or two was good, but then the difficulties in our life together became too much. It's hard to have a mixed marriage."

"Mixed marriage? What do you mean?"

"Your mother's name wasn't Catalina," he said. "It was Katalin

70

with a 'K.' When I married her, she was Kati Balog from Cluj—which her family called Kolozsvar."

Corina felt her mouth spring open. "Mami was Hungarian?"

"Yes." He cleared his throat.

"Why have you never told me this before?"

"I never minded that personally—I didn't have anything against Hungarians, but I minded what it meant for us. She was constantly scrutinized by the government, more than the rest of us are." Corina's father quickly looked up at the ceiling light fixture, as though he expected a microphone to be there.

He lowered his voice. "I was starting out in my career at the Dacia factory and trying to make a good name for myself. Kati's family had always suffered prejudice as part of a minority in Romania, but when you were a baby, the persecution stepped up. An informer followed your mother everywhere she went. She was forced out of her job at the beauty salon before you started school."

"She died before I started school," Corina said, her voice thick with emotion.

"Yes, she did. But it wasn't a car accident, Corina," her father said softly. "Two men in suits came to the apartment one night and forced her into a black Dacia. They told me they were taking her in for questioning." He took a breath and closed his eyes. "I'll never forget that night. Kati was sobbing. You were screaming. I had to stay with you, of course. I never found out where they took her. I was a wreck. I didn't know what to do, where to turn. I tried to find her, but the government isn't very forthcoming about people taken in for questioning."

Tears collected in Corina's eyes.

"Two nights later, one of those men came to the door. He said he regretted to inform me that my wife had had an accident in interrogation. Kati was …" Tata's voice caught. He didn't finish his sentence. The word "dead" suspended in the air, filling the empty space between them.

A sob escaped from Corina. She felt so many emotions at once, all jumbled up together: anger, sadness, confusion, grief.

"Why have you lied to me all these years? You know I've always had questions about Mami. How could you keep this from me?"

"You didn't need these burdens. Of who she was. Of how she died. It was safer for you to think of yourself as a full-blooded Romanian. A car accident just seemed like it would be easier on you. However it happened, the fact was that you had lost your mama. And you were stuck with a father who didn't know how to raise you." He looked at her and spoke in a husky voice. "I'm sorry."

Corina could sense her father's pain, but he was right; she'd always felt like she raised herself.

Her father continued. "I didn't know the first thing about taking care of a daughter, but I knew I had to keep you safe. And the best way I knew to do that was to join the Party. The very organization that brought all the misery into my life." He looked up at the light fixture again and lowered his voice. "I never believed in the Party's values, and certainly not in their tactics. But after my wife was killed, I had to make sure my daughter would be protected. And so I joined. I went along."

"So you joined the organization that *killed* her?" Corina stood up and walked to the balcony window. "How could you?"

Her father sat with his head down. When he looked up, Corina saw moisture in his eyes. "All I could think about—the only thing—was keeping you safe. I hated doing it, but please believe me, I did it for you. Because I ... I do love you, draga."

Corina let his words sink in a few moments. Had she ever heard her father say he loved her? She couldn't remember.

"I don't understand how Alex fits in with this," Corina said.

"Honestly, Corina, he seems like a nice enough boy. But I am convinced that he is a courier. I didn't lie to you about that. And if he's a courier, he will be followed, and he may be caught and thrown in prison." Tata picked up his cigarette and took another drag.

"And what would that mean for his girlfriend? Of course they'd be watching you too. Because of your mother's ethnicity, you already have several strikes against you. You're both under suspicion. Associating with Alex could pull both of you down. It could ruin your life." When he looked at her, his eyes seemed softer. His voice was softer too. "I don't want that for you, Corina. And I'm guessing you don't want that for him either."

She had to let those words settle in. "So did you mean it when you threatened to turn him in to your Party bosses?"

Tata exhaled a puff of smoke. "No." He shook his head. "I wouldn't do that. I just wanted to scare you enough that you would do what I asked." He looked at Corina. "I *do* want you to break up with him. I know you think you care about him, but other boys will come along. I promise."

Corina shook her head.

"Look at it this way: if your relationship progresses and he finds out you're half Hungarian, well … he may not be as fond of you after that. Prejudice is hard to come to grips with, but it's reality, draga."

Corina wanted to think that wouldn't matter to Alex. But it wasn't a conversation they'd ever had. She didn't know any Hungarians in Bucharest; they mostly lived in Transylvania. She doubted Alex knew any either. Did he dislike Hungarians? What would he think of her if he knew the truth?

"Please, Corina, consider your safety." Tata looked at the line of ash about to fall from the tip of his cigarette and put it out. "Consider me. Please don't break my heart again."

Corina walked into her bedroom without saying goodnight and closed her door.

When she crawled into bed, Corina picked up the tiny, framed photograph of her mother that sat on her night table. It was the only photo she'd ever seen of her. She kissed the photo.

"I'm so sorry, Mami."

When Sunday morning had dawned and Corina decided not to go to the training, she tried to dial Gabi's number to tell her she was sick. Gabi's phone didn't ring. Why did telephones have to be so unpredictable? Corina kept trying Gabi up until the time the training started. There was nothing more she could do, so she went back to bed.

She'd hardly slept last night. When she did finally drop off, she dreamed of her mother. Mami was sobbing and reaching for her as she kept fading more and more into the background.

Corina was still in bed when she heard her father leave. He usually visited Marta on Sundays. Corina got up and walked into his bedroom and started searching through his wardrobe. Surely there were more photos of her mother somewhere. Finally, she felt something with hard edges stuffed in the back and wrapped in a blanket. It was a small photo album.

She flipped the pages. It was easy to pick out her mother; it was like looking into a mirror. She saw her mother as a child, with people who must be her sister and parents. She found the photo of her parents on their wedding day. Her mother had the same glossy, straight black hair that Corina had. Mami looked happy. Corina turned the page and saw Mami holding her when Corina was a baby, Tata standing behind with his arms around Mami. She gently rubbed her finger over her mother's face.

Oh, Mami. How you suffered.

As Corina looked into her mother's eyes, another thought pressed itself into her consciousness. *How we suffered too. I suffered, and Tata suffered.*

She was still angry with her father, for all the years of lies, for not being better at raising a daughter, for asking her to do something as difficult as break up with Alex. But she began to understand why he asked.

That evening, when she knew Gabi would be home from the training, Corina tried to call again. She had to get a message to Professor Filip that she wouldn't be in school tomorrow. Still no answer. Gabi's phone must be broken.

She couldn't just not show up for school without calling someone. She couldn't call Alex, so she had to try Adriana's number next.

Corina liked Adriana, but they had a complicated relationship. Adriana always seemed to compete with Corina; first, with her friendship with Gabi, and now, her relationship with Alex. Corina was the perennial third wheel. Gabi and Adriana had called each other sister-friends since childhood, but neither of them used that term for Corina.

And then with Alex, Corina never knew if he only liked her because Adriana was out of reach. Corina knew how she felt about him, but Alex had never told her he loved her. When they were around Adriana, Corina felt like an outsider. Girlfriends shouldn't feel that way. Alex and Adriana shared such a special bond since childhood that if he had to choose between the two, Corina feared he'd pick Adriana. Corina had assumed, like everyone did, that Alex and Adriana would end up together, so she had asked permission from Adriana to even *like* him.

She should hate Adriana, but she didn't. She wanted to *be* Adriana.

Lately, she and Adriana had come to a new appreciation for each other. As she dialed the phone, she knew she had to count on that.

Adriana's mother picked up the phone. Corina tried to make her voice sound sick and weak.

"Corina! Where were you today?" Adriana asked when she got on the line.

"I'm really sick. I have the flu. I won't be in school for a while," Corina said.

"I'm so sorry to hear that."

"I may be out several days. Please explain to Professor Filip. And Alex."

"Do you want me to come by tomorrow and tell you what you missed—"

"No, please don't." She paused. "And please ask the others not to. Thank you, Adriana."

Then Corina hung up the phone. She knew what she had to do.

She cared for Alex too much to let his life be disrupted by her drama. She would do what her father asked. She would break up with Alex, for his sake, not hers.

CHAPTER THIRTEEN

ADRIANA: AUSTERITY

ADRIANA PASSED ON CORINA's message to Professor Filip as soon as she arrived at school Monday morning. She also told Alex and Gabi that Corina had the flu and may be out for several days.

"Should we go visit her tonight?" Gabi asked.

"She said no when I asked," Adriana said. "And she seemed pretty adamant about it."

Alex didn't say a word, but Adriana could tell he was upset. It must have bothered him that he wasn't the one his girlfriend called.

Adriana had known for a while that she had feelings for him. When Corina was present, she stuffed those feelings. But now that Corina was gone, Adriana felt more confused than ever.

All day at school, she couldn't get Alex out of her mind. As she walked home, she told herself she had to stop this craziness, to stop thinking about him. But the sterner she got with herself, the more she found she couldn't think about anything else. She had to do something.

She knew where she needed to go to get some answers. Last year, Jane Austen's novel *Pride and Prejudice* helped her sort out her feelings and discover something about boys: that she didn't really understand them at all. Aunt Violeta told her she had another Jane

Austen novel in the secret room. Adriana headed there. Besides, she needed a break from all the heavy novels she'd been reading. A love story sounded perfect.

Adriana entered her aunt's flat with her own key. She walked straight to the bedroom, opened the flowered doors of the bright blue wardrobe, and walked into the chamber hidden in the wall— her favorite place on earth—and started to sift through one of the piles of books.

She didn't have to look far. *Sense and Sensibility* sat near the top. She picked up the book, closed the secret doors on her way out, and snuggled into her aunt's wingback chair by the living room window, ready to get lost in another world.

As she read, she could see bits of herself in both Dashwood sisters. After their father's death—another way Adriana could relate—the older sister, Elinor, had to help her mother make all the family's decisions, but Elinor was only nineteen. Adriana discovered why Elinor took on this responsibility: she was the sensible one.

> *She had an excellent heart; her disposition was affectionate, and her feelings were strong: but she knew how to govern them: it was a knowledge which her mother had yet to learn, and which one of her sisters had resolved never to be taught.*

That sister was Marianne. Marianne loved the idea of love and listened to her feelings above all else. She did everything with her fullest energy and passion, without any moderation. Marianne never held back. She hadn't learned to control her feelings as Elinor had, and as Adriana was just beginning to learn.

Adriana kept reading until she met the girls' suitors. Edward Ferrars, the one who seemed ideal for Elinor, reminded her of Alex. He was a good man but not handsome or exciting. Adriana learned last year, through heartache, that other qualities surpassed handsome and exciting.

Marianne falls hard for a dashing man, John Willoughby, blind to his charms. He sounded a lot like Liviu, and she suspected he'd turn out to be a rogue.

Already, just a few chapters in, the novel had hooked her.

Adriana glanced out the window. The sky had darkened to the point that she would have to turn on a light to continue reading. The autumn days had begun to grow cooler and turned dark much earlier. Curfew would soon be upon her. She should use that good judgment Elinor had to call it a day. She stuffed her novel inside her coat pocket and left for home.

Adriana walked as briskly as possible, partly to keep warm, but mostly to get past the armed soldiers stationed at every corner. Recently, the number of soldiers had multiplied. They patrolled the streets and seemed to enforce the mandatory curfew with glee, as though they lived to catch some young person who was running late. She didn't want to make them happy.

Lately, life in Bucharest had become much more difficult. President Ceaușescu referred to it as the Austerity Policy. He coaxed people with the promise that loyal comrades would be rewarded if they did their part and embraced this more severe lifestyle, for the good of the state, naturally.

Romanians had lived under hardship measures all decade, but nothing in comparison to the government's recent crackdown. Nobody knew exactly why, but Adriana had heard Uncle Mihai whisper that it probably had to do with the Communist regimes thawing in nearby countries.

Poland was free. Even Russia had instituted vast changes politically and economically. Mikhail Gorbachev called the programs *glasnost*—meaning openness—and *perestroika*—restructuring. And there were rumblings of changes brewing and building to a crescendo in other countries, like Hungary. That had to make the Ceaușescus nervous, with many ethnic Hungarians living in Romania.

Adriana flashed her identification papers to a leering soldier at the park entrance. The soldier laid his chapped hand on top of hers as he read her name and address. His nails were caked with dirt. Adriana felt uncomfortable, but didn't want to let it show by wriggling her hand free. Finally, he nodded and let her pass.

Did people in the other Eastern Bloc countries have to put up with this kind of treatment? The newscasters on Romania's only channel completely ignored the momentous events taking place in countries close by. They read the scripts the state wrote for them, like marionettes controlled by unseen hands and voices. Propaganda films in classrooms across the country had become weekly events. Timo said that Romanian citizens were almost completely cut off from whatever went on outside of their isolated little world.

Rations had grown stingier. For all of Adriana's life, the main goal each day was to find food. Now food had become much scarcer, and the hunt for it more difficult.

The nightly water "hour" had shrunk to 45 minutes; sometimes just half an hour. As soon as the clock chimed 8:00 each evening, everyone would drop whatever they were doing to fill every available pot or bucket with precious water, and then dole it out to last until the next evening.

Now that they were in the middle of October, the chilly weather had dug in its heels. People needed heat inside, but the heat hadn't been turned on yet. There was talk that it wouldn't be turned on all winter. Every winter, the elderly and babies froze to death in Bucharest. Would the toll be higher this year than ever before?

As Adriana thought about all this, she increased her pace. When she made it to her flat, she saw Mrs. Petrescu in the lobby downstairs. She'd rarely seen more than the top of her neighbor's head as Mrs. Petrescu peered around her doorway. It always surprised her that she was so tall.

Adriana spotted Mrs. Petrescu leaving the flat where the chief informer for the whole building lived. The lady seemed embarrassed that Adriana saw her. Mrs. Petrescu, as the eighth-floor snitch, reported to the chief informer. She must have brought important news today, because she clutched a box of cigarettes in her hand.

That could only mean one thing: Mrs. Petrescu had been bribed.

CHAPTER FOURTEEN

ALEX: CONFUSION

A LEX STOPPED BY CORINA'S flat on his walk home from school. He knew Corina had said she didn't want anyone to come by, but he wasn't just anyone. He was her boyfriend. And he was concerned about her.

At first, nobody answered when he knocked on the door.

Then Corina opened the door. She just stood there staring, not inviting him inside.

She appeared to be really sick with this flu. Her eyes were red and puffy and she looked pale.

"Corina, I came to see how you're doing," Alex said. "Please let me inside. I'm not afraid of catching your germs, if that's what you're worried about."

Corina stepped aside and let Alex enter. He laid his hand on her arm. "How are you feeling? What can I do to help?"

"I'm surviving," she said. She took a deep breath and then exhaled it slowly. "But I do need to talk to you, so it might as well be now. Come on into the living room."

Corina led the way. She sat in her father's armchair, and Alex took the sofa. An awkward silence hung between them.

"Do you want to know what you missed in class today? Or about the training yesterday?" Alex asked.

"No, not now." She smoothed her hair. "Alex, this is hard for me to say, so I might as well jump right in." She gave him a small smile that didn't quite reach her eyes. "I think you're great, but I just don't see our relationship going anywhere. It's not fair to you for us to keep dating. Alex," she looked squarely into his eyes for just a second, then quickly looked down at her hands, "I think we should break up."

Alex sat, stunned. What? A dozen thoughts sprang to his mind, but his mouth couldn't utter one of them. He closed his eyes for a moment to help him focus, then he picked out one of his swirling thoughts. "But Corina, I thought we were getting along so well. I've been really excited about our relationship." He gazed into her eyes, forced her to look at him. "I know I'm not the most intuitive guy, but how could I be so wrong? Tell me what I've missed."

"It's not you, Alex, it's …" Corina hesitated, "you're fine just as you are. It's just … the future, I guess."

"I don't understand." Alex raked his hands through his hair. "You mean, *our* future? Are you asking how serious I am about you? Because I do see a future for us. I see us going somewhere."

"Well, I don't," Corina said, more abruptly than she usually spoke. "So I guess that's the problem."

"I … I," Alex stammered. "I don't get it. Help me understand."

Corina didn't respond for a moment. Her eyes looked up as though she was searching for an answer. "It's Adriana. I just don't think you and I will ever be as close as you are with her—"

"That's not true. Adriana and I are just friends. Really. We're close because we've been friends a long time, and we got closer when I was there when her father died. But believe me, there's nothing there."

"How can you be sure?"

"What can you possibly mean? Can you give me an example?"

"At Professor Filip's flat, the way you and Adriana laughed together. You never laugh like that with me."

"That was like a bratty sister and brother competing with each other. It's not the same—"

"Look, Alex, maybe you'll never understand. But this is just how it is." Corina stood up. "We need to break up."

Alex rose from the sofa. He nodded, afraid that if he opened his mouth, he might cry. And he did not want to do that in front of a girl who was breaking up with him.

"I'm sorry, Alex," Corina said. "I still want to be friends."

But Alex was already opening the front door to leave as she said that.

CHAPTER FIFTEEN

ADRIANA: LOVE

THE MORE ADRIANA READ in her new novel, the clearer it became. Love was something out of reach for her, at least for now. She might as well make her peace with that.

As she crossed the river on her walk home after school, the river called to her, and she decided to answer. She didn't need to hurry home. Gabi had to babysit—again—so she walked alone. She put her hands on the black iron fence, leaned over the railing, and gazed into the shallow river. The temperatures had dipped even lower lately; the chilly air helped clear her mind so she could think.

All day, she'd been thinking about one thing. One person.

Alex, not usually chatty, had been even more withdrawn today. Adriana didn't want to be a stand-in for Corina, but with her being out sick, she'd hoped to fill some of the space Corina left behind. That sure wasn't happening. Something seemed to be bothering Alex.

Anyone who read *Sense and Sensibility* could see how perfectly suited Elinor Dashwood and Edward Ferrars were for each other, just as she was with Alex. Adriana felt almost as crushed as Elinor did when she read that Edward was committed to someone else. Again, like Alex being in a relationship with Corina. What good did it do, in the long run, for Elinor to be so sensible? Elinor ended up with a broken heart, the same as impulsive Marianne.

Adriana felt a hand on her shoulder. She jumped.

"I'm sorry," Professor Filip said. "I didn't mean to startle you. I just saw you standing here and thought we could walk together."

"I shouldn't have jumped—" Adriana caught her breath. "I'd love to."

"I'm going to the Telephone Palace," Professor Filip said. "Sending a telegram to my mother. Are you going that way?"

Adriana nodded.

"You seem very pensive today. Do you mind telling me what's on your mind?"

"Boys … love … nothing big."

Professor Filip laughed. "Have you come to any conclusions yet?"

"Not really. I have questions, that's all."

"Such as?"

"People say that the most important thing for a woman to do is get married. My mother says that. But why? What's wrong with a woman taking care of herself, by herself?"

"Nothing at all is wrong." Professor Filip winked. "But I do have a bias here."

"You said before we can ask you anything."

"You want me to drop my pearls of wisdom on you?" Professor Filip asked. "I'm sorry, but I'm no expert on the subject."

"But you know more than me," Adriana said. "How did you decide it's better not to marry—ever—than to marry the wrong person?" She cleared her throat. "I think that's what you said."

"That will involve telling you my story. Do you have time for a slow walk home?" Professor Filip asked.

"If you don't mind …"

Professor Filip tucked her loose hair back into her messy bun and looked off in the distance, as though she saw mountains there, instead of ugly apartment blocks. She started walking slowly, and Adriana fell in step with her. "I was in love once. It didn't end well."

"I'm sorry."

"To tell my story, I need to take on my teacher role and start with a little history and geography. You know I'm from the Romanian side of Moldova. Do you know anything about the Russian side?"

"Just what you've told us."

"After the October Revolution of 1917, the one with the Bolsheviks and Lenin, Russia swallowed up half of Moldova. They sent ethnic Russians there to populate it and subdue the locals, and changed the official language from Romanian to Russian." She paused.

"Now on to the story. After I graduated from the university in Iaşi, on the Romanian side of Moldova, I took a teaching job there. That's when I met a guy from Chişinau, the capital of the Russian Republic of Moldova. His city was just on the other side of the Prut River from Iaşi, but it was another country. Oleg was tall, blond, nice-looking, obviously of Russian heritage. We enjoyed talking together—he knew Romanian—and, at first, we were just friends. I didn't have any women teacher friends my age and I was lonely. We enjoyed the same music. We loved taking walks. We both were curious and liked to learn new things. You'd never know he didn't finish high school. Looking back, I guess I always had reservations. Whenever I'd thought about getting married someday, I pictured a professor or a doctor or an engineer; not someone like Oleg. But we spent so much time together, it was inevitable."

Professor Filip pulled a necklace out from where she'd tucked it inside her blouse. She fingered a gold ring that hung on the necklace. "He gave me this when he asked me to marry him." She sighed. "I was so in love with the idea of love, I blurted out *yes* before I even thought about it. I hesitated to tell my family—I knew they wouldn't be happy with me marrying a Russian—so when Oleg suggested we elope, it sounded like a good idea. Once we were married, my parents would just have to accept him. But until then, they would only see the differences in our backgrounds—not only our nationalities, but also our education level. Oleg was the only one who could make money in his family—his father was dead and his mother was crippled—so he'd taken on a really risky job, something illegal my parents would never have approved of." Professor Filip lowered her voice. "He sold things on the black market."

Adriana sucked in her breath. By now, their steps had become so slow they'd practically stopped walking.

"He's the one who gave me my *bluj*. The first time I went to his flat, it was filled with stacks of blue jeans and coffee and cigarettes." Professor Filip cleared her throat. "I never liked his job, but I was willing to overlook it for a pretty face and a hope of romance."

Adriana nodded. She understood.

"One day, Oleg had to pick up a shipment in Constanța, on the Black Sea. He promised me this would be his last time to be involved with the black market. He was supposed to meet some Russian sailors who smuggled the goods in from Ukraine. After that, he'd be finished, and we'd elope when he returned." She looked into Adriana's eyes. "But he never came back."

Adriana gasped. "Did you ever see him again?"

She sighed. "I had to know if Oleg was alive or dead. I could only think of one option. I wrote a letter to his mother's address, explaining I was a friend of Oleg's. A woman wrote back, claiming to be Oleg's wife. They had just gotten married."

"I'm so sorry," Adriana said. She bit her lower lip as she thought of Mr. Willoughby in *Sense and Sensibility*.

The silence between them grew, but Adriana did not want to be the one to break it.

Finally, Professor Filip continued. "I was devastated; I didn't know what to think. A few months later, Oleg appeared outside my school one day when I was walking home. He apologized, said he still loved me. I didn't believe him. When I confronted him about his wife, he didn't deny it. He just shrugged his shoulders and smiled a stupid sheepish grin. He didn't see anything wrong with having a wife in Chișinau *and* a wife in Iași."

"What'd you do?"

"I slapped him. Screamed at him to go. And to never come back. If I hadn't asked him myself about the wife ..."

They'd stopped walking altogether by now. They stood facing each other on the sidewalk, under the shade of a tree.

"At the end of that school year, I asked to be transferred. I needed to start over in a place where I wouldn't have memories of Oleg. It took a couple years, but they finally let me come here. I arrived in Bucharest determined to devote my life to teaching. I love teaching; I really do. And this year, I have an especially fine group of young minds." She winked at Adriana.

"Believe me, I'm not settling for something by doing this job. I feel like I've finally come into my own, and I just want to live my life and be who I've become: a strong woman. One who's not swayed by what other people—especially men—think of me. Besides, I don't trust my own judgment when it comes to men. Not anymore." Professor Filip blew out a long breath.

"Thanks for telling me—"

"Look, I'm sorry if this was too personal for a teacher to tell you, and I don't mean to sound totally down on love. I've seen it work for some people. My parents for one. I'm not saying I'm completely closed off to the possibility. But personally, I'm just more content when I put it out of my mind. It's a distraction that I don't need right now."

"It wasn't too personal. It's just what I needed to hear." Adriana studied her professor's eyes. "Can I ask you one more thing?"

"Sure."

"Why do you still wear his ring around your neck?"

Professor Filip smiled with her lips, but her eyes didn't smile.

91

"To remind myself to think before I act. To not let a handsome face knock all the good sense out of my mind. If the opportunity for love ever presents itself again—and I'm talking several years from now, I just need to be sensible about it."

"I can't imagine you being anything but sensible."

"Now you know the truth. I was foolish once," Professor Filip said. She started to leave, then turned back. "Adriana, my biggest piece of advice to you is this: don't worry about love or finding a husband. Not now. Not yet. Just be yourself. Get to know who you are, what makes you uniquely you. When the time comes, I'm confident you'll know what—or who—you need. Live your life and don't go searching for love, but please, don't run away if it comes knocking on your door."

As Professor Filip walked away, Adriana made a new resolve. Starting now, she'd loosen up and stop analyzing every single thing in terms of a potential relationship with Alex. Why couldn't they go back to the way it used to be, in the old days, when she felt free to just be his friend? She would put thoughts of anything else with him out of her mind.

And she'd go a step further. Adriana Nicu decided to put love on hold until she graduated from university. She had more important things to concentrate on and, like her mentor, she didn't need the distraction.

It was with this new determination sealed in her mind that Adriana walked into class the next day. As soon as she crossed the threshold, her resolve was tested. Corina had returned.

CHAPTER SIXTEEN

ALEX: TUTORING

CORINA HAD BEEN OUT sick for three days. It had been two days since she broke up with Alex, and he hadn't been able to focus on anything since then.

On the fourth day, when Alex walked into class, the first thing he noticed was that Corina was back.

He tried to greet her, but she didn't look his way. They had to learn how to *be* around each other. They were still classmates, after all.

Adriana leaned across Gabi's desk to say hi to Corina. When Professor Filip entered, she stopped to talk to Corina.

Alex overheard Corina say, "No, I thought my flu might take a week to get over, but I guess it wasn't as bad as I thought."

"We started studying thermodynamics this week, and we'll be on this subject for a while. We need to get you caught up now," Professor Filip said. She turned to include Alex in the conversation. "Alex, Corina, I want you both to come talk to me after class to schedule Corina's tutoring."

"I don't want to put Alex out …"

"Nonsense," the professor said. "He agreed to be your tutor earlier. This is all part of it. Right, Alex?"

Alex cleared his throat. "Yes, of course. I'm happy to do it."

That is what he said out loud. But he had no idea if he'd be able to handle being around Corina again.

During the break, when everyone filed downstairs to the cantina to get tea, Alex waited to the side of the line so he could talk to Corina.

She spotted him and started to turn away.

"Corina," he called, "we can't avoid each other. Please, let me talk to you for a minute."

She turned back around and faced him.

"If it will be too hard for you to be tutored by me—" Alex said, noticing Corina wince, "I understand—"

"Oh, Alex, don't be silly. I said I wanted us to be friends, didn't I?" Corina's voice sounded breezy, but her face didn't match her words.

Gabi walked by when Corina said that. Alex wondered if she heard. Of course she heard.

He nodded. "You did say that." But how would he do that?

"Besides, nobody else knows the material like you do."

So she didn't want him as her boyfriend, but Corina wanted to use him for what he knew. That stung.

Alex got into line to buy tea and left Corina standing behind.

Gabi turned around and gave Alex a sympathetic look. Yes, she had heard. At least she didn't ask any questions.

After Professor Filip dismissed class for the day, Alex got up and stood at the edge of her desk. Corina followed him.

Professor Filip laid her papers down. "Corina, I noticed you looked lost in class. We need to get you up to speed right away so you don't get further behind. Alex, do you have time today?"

"Uh," Alex stammered, "yes, I do."

"Corina, does that work for you?" Professor Filip asked.

"Da," Corina said.

"You'll meet at Corina's flat, I assume?"

Alex noticed Corina's face. Her eyes widened. She looked worried. Alex assumed she didn't want him to come to her flat but didn't know how to say "no."

He jumped in. "We can meet at my place."

Corina's expression seemed to relax when he said that.

"Alright then." Professor Filip picked up her record book. "Glad that's settled so quickly." She opened her book and started to flip the pages. "Go and get started."

Alex and Corina donned their jackets and scarves and started walking to Alex's. In silence.

The more steps they took, the more uncomfortable Alex felt. *This is ridiculous. Why am I afraid to talk to her? We said we're still friends.*

"Corina, look, we need to get past this awkwardness, don't you think?" Alex asked. "I mean, we have to see each other every day."

He heard Corina sigh. "You're right."

Alex talked about the weather. Their study group planned for Sunday. What the defense of the motherland training had been like. Corina gave polite, short responses.

When they neared Alex's building, Alex paused outside the front door. "If there's something I did, or something I didn't do, please let me know. I can fix it. I just …"

Corina looked at him for an instant. Then she averted her gaze to her hands. "I meant what I said before. It's not you. Please don't think you did anything wrong." She cleared her throat. "And I also meant it when I said I want us to be friends. Your friendship is very important to me, and I'd hate to lose it. I'll try my best to act natural, especially around the others."

Alex nodded. "I'll try too." He opened the outside door. "Now let's see what you missed." He held the door for her. "Thermodynamics deals with heat, work, and temperature. Sound fun?"

"I can't wait to dive in." Corina giggled. Her hand hovered above Alex's arm before it settled on the door frame. "Thanks, Alex."

CHAPTER SEVENTEEN

ADRIANA: CROSSED WIRES

November 1989

THE FIRST FRIDAY IN November, Professor Filip walked to the front of the class and cleared her throat. "All educators in Bucharest have been called away for a special meeting tomorrow," she announced. "You are authorized to have a two-day break. No class tomorrow and no study group on Sunday."

Gabi nudged Adriana, her jaw springing open. Their classmates smiled, but nobody made a sound. They had years of training in how to not react.

It was so mysterious. What was the meeting about? Adriana couldn't remember school ever having been cancelled so teachers could meet. And too bad it included cancelling study group and not their military training. Something must be up.

And what was up with Corina? She'd been acting so strangely—subdued, and even sad—for days now. Adriana tried to talk to her and draw her out when she returned after being out sick, but Corina kept giving her short answers, so Adriana just gave up. She hadn't said more than a handful of words to Corina all week. Today she didn't even say hello to her. Their friendship didn't seem to be worth the effort.

These topics weighed on Adriana as she and Gabi walked home together at the end of the day.

"Gabi, have you found out anything yet about what's bothering Corina?"

Gabi bent to pick up a fallen leaf, deep red in color. "Nope."

Adriana knew Gabi too well. She was holding something back.

"But you know what's wrong, don't you?"

Gabi twirled the leaf in her fingers. "I didn't ask. I have a feeling we might never know. Subject closed."

"She sure got over the flu quick. I bet she was never sick in the first place."

"I can't even guess at that. Nor do I want to." Gabi rolled her eyes. "Look, you and I both have had our share of secrets. It's best we don't pry."

"But if she talks about it, she might feel better."

"I don't know the answer to that. But I do know one thing: you need to give it a rest. Just drop it, Adri," Gabi said. "If she tells us, it'll be when she's ready."

Adriana's face stung. "You're right …" She said those words out loud, but she didn't mean them. Gabi seemed so testy today. "Are *you* okay, Gabi?"

"I'm just … I'm so tired of having my little brother monopolize my life. I'm always taking care of him. It's just not fair."

"Maybe I can come over more, and we can watch him together."

"It's more than that." Gabi hung her head. "This morning, I—"

A tram a block ahead pulled to a stop.

"That's mine. Gotta go," Gabi yelled over her shoulder as she raced to the tram.

Adriana watched the tram door close seconds after Gabi made it inside. She hadn't even had a chance to ask Gabi what she thought about their professor's news. Or what she planned to do with her free day tomorrow.

No matter. If Gabi's foul mood continued, Adriana would be happy to spend tomorrow alone. She knew exactly what she wanted to do, and there was no time like the present to start doing it.

Adriana headed to her aunt's flat. She wanted to get lost in the complicated lives of her novel's characters and leave her own behind.

When she entered Aunt Violeta's flat, something seemed amiss. Violeta always had a basket of slippers of all sizes sitting inside the door. There was no basket. How curious. Her aunt had to have a good explanation.

Adriana hung her coat on the hook and slipped out of her shoes, tucking them neatly underneath the bench. Then she set her book bag on the kitchen table. She walked into the bedroom, opened the blue wardrobe, and entered the secret room. There she settled onto one of the cots. Her feet felt cold, so she covered them with a blanket.

When she last put her book down, the plot was at a low point. Both the Dashwood sisters were devastated, their hearts broken seemingly beyond repair.

As Adriana devoured the novel, hungry to finish it, it became progressively harder to see the words. The sun coming through the tiny window at the top cast long shadows on her book. Adriana noticed that light still illuminated the other side of the rectangular room, where the table with the banned books and the illegal typewriter sat. Adriana wondered if the sparse furnishings in the room could be rearranged so she could sit in the light.

She decided to try it. She could surprise her aunt and uncle.

She scooted the first cot down to clear the space. Then she started to swing the table around. It was too heavy to budge with all the books, so she carted the stacks of books and the typewriter to the cots.

She had to make a series of small pivots, pushing and pulling. It took a while, given the tight quarters, but if her measurements were correct, the table promised to squeeze in snugly. However, with her final pivot, one of the legs of the table seemed stuck.

Adriana bent down to lift the leg by hand. She saw the problem right away. One of the squares of wood on the parquet floor was raised and the leg was caught on that. She freed the leg and slid the table easily into the space she'd made for it. Then she pushed the first cot into the empty space where the table had been and centered the other cot on its wall.

She stood back to survey her work. It looked good. The rays from the waning sun zeroed in on the first cot, like a beam from a spotlight. But her aunt and uncle might not like that bit of flooring sticking up. So Adriana knelt down on the floor to inspect the problem square. It had probably warped somehow. She wondered if she could just hammer it back into place.

As she ran her fingers along the edge of the wood, she felt it lift up even more on one side. The whole square started to move.

Instantly, her eyes went to the spot in the wall, the loose brick that hid official papers proving her uncle's royal pedigree. When she'd discovered those birth certificates and family trees, she'd been told that something else had been hidden in the secret room. The architect, Uncle Mihai's great-grandfather, thought a hiding place might come in handy as Europe geared up for the first world war. The family didn't need a safe place then, but they did thirty years later, after the second world war, when the Communists forced Romania's royal family out of the country to live in exile. Some relatives escaped by hiding and changing their identity. However, Mihai's family kept a few proofs in case they might want to claim their heritage someday. One piece of evidence had never been found.

What if this was where it had been hidden?

She worked her fingers around the wood, prying with all her strength. Three sides came up easily, but the last one was wedged tight. Adriana looked around for something she might use as a tool.

On the table, her eyes fell upon a letter opener. She shimmied it under the stuck part like a lever and pushed down on the handle. The wood started to move upward.

She reached her fingers in and lifted the wood straight up. She saw something inside: a small wooden box, inlaid with pearls that depicted a palace with a backdrop of mountains. It looked like the royal palace in Sinaia, Peleş Palace. She pulled the box out and started to open it, but as she did, she heard the unmistakable squeak of the front door.

She looked at her watch. Right on time. Aunt Violeta closed her grocery store, like all the state-run shops, like clockwork. Adriana pushed open the chamber door and stepped through the wardrobe, eager to show Aunt Violeta what she had discovered.

But when she opened the wardrobe's double doors and stepped into the bedroom, the person she spied in the hallway was not her aunt. It was the neighbor, Mrs. Stoica. The gray-haired lady faced the living room, her back to Adriana and the bedroom.

Adriana quickly jumped back inside the wardrobe and silently closed the doors. She hoped Mrs. Stoica hadn't seen her. Or heard her.

"It's done," Mrs. Stoica said, to someone Adriana couldn't see.

Adriana heard a muffled male voice, followed by the front door clicking shut. Adriana didn't dare move.

A few minutes later, the door opened again.

"What happened exactly?" That was Aunt Violeta's voice.

Mrs. Stoica answered, "There was a short in the wiring. In the whole building. I let myself in and just now finished wrapping your fuses with tin foil." Mrs. Stoica must have followed Violeta back into the apartment.

"You could have left that for my husband to do," Aunt Violeta said.

"Now, now. We don't want to start a fire, do we?" Mrs. Stoica said.

"You keep such a careful eye out for us," Aunt Violeta said. Adriana could hear the sarcasm in her voice, but she doubted Mrs. Stoica noticed.

When Adriana heard the door close again, she remained inside the wardrobe, holding her breath, just to be sure. Why did Mrs. Stoica really come in? The fuses could have waited for Uncle Mihai. The authorities had been trying to pin something on Mihai Zaharia for quite a while. Had they asked the floor informer to plant evidence?

Adriana could no longer count the number of spies she'd encountered, and especially here, at her aunt and uncle's. All she had to do was enter the secret room, and spies would freely come in and walk through her aunt's flat, or so it seemed. She'd found hidden microphones, heard people listening in over the phone lines, and spotted shady characters lurking nearby—both here and in her own flat. Whenever she started to feel normal and let down her guard—for even a minute—something happened to remind her that paranoia held her country in its death grip.

After a few moments, Adriana opened the wardrobe and padded soundlessly into the kitchen. Her aunt had clicked on the gas burner on the stovetop. It didn't light; Violeta bent down closer and struck a match.

Suddenly, Adriana had a bad feeling. "Watch out!" she cried.

Aunt Violeta jumped. The lit match fell from her hand as Adriana pushed her away from the stove.

Adriana expected to hear a boom, or smell burning hair, or see her aunt be blown across the room from a gas explosion.

But nothing happened.

Aunt Violeta suffocated the match with her dishtowel, her hand on her heart.

"Adriana! You scared me to death." She took several rapid breaths. "What's wrong?"

Adriana stood there, shaking.

"I thought—" she said, pointing into the bedroom. Adriana whispered, "I was in there when she came in."

Aunt Violeta strode into the living room and opened the fuse box. "It's as she said. She wrapped the fuses in tin foil."

Adriana's face must have still been white with fear, because her aunt came over and wrapped her arms around her.

"You know what they say. Give a Romanian a box of tin foil and a ball of twine, and we can fix anything," she said.

"I didn't mean to scare you. I just thought the gas—"

"Come sit. Let me fix us some tea."

"When's Uncle Mihai due home?"

"Not till late tonight. Why?"

"I have to show you something."

She beckoned her aunt to follow her into the secret room, where the square hole in the floor sat exposed. Adriana had laid the wooden box with the inlaid pearl lid beside it.

"I thought I'd surprise you and move the bed so it'd get better light, but the table leg got caught on this square. And then I found this box."

Aunt Violeta picked up the box. Her eyes opened wide. "Is this what I think—"

"Maybe," Adriana smiled.

Violeta lifted the top off the wooden box. Then she sucked in her breath.

The waning light caught the edge of what was inside and reflected a brilliant green light across the room. Adriana leaned in to see better.

A green velvet cloth lay inside the box. Two exquisite emerald earrings were situated at either end of the cloth.

"The princess's earrings!" Violeta said, her voice almost reverent.

"Earrings?" Adriana asked. "Wasn't it supposed to be a necklace?"

"Look." Violeta touched an empty circular imprint in the middle of the velvet.

"Is this the proof that Uncle Mihai has royal blood?"

"It has to be. You found it!" Violeta hugged Adriana. "But the necklace is missing. Where …"

Violeta carefully picked up the earrings and lifted the velvet cloth. A small piece of paper was underneath.

Adriana couldn't sit still. "What's it say?"

Violeta read the note. "*Given to O. Grigorescu for safekeeping.*" She looked up. "It's signed *Z*. That must mean Zaharia, Mihai's grandfather, since he's the one who hid the jewels and the papers. You know Octavian Grigorescu is Bunica's father, the one who built the wardrobes."

"Do you think it's at Bunica's? The necklace?" Adriana bit her lip. A plan began to form in her mind. "We have tomorrow off school—"

"You do?"

"Long story, but I'm going to hop on a train and go visit Bunica."

"Well, if anyone can find it, it's you." Violeta beamed at Adriana. "Just be careful, okay?"

Adriana took a deep breath. "I'll be fine." She picked up *Sense and Sensibility* where she'd left it on the cot. "I'll take this home. I'm almost finished. It'll take my mind off everything else."

She kissed her aunt and went to the kitchen to retrieve her book bag, but it wasn't there. "Where—"

"Where what?"

"My book bag."

"Where'd you put it?"

"On the table." Adriana stepped into the foyer. Her book bag was hanging on top of her coat. "But I thought for sure …"

As Adriana laced up her shoes, she remembered the slipper basket. "And where's—"

The basket was there, in its usual spot.

"Where's what?"

104

"Nothing." She rubbed her eyes. Her mind must be playing tricks on her. "Good night, Aunt Violeta."

As she walked home, Adriana figured she must be even more tired than she thought. She'd started seeing things.

CHAPTER EIGHTEEN

GABI: WORDS

G ABI HELD ONTO THE overhead bar in the tram, watching the stops go by. She didn't care where it took her.

She wished she could do this morning over again. When she was hurrying to leave for school, her mother had reminded her she needed to babysit Teodor after school.

"How could I forget? That's all I ever do," she had snapped back.

Her mother hadn't said anything; she didn't need to. She just looked at Gabi with those wounded eyes of hers. "Is anything wrong?" she had asked calmly. Sweetly, even.

"Yes, *everything's* wrong," Gabi had said. "I'm so tired of always watching him. I can't do anything with my friends, like kids my age are supposed to do. I'm always tied down with *your* baby. I can't have anybody over because of what you and Papa do here, our big secret." She flung her arms out to her sides. "What about me? I didn't ask for any of this. Why does my life have to change because of all this?"

Mama had laid a hand on Gabi's shoulder. "I'm sorry you feel this way, Gabriela. I'll get Mrs. Goga to watch him today. We'll talk tonight, okay?"

"Talking, that's all we do is talk," Gabi said. "It won't fix anything."

"We'll work it out."

Gabi looked down, grunted, and stormed out of the apartment.

That only marked the beginning of the bad day. Yes, Professor Filip gave them an extra day off from school, but her friends' behavior eclipsed that news. Gabi knew Alex and Corina had broken up since that day she overheard them talking at the cantina, but since neither of them had confided in her, she felt she should pretend she didn't know anything about it. And then Adri was so nosy and just kept pushing and pushing …

Gabi couldn't handle Adri's questions, so she'd jumped on the first tram. With Mrs. Goga watching Teodor, Gabi had no reason to go home. Not yet.

She hoped her mother wouldn't tell Papa about the words they'd had, but knew that was an unrealistic wish. Her parents discussed everything. But the talk her mother had planned for her tonight? Gabi dreaded it. She wasn't afraid of her parents. They were fair and kind, and they'd never strike her. They played a more effective card: disappointment.

Gabi got off the tram when it reached Piața Unirii, and started walking as though her legs had a mind of their own. Before she knew it, she'd arrived at Uri's neighborhood. Her worries about Uri must have pulled her to this place.

Whatever brought her here, the old Jewish Quarter would be a peaceful place to sort things out. As she walked the perimeter of the cemetery, she spotted him, her white-haired friend in his unmistakable black wool coat and fedora, walking down the path with his arms folded behind him. The next moment, Uri turned the corner and saw her himself.

"Grațiela!" he called. "Where's your friend today?"

She felt relieved; he seemed much more himself today. "She's home."

Uri peered into Gabi's eyes. "I'm not always astute, but I think something might be bothering you today. Do you care to talk about it with an old man?"

Gabi shrugged. She kicked at a pebble on the path.

"Come. Let's go to our favorite bench."

Uri led the way to the bench hidden in a windowless corner of a nearby building, the place he always called the safest spot in all of Bucharest, where no eyes could watch.

"Do you want to tell me what is troubling you, dear one?"

"I feel like the walls are closing in on me. I have no life. After school, I have to hurry home to take care of Teodor. My friends can't come over to visit, because, you know—"

"Ah! Because of the church."

Gabi nodded. "How am I supposed to be a normal teenager? The other girls always talk about boys, but I don't have any time for them." She exhaled. "I just don't have a normal life. I never have, but I'm tired of it."

Uri studied his hands so long Gabi began to wonder if he'd heard her.

"Normal—is this what you want?"

"Yes."

"I think normal is overrated. Normal is boring, and you, my young friend, are anything but boring." He peered into Gabi's eyes.

It felt to Gabi as though he could see all the way through to her soul.

"Tell me, why do you want to stoop down to become ordinary, when you are already so much more than that?"

Gabi shrugged. She looked down at her feet.

"Perhaps rather than look down, you should look up. When your troubles seem overwhelming, and even when they seem light, you should cast your eyes above."

"I know you mean look to God. But I can't. I'm too ashamed."

"And why are you ashamed, my young friend?"

"I snapped at my mother. I do that a lot lately, and I don't mean to. Then I did the same thing with Adri."

"Have you explained to your mother how you're feeling?"

"Yes. I told Mama the same things I told you, but I kind of yelled it. I made a mess of it. I said I refused to watch Teodor—"

"I never would have guessed, but it appears you are human after all." Uri smiled.

"Uri, I feel stupid complaining about any of this stuff to you, of all people. What kind of normal life did you have as a teenager? You wandered—all alone—and hid out all those years during the Holocaust. How can I tell *you* I don't have a life? You must think I'm foolish. And you didn't even have a family—" Gabi started to cry. "Now I really am ashamed."

Uri placed his arm around Gabi's shoulders. She turned her face into his scratchy wool coat.

"Now, now. I don't think you're foolish at all. Just young. Nothing to be ashamed about in being young," Uri said. "It was a long time ago for me, but I can remember."

Gabi's tears had stopped. She pulled away from Uri's embrace and sat up straight.

Uri started to hum. "Let me teach you a song. Actually, it's a psalm. In Hebrew, we sing the sacred words so we can remember them. This one helps when you need to remind yourself to look up."

> *I lift up my eyes to the mountains—*
> *Where does my help come from?*
> *My help comes from the Lord,*
> *the Maker of heaven and earth.*

"That's beautiful," Gabi said. She could feel wetness clinging to her eyelashes.

"This is one of King David's psalms. People sang it on their way to Jerusalem for the feasts. When they needed help, they knew better than to look for it in other people or in anything here on earth. They looked up to the mountains, to the Lord. You told me before that you believe, Graţiela. That your parents' faith is now your own. Am I right?"

"Yes," Gabi said softly.

"Then you sing this psalm as you go on your way, as you find your path in life. Remember, don't look down; look up. It's when you feel farthest from God that you need to run to him the fastest." Uri paused. "He'll be there."

Gabi nodded. "Thank you, Uri."

"You can come talk to me anytime," Uri said. He stared into the middle distance, into a place only he could see. "One day I won't be here any longer, but someone far greater than me is always here for you, waiting for you to talk to him about whatever troubles you."

Gabi leaned over and kissed Uri's bearded cheek.

"We've been talking all about me. I didn't even ask how you're doing," Gabi said.

Uri put his finger on his lips. "Shhh! I've been hiding."

Gabi tilted her head. "Hiding?"

"Hiding! You watch out for the Iron Guard, alright? Those Nazis are everywhere."

"I will ..." *Oh, no, not that again.*

"And where's my hat? Can you help me find my hat?"

Gabi tugged on his fedora. "Can I walk you home?"

"I'd like that. Thank you."

After Gabi got Uri settled in his flat, she thought about his words as she returned home to talk with her mother. She had a sense that those words from an old man she loved would become very special to her.

CHAPTER NINETEEN

ADRIANA: THE RED WARDROBE

Armonia, Romania

ADRIANA KNOCKED ON HER grandmother's door early in the morning. It had taken some convincing before her mother finally gave her permission, but when she did, Adriana took the first train of the day to the village of Armonia.

Bunica opened the door. Her mouth sprung open but no words emerged.

"Surprise!" Adriana said.

"Draga, what are you doing here?"

Adriana kissed her little grandmother on each cheek. "We have today off from school, so I came up to see you—just for the day."

"I'm so happy," Bunica said, ushering Adriana inside. She closed the door. "But you're not spending the night?"

"No, I'm sorry. I came for a very particular reason."

Bunica walked to the water pump to fill the kettle with water. "Well, you can tell me about this 'particular reason' over a cup of tea."

"I'm looking for that emerald necklace. I found the earrings and a note that said it was given to your father. Do you know where it would be?"

"No," Bunica said, setting the kettle down on the table. "I don't."

"You've told me that your father built secret back panels in each of the three wardrobes," Adriana said. "The blue one opens to Violeta's secret room. And the books." She smiled. "The green one was meant to provide a way of escape for your friend Ester and her family." She tapped her lip. "But this one here—the red one. If the back panel opens, are you sure there's nothing behind it? No secret room?"

They both turned to study the massive tomato red wardrobe, painted with light gold and white flowers, green leaves, and dark blue swirls.

"If you walk around the cottage, you'd see that is impossible."

Bunica was already on her feet, running her hands up the back of the wardrobe, as far as she could reach, then tapping the wall behind it. She shook her head.

"Can we budge this?" Adriana asked. She opened the wardrobe door and started to pull. It didn't move at all.

"No, draga," Bunica said. "That is a solid piece of wood. And this is something we can't ask help with."

"Let's empty it and look it over."

A wooden partition divided the interior of the wardrobe in half. On the right, clothes hung from a rod, with a shelf above them. Four shelves were stacked on the left side. Adriana picked up the hanging coats and dresses and laid them gently on Bunica's bed. Then she and Bunica grabbed stacks of quilts, knitted sweaters, books, and photographs, emptying all the shelves one at a time.

Adriana moved her hands over every square inch of the interior, tapping and pounding. She climbed inside the wardrobe on the right side. She stomped her feet on the floor of the wardrobe. Nothing.

Adriana climbed back out and got on her knees, tapping the floor of the wardrobe on the left side. There was a spot, in the back below the lowest shelf, that sounded different. Hollow.

She looked, wide-eyed, at Bunica.

As she pressed her fingers hard against the wood at that spot, she heard a creaking sound, like a rusty latch springing to life. Adriana kept pressing but didn't see anything move inside the wardrobe.

"Look!" Bunica cried. "Over here!"

Bunica grabbed Adriana's arm. They both gazed in wonder at a piece of wood that had popped out of the side of the wardrobe, down at the bottom.

"It's like those wooden puzzle boxes Father used to make!" Bunica said. "I loved trying to figure out how to open them. I'd press all over and ask Father the secret. He always refused to tell me. Finally, after days or weeks of trying, I'd get lucky."

Adriana got down on her knees and tugged on the piece of wood. A shallow red drawer emerged from the side of the wardrobe. She looked at Bunica and smiled.

"This is it!" Inside the drawer sat another wooden box, identical to the one in the secret room, inlaid with pearls in the design of Peleş Palace. She pulled the box out and handed it to Bunica. "You open it."

Bunica fingered the pearls on the lid. She turned the box over. *Grigorescu* was engraved on the bottom."

Gingerly, Bunica lifted the lid. A brilliant emerald necklace was nestled inside atop a green velvet cushion. The light from the fire caught a couple facets and made them shine a dazzling green. The necklace sparkled more than both the earrings combined.

Bunica stared at it. "That's the most beautiful thing I've ever seen."

The necklace, set in gold, had one giant emerald in the center with two other large emeralds on either side. Two rows of draped chains, covered with small emeralds interspersed with diamond chips, extended to the clasp.

Adriana lifted the necklace reverently and held it up to her neck. The weight was heavy against her skin. Her eyes filled with tears. "This is Uncle Mihai's proof."

"You found it!" Bunica said. "Once again, draga, you did it."

Adriana smiled. "So what do we do with this necklace?"

"We'll put it back where it was," Bunica said. "It's the only thing we can do. The necklace has been safely hidden here for over forty years, so there's no better place."

"You're right." Adriana tenderly placed the necklace back inside its box. "Ready?"

Bunica nodded.

Together, they put the box inside the small drawer and pushed it back into the red wardrobe until they heard a click.

"We need to keep this secure for a little while longer. Someday we can let the world know Mihai is related to royalty, but not quite yet," Bunica said. "Now can we sit down and have some tea?"

CHAPTER TWENTY

TWO BOOKS

Bucharest, Romania

ADRIANA COULDN'T SLEEP WHEN she returned home after all that happened in Armonia, so she stayed up late and finished *Sense and Sensibility*. She had so much on her mind, she woke up early Sunday morning. Timo had said he had another book for her. She decided to pick that up and then return *Sense and Sensibility* to her aunt and report about her trip to Armonia.

As she stepped out of the metro at Grozaveşti, she noted that the cool morning looked like it could turn into a pretty day. The November sun played hide-and-seek among the clouds. When she crossed the street to walk to Timo's dorm, she spotted Timo coming toward her with one of the guys from that secret meeting.

"Hey, Adriana, do you remember my friend Beni?" Timo said. "Beni Barbu, this is my *little* cousin, Adriana. She's in high school."

Adriana swatted his arm.

Timo rubbed his arm and acted like she hit him hard. "You've got some muscles there, Green Eyes."

Adriana squinted her eyes at him. "Don't call me that," she said with gritted teeth.

"Don't worry," Beni said. He turned to Adriana and bowed slightly at the waist. "I never pay any attention to him. Sorry, but I have to run."

Timo called to Beni, "Don't forget. Friday night, *La Bohème* at the opera house."

Beni nodded. "I'll be there."

Timo took Adriana's hand. "You should come with us. It's an opera set in Paris. A few of my friends, guys and girls, are going."

"I don't know. I'll feel kind of out of place—"

"Look, I was kidding about the high school thing. You're only one year younger—"

"But it feels like more now that you're a college man."

"True." Timo smiled and shrugged. "But will you come anyway?"

"Can I bring Gabi?"

"Sure. I'll get two more tickets."

Adriana grabbed Timo and kissed his cheek. "Thanks. This will be fun."

She was his cousin, but Timo seemed embarrassed by the display of affection. "So, what brings you here today?"

"I came to get that book. I'm on my way to Aunt Violeta's."

"Oh, good. I need you to give Uncle Mihai a message. Can you do that?"

"Of course."

"Let's walk down to our usual spot." Once they were seated along the riverbank, he said, "Exciting things are happening these days. Nobody in Timişoara had been able to get a radio signal for a week or so, but now they've finally picked up the chatter. My friend passed on some big news to me that occurred almost two weeks ago."

"Sounds important."

"Extremely important." He lowered his voice. "Another country is now free."

Adriana covered her mouth with her hands. "Another! Which one?"

"Hungary."

"When?"

"Sometime at the end of October."

"Hungary is our neighbor. Do you think—"

"It's still a long way to go before it's our turn. Don't be surprised if things keep getting worse before they get better. But our turn's coming, and when it's here, we must be ready to act." He thumped his right fist in his left palm. "That book I promised. It'll inspire you."

"What's it about?"

"Revolution and ideals," Timo said. "Get this. Not only is it banned here today, but France forbade it when it was first published there. The emperor Napoleon even forced the author, a man named Victor Hugo, to live in exile in England." He started to stand. "And it's big. The original is over 900 pages, but mine is abridged. It's only 300-some pages."

"I'm glad."

"You wait here. I'll run up to my room and get it."

Adriana tried to digest the news about Hungary. What might her life look like if change ever came to Romania?

In no time, Timo returned with the book. He didn't bother to sit down. "I know you have to hurry …"

Adriana took her cue and grabbed the book, stowing it in one of the hidden pockets in her coat. Then she left for her aunt's, patting both pockets as she walked. One held *Sense and Sensibility* and the other a thick paperback named *Les Misérables*.

Uncle Mihai answered the door when she rapped. "Scumpita! Come on in."

Adriana noticed he had his shoes and coat on. "Were you going someplace this morning?"

"Yes, but it can wait a few minutes."

"I brought this back," she pulled *Sense and Sensibility* out of her pocket. "And I have a couple messages, one for each of you."

"Let's put that away first, then we can talk outside on our way to see Violeta."

When Adriana entered the secret room, she noticed that the warped square in the floor was covered with a small rug on top of the parquet. She pointed to the rug and smiled at her uncle.

Mihai smiled back and pumped his fist.

She placed her book on the stack on the table and carefully closed every door behind them as they exited the wardrobe and then the flat.

Once safely on the street, Uncle Mihai took Adriana's arm. "So how was Armonia?"

"Great. But first, a message from Timotei." She kept walking, her eyes focused straight ahead. A man strolled slowly in front of them. She tugged at her uncle's arm to lead him around the man.

After they'd passed him, Adriana turned to her uncle. "The radio was down for a while, but Timo's friend in Timişoara has heard that Hungary is free. He doesn't know any details."

"Hungary?"

"Yes."

Mihai whistled. A big grin spread across his handsome face. "That's two!"

"Two countries?"

"Yes. Wonder who's next?"

Adriana grinned. "Maybe us?"

Mihai shook his head. "I don't know. Sometimes I can't dare believe it could happen here."

"So ... about Armonia. I found it."

"You did?"

"Yes, I found the proof. The emerald necklace, the one that belonged to Princess Maria Hohen—"

"Hohenzollern." Mihai's eyes flashed. "Is it beautiful?"

"More exquisite than anything I've ever seen. Including the earrings."

120

He put both hands on his heart. "I don't know that I can take all this good news!"

"So does this mean you're like a prince now?"

Mihai laughed.

"Do I have to call you Your Highness?" She raised her eyebrows.

"As long as you curtsy, I think we're fine," Uncle Mihai said.

Adriana curtsied, right there on the sidewalk. Then she punched her uncle's arm. "Aren't we going the wrong way?"

"That's because Violeta is not in her shop. We're going to my office. At the concert hall."

"I've never been to your office before," Adriana said.

"Violeta is there, waiting for my cousin."

"You mean—"

He put his finger to his lips. "My royal cousin."

.

CHAPTER TWENTY-ONE

SECRETS AND SPIES

U ncle Mihai and Adriana crossed onto Calea Victoriei. They walked down the broad street to Palace Square, where Adriana pointed to the National Library. "That's where Timotei spends all his time."

"Just think, Scumpita. Libraries house books that contain ideas—ideas that can enlarge our world and open it to a sea of possibilities. But this one is situated beside two places that do the opposite, that squelch ideas: the headquarters of the Securitate and the Communist Party's Central Committee. They've effectively closed our world off and made it small."

Adriana shuddered. The places of spies and secrets. She'd never forget being interrogated in the Securitate building.

When they had passed those massive buildings, they arrived at the Atheneum, Romania's ornate circular concert hall, fronted by a portico of Ionic columns and a long green lawn sporting a large statue of beloved poet Mihai Eminescu. Uncle Mihai led Adriana along the side of the building to a nondescript entrance in the back. They entered a dark narrow hallway that he said ran along the backstage area, climbed down a flight of stairs, and followed a cavernous path of short hallways with enough turns that Adriana didn't think she'd ever find her way back by herself. They arrived at Mihai's office, the last door in the hallway. The sign on the door read "Concertmaster." Even though Aunt Violeta was supposed to be there, Adriana noticed no light spilled out underneath the closed door. It was as silent as the tomb it felt like they'd entered.

When Mihai opened the door, it took a few moments for Adriana's vision to adjust to the dark. The large office was filled with messy stacks of music scores, various instruments and music stands against the wall. The walls were covered with wooden panels bearing framed programs and photos from significant symphonies. Mihai's massive oak desk faced the door, his leather chair behind it and several wooden chairs scattered around.

But Violeta was not there.

Adriana looked at her uncle and raised her eyebrows.

He whispered to Adriana, "There are several perks to being the concertmaster. I get not one but two offices." He gave her a smile that was all in the crinkles around his eyes. "But only a few select people know about the second one."

Mihai pressed on one of the wall panels behind his desk. The panel swung in, toward his desk. He leaned into the hidden space. "It's Mihai. You're safe," he said. Then he motioned to Adriana to follow him.

They stepped inside an unlit space. It felt like the secret room. Before Adriana could see clearly, she felt a fur coat brushing against her skin and smelled perfume. It was rare for anyone to wear perfume.

Mihai struck a match and lit a sconce on the wall.

Adriana could see her aunt and another woman. The space was about half the size of Mihai's office. More wooden chairs sat in a circle. The opposite wall held another door.

"Adriana! I didn't expect to see you here," Violeta said. Her gaze traveled from her niece to her husband.

"It's okay," Mihai said. "She's with me."

The woman who stood next to Violeta had perfect posture. Her flawlessly coifed hair was swept back in a French twist.

"My cousin, Ofelia," Mihai said, indicating the woman. "Ofelia, please meet my niece, Daniel Nicu's daughter."

Ofelia graciously offered her manicured hand to Adriana. "I'm very sorry for your loss."

"*Mulțumesc.*" Adriana had never met a royal before, unless she counted Uncle Mihai.

"Adriana's the one who found … what you were discussing," Mihai said.

"I'm grateful to you for that," Ofelia said. Her tone was formal and her enunciation crisp.

"We were composing a message for your relatives, Mihai," Violeta said.

Adriana knew she referred to King Mihai, exiled in Switzerland.

"What do you have so far?" Mihai asked.

"That the Resistance is alive and strong. The monarchists are organizing and are willing to do whatever's necessary to restore the family to their rightful throne. If they will ever be in a position to return, there is a groundswell of support for them."

"Good, good." Mihai stroked his chin. "How will this be delivered?"

"It will be encrypted and passed along several links. That's all you need to know," Ofelia said. "For our mission to be successful, the fewer people who know the links in the chain, the better. It's for your own safety."

Violeta smiled at Adriana. "We will also tell them that we've found *some* proof of your identity as their relatives. Unless …" she looked at Adriana, "do you have more news?"

Adriana felt herself beaming. "I found the necklace!"

Violeta's face lit up. "Where?"

"In Bunica's wardrobe."

"Superb!" Ofelia murmured.

Mihai's low voice became even softer. "This is a day for wonderful news. There's more. Just in from Timişoara."

"About Hungary?" Ofelia asked.

Mihai nodded. "Hungary is now free," he said.

Violeta gaped at him.

"Tell me," Ofelia said. "How did you hear?"

"Adriana told me," Mihai said. "How long have *you* known?"

"I've only just received the intel myself," Ofelia said. "But we can see how the word is spreading. The Ceauşescus won't know how to handle this."

"Any details?"

"It happened on 23 October," Ofelia said. "It was a peaceful exchange of power. The Communist regime simply turned over control." She smiled. "Hungary is now a democracy!"

"I don't know how to react. I think I'm stunned," Violeta said.

"It's interesting that the Hungarian people intentionally delayed finalizing the exchange until that particular date," Ofelia said.

"Why'd they wait?" asked Adriana.

"It's the anniversary of their twelve days of freedom in 1956, when they captured Budapest back from the Soviets," Ofelia said. "It was short-lived, but none of the other Eastern Bloc countries managed to do that."

"And now I must leave to pass the news about Hungary on to my contact," Mihai gestured toward the other door. "It might be better if you all leave before me."

"Ofelia, can you come sometime to see the jewels for yourself?" Violeta asked.

"I'm afraid not." Ofelia shook her head. "I trust you to take good care of them."

With that, Ofelia took her leave. She opened the door on the far wall and entered a dark space.

"She leaves a different way than you will," Mihai whispered. "This old building has its share of secrets. When it was built in

1888, the royal family often brought clandestine guests to sit in their private loges in the balcony and watch the performances. They wanted them to exit without a lot of fanfare, so they had secret hallways and underground tunnels built that lead to entrances far from the building itself. This is how Ofelia comes and goes."

"But doesn't the Party now use the tunnels the royals used to use?" Violeta whispered back.

Mihai nodded. "Probably. But Ofelia moves around like a ghost. Nobody will spot her. Trust me. She's skilled at disappearing."

Violeta looked skeptical.

"Uncle Mihai, will you tell me the truth about something?" Adriana asked.

Mihai looked surprised. "Always."

"When you were arrested before, I thought—I was certain—you were innocent …"

He smiled. "I've been part of the Resistance for some time now. I guessed I was probably passing along important intel, but I honestly didn't know. So, yes, technically, I was guilty, but no, it wasn't wrong to do it."

"I'm glad you did it," Adriana said softly.

Mihai hugged Adriana. "Now it's your turn to leave. You don't need to hide," Mihai said. "If anyone sees you two leaving, just say you came to visit me at work."

He blew out the candle and led the way through the wall panel back into his office. Then he kissed Violeta goodbye.

Violeta and Adriana left, arm in arm, walking out the back door, wide open for anyone to see.

Once they were outside, as Adriana waited for her eyes to adjust to the light, she looked over at Athenee Palace Hotel, next door to the Atheneum. It was the classiest hotel in Bucharest and a hot spot for espionage and intelligence gathering. Everyone knew that a Securitate colonel managed the hotel and all employees were Securitate agents. The maids photographed every item inside the foreign guests' suitcases, even poking through their trash, while every room and restaurant table held hidden microphones.

As Adriana gazed at the hotel doors, she saw something—somebody—that made her freeze. Coming out of the Athenee Palace Hotel was Captain Zugravescu.

Adriana grabbed Aunt Violeta's arm. "It's that man," she whispered.

Without discussing it, both of them intuitively turned and put their heads down. They stood perfectly still. Any movement might catch his eye.

Adriana hoped Zugravescu didn't see them, but if he did, so what? They'd done nothing wrong. There was no reason they couldn't visit Mihai at work on a Sunday. Instinctively, she reached for her coat pocket with the new novel hidden inside, patting it to be sure the book was still there. Suddenly, she had an irrational fear that Zugravescu would be able to see it through the thick fabric of the coat.

Even with her eyes downcast, she watched Zugravescu out of the corner of her eye. When he climbed into a black Dacia and left, she exhaled relief.

"Are you okay?" Violeta reached over and tucked Adriana's bangs behind her ears, leaving her hand there a moment.

Adriana nodded.

"Now I know who to look out for."

Adriana clung to her aunt's arm as they walked away.

When they reached Violeta's street, Adriana split off to walk home alone, cutting directly through the park. She felt on edge as she walked, constantly looking back over her shoulder. It had been an intense couple of days, starting with her trip to Armonia and finding the necklace. Everywhere she turned, she encountered more secrets and more spies, both good and bad. It's no wonder she jumped when the guards at Cişmigiu Park asked to see her papers.

When she arrived back home and climbed the steps to her floor, she spied Mrs. Petrescu stepping inside her own flat with a box of chocolates in her hand. Another spy. Mrs. Petrescu seemed surprised to see Adriana. She whipped the chocolates out of sight as quickly as she could. The only way people got chocolates was if they'd been bribed by someone with black market connections.

Adriana opened her door and called out to her mother. No one answered. She stepped out of her shoes, hung up her coat, and removed her latest novel from her coat lining.

She walked into her bedroom to stow the book out of sight. When she lifted her mattress to slide the book underneath, she noticed a blank spot on her nightstand where the photo of her father always sat. She felt a sense of panic. She couldn't have lost that precious photo. Where could it be?

While she puzzled it out, she noticed a picture frame sitting on her windowsill on the other side of her bed, facing the window, like it belonged there. She turned it around. It was the picture of Tati. What was it doing there?

Adriana looked closer at the nightstand where the photo should have been. A few days ago, she'd noticed a layer of dust on the table, her signal to get busy cleaning her room. But she hadn't gotten around to that yet. There should be a mark in the dust to show where the photo used to be. But there wasn't even a speck of dust on the table's surface anymore. Her mother must have dusted and, for some strange reason, moved the photo. That was the only explanation. The only explanation she wanted to entertain.

If it hadn't been Mama, then someone else broke into their flat. Adriana shivered at the thought. Did this person pay Mrs. Petrescu in chocolate to move the photo?

The alternative was that she'd moved it herself, without being aware that she did it.

Adriana had to forget about it until her mother came home and she could ask her about Tati's photo. She decided to make a cup of tea, always a good idea when she felt stressed, so she put the teakettle on the stove. She opened the tin to get a bag of black tea, but instead she found green tea. Last night, when she made tea for her mother, she was certain they had about ten black tea bags in the cannister, and only black tea bags. They would never have been able to find any other kind of tea in the store. But now, the tin contained three bags of green tea. No black tea bags.

Who put them there? And why?

CHAPTER TWENTY-TWO

ALEX: RESISTANCE

ALEX WAS GLAD HE had something important to do today. He needed to try to clear his head of all the confusing emotions swirling inside since Corina had broken up with him.

Something about Corina had changed. She'd only been sick for three days, but she seemed different. Preoccupied.

He still couldn't believe it. He'd thought things were progressing well between them; what did he know? Shouldn't *Alex* be the one to decide what was best for him? He knew what he wanted. He promised himself he would wait for her, no matter how long it took.

He just didn't understand girls at all. For years, he'd thought he and Adriana were meant for each other. They made sense together, and he liked things that were logical. But then Adriana fell for Liviu, of all people, and it turned out she just saw Alex as a brother. He figured he just wasn't the kind of guy girls thought twice about. Then one day, he woke up and wham! He realized he had feelings for Corina. The best part: she liked him as much as he liked her. At first, she seemed less complicated than Adriana, until he discovered he didn't understand her either.

It was all so confusing. Now Alex felt awkward around two of the three girls in his study group. He couldn't avoid them forever. At least today they'd get a break from their group. He needed time to figure out how he should act around them.

He wished he had somebody to talk to about all this. He didn't really have any guy friends. Everyone just hung out with the kids who sat next to them in class, and he'd always been in a row of girls. He wished he could talk to his mother, but she was snoring on the sofa with an empty bottle of vodka on the floor next to her. Besides, what could she say that would help?

He'd just about decided to broach the subject with Gabi—spunky Gabi who always knew how to cheer him up, safe Gabi too busy being a second mama to her baby brother these days to even think twice about boys—when the phone rang.

He picked it up. "Da."

A strained voice spoke. "May I speak to Aurel?"

"You have the wrong number," Alex said.

"I'm sorry. I must have dialed your number by mistake." Then the line went dead.

That was Alex's signal to pick up a message from his operative at the *farmacie* on Strada Aurel Vlaicu. Usually when Alex walked to the secret meeting place, it was late at night, so he'd creep along city streets under cover of darkness, hugging the buildings, bending low whenever he came to a window, until he reached the alley behind the closed-down pharmacy. But today was a Sunday that everyone had free, and a particularly sunny one on the heels of the recent preview of winter. When he stepped out onto his street, he could see that the whole city's population seemed to be outside.

He sauntered on his way, right out in the open daylight, as though he was merely taking a stroll. When he reached the pharmacy, he tried to act nonchalant as he walked around to the back. Once there, he looked all around to be sure that no eyes were watching.

When he felt convinced, he opened a window and climbed inside, making his way to the office behind the old storeroom.

He waited, alone with his thoughts.

Alex didn't hear a thing. Ofelia entered so quietly, it seemed like she must be a ghost. But as always, he knew she had arrived by the scent of her perfume. It was her giveaway.

"Did anyone see you?" Ofelia asked, stepping out of the shadows. As always, she looked polished and unruffled.

"No." He shook his head. "I don't think so."

"I received a message today from our operative. You must deliver this message to your contact immediately. Tell him that Hungary is now free as of 23 October."

Alex gasped.

"We must be extra careful now and increase our alert level. Our government is afraid, and they'll clamp down even harder. Tell him that part too."

"I will."

"He will know what to do with the news. Now go."

Alex walked faster on his way to Gabi's than he had to the pharmacy. His contact was Gabi's father, Constantin Martinescu, one of the many people from all walks of life who had joined the Resistance. Alex had been recruited to be a courier along with Adriana's bunica.

As he walked, he thought about the significance of the news. Hungary and Poland were both free! News like this was exactly what he needed to snap him out of his despondency about Corina.

He knocked on Gabi's door. Shuffling noises came from inside, but nobody opened the door. They couldn't pretend they weren't home; he'd heard them. Alex had to deliver this news to Gabi's father personally, but if no one answered the door, where should he go?

As he debated what to do, the door opened. Mrs. Martinescu stood there with a scarf covering her hair.

"Are you here to see Gabriela?" she asked.

"Yes, but first, if it's not a problem, I would like to speak with Mr. Martinescu."

Gabi's mother invited Alex into the foyer, while she called, "Constantin, can you come here?"

He noticed that the flat was completely dark. That seemed strange since it was full sun outside.

Mr. Martinescu appeared a few seconds later. He merely looked at Alex's face and seemed to know why he was there. He bent down and whispered, "Do you have some—"

Alex whispered directly into Mr. Martinescu's ear, "Hungary became free on 23 October. The government's scared, so be extra careful."

Mr. Martinescu put his broad hands on each of Alex's shoulders. His smiled with his whole face. "Thank you, son."

Alex cleared his throat. "May I speak with Gabi now?"

"Of course." Mr. Martinescu turned. "Gabriela, you have company."

As Gabi came to the door, Alex caught a glimpse of the living room. Thick drapes completely covered the windows. His eyes had adjusted enough that he could see that a couple sat on the sofa. He noticed the other woman with a scarf on her head like Gabi's mother wore.

"Can we go outside?" Alex asked "I didn't realize you had people—"

"Yes, let's go." Gabi stepped into her shoes, grabbed her coat, and practically pushed Alex out the door.

She took his elbow and led him down the steps rapidly. They were out on the street before Alex could think.

"What was that all about?" he said.

Gabi put her index finger to her lips and pulled him with her in the direction of the river.

Once they were safely away from anyone who might hear, Alex asked again. "Was that a secret meeting? Part of the Resist—?"

"What do you mean?"

"The curtains drawn. People inside. You in such a hurry to leave."

"Shhh," Gabi said. "I shouldn't tell you this, but you already suspect something. My father's the connection between the group you just tried to name and an even more subversive group."

"What can be more subversive than the Resistance?"

"Think about it. What did Karl Marx say was the opium of the people?"

Alex felt his jaw drop. "You mean … religion?"

Gabi smiled. "You got it. You, my friend, just stumbled on an underground church."

Alex didn't know what to say. He just stared at Gabi.

"Did you have something specific you wanted to talk to me about, or did you just want an excuse to get out of there?" Gabi asked.

"I do have something." Alex ran his hands through his hair. "I need to ask your advice, if that's okay."

"Sure. About what?"

"Girls."

Gabi laughed. "You've come to the right place. There's a nice bench up ahead. Let's sit and talk and I'll tell you everything I know."

CHAPTER TWENTY-THREE

ADRIANA: FRANCE

Before Adriana poured her green tea, she heard a knock at the door. She opened it cautiously.

"Gabi!"

"Hi, Adri. I can't stay long—curfew. But I have something to tell you."

Adriana opened the door wide for her to enter. They stood in the hallway.

"Alex came to visit me today."

"Alex?"

"Yes. He wanted advice. He said Corina broke up with him."

Adriana's eyes opened wide. What timing, now that she'd decided to put love on hold. Could this be what Professor Filip meant about love presenting itself to you when you're not even looking for it?

"I know what you're thinking," Gabi said.

"How do you know?"

"For one thing, you're biting your lip, and you always bite your lip when you're deep in thought." Gabi crossed her arms. "For another, I know you, Adri. You're my best friend."

"So what am I thinking?"

"That you might have a chance with Alex after all."

Adriana shrugged. *What was wrong with that?*

"Just remember that Corina's our friend."

"Some friend. She won't even say hello to me these days."

"Look, they're both hurting."

"Well—"

"I told Alex to try to act normal and the same goes for you. You two are like brother and sister, and you can't let anything weird come in to mess that up." Gabi cleared her throat. "He didn't say it was a secret, but still, you can't let him know that I told you any of this."

"I won't. I promise," Adriana said.

Gabi put her hand on the door handle.

"Before you go," Adriana said. "How'd you like to go to the opera on Friday night? It's *La Bohème*."

Gabi squealed. "I'd love to!"

"Can you get away? What about Teodor?"

"My mother … well, the other day, I got upset about always watching him. My mother and I had a big talk. She said she doesn't want me to resent my baby brother. So, she talked to a friend who agreed to come over every afternoon to babysit."

The relief was written all over Gabi's face.

"Nice." Adriana smiled. "So, you can go?"

"Yes." Gabi's whole face lit up.

"My cousin Timotei invited me. And get this," Adriana lowered her voice. "We're going with some college friends of his."

"What? I've never done anything with college students before."

Adriana laughed. "Me neither." Unless she counted that secret meeting she'd crashed.

Minutes after Gabi left, Adriana's mother returned from her extra shift.

Adriana poured two cups of tea, still warm, and sliced some bread. She brought it on a tray and set it on the coffee table.

Her mother had already clicked on the TV and curled up on the sofa.

"You must be tired. You never have a free day off work."

"I am, draga. Exhausted, actually."

The state news was on. They both watched and ate without speaking.

Adriana wasn't surprised by what she saw, or rather, didn't see. The commentators said nothing about Hungary, just like they'd said nothing about Poland.

When the show was over, the broadcast went to static. Adriana turned it off.

"Mama, did you dust my room?"

"Are you asking me to clean your room? When I just said how tired I am? You know that's your responsibility. I refuse to do your chores for you."

"That's not what I meant …"

If her mother didn't move it, then who moved her photo? Adriana *knew* where she'd put the photo, just like she knew where she'd put her bookbag at Aunt Violeta's. She had no doubt. She felt like she must be losing her mind.

"Well, I'm too tired to get into a discussion tonight," Mama said. "If you can clean the dishes when the water comes on, I'm going to get ready for bed. *Noapte buna.*"

Adriana went into her room and turned on her bedside light to read *Les Misérables*.

She knew she'd agreed to let Mama approve all the novels she read. She'd had no problem getting her to say yes to *Sense and Sensibility*. After last year when Adriana lost her head over Liviu, her mother had seemed thrilled that she might learn how to be more sensible when it came to boys.

But the books Timo gave her were too political for her mother. Adriana couldn't imagine her ever approving those. She'd successfully kept *Animal Farm* hidden from Mama, and she'd do the same with *Les Misérables*.

Adriana loved nothing more than the prospect of a new novel, so she burrowed under her duvet and started reading.

The story began in the French countryside in 1815. Jean Valjean is released from a horrible prison where he served nineteen years—for the terrible crime of stealing a loaf of bread. As an ex-convict, he's turned away everywhere he goes, until he comes to a bishop who invites him in. Valjean repays the bishop's kindness by stealing his silver. The police capture Valjean and haul him back to the bishop to verify that the silver belongs to him. The bishop covers for Valjean. He claims he'd asked Valjean to sell his silver, and Valjean had forgotten to take his candlesticks. The police release Valjean and the bishop adds the silver candlesticks to Valjean's loot, an undeserved gift.

> The bishop approached him, and said, in a low voice:
> "Forget not, never forget that you have promised me to use this silver to become an honest man."
> Jean Valjean, who had no recollection of this promise, stood confounded. The bishop had laid much stress upon these words as he uttered them. He continued solemnly:
> "Jean Valjean, my brother: you belong no longer to evil, but to good. It is your soul that I am buying for you. I withdraw it from dark thoughts and from the spirit of perdition, and I give it to God!"

Adriana couldn't wait to find out if Valjean keeps the promise he never made. She decided to stop there. She had a lot to think about.

Life for Romanians meant being punished for wrongs they never committed. How freeing would it be to be forgiven of bad things you did do? She could not fathom what that would feel like.

On Friday, Adriana and Gabi hurried to their respective homes after school to get ready for the opera. They'd discussed what to wear, which hadn't been that difficult since each of them had only one nice outfit, but they wanted to add a few touches to make it special. Adriana put on her faithful green dress with the flouncy skirt, the one her father had always said perfectly matched her eyes. Her mother let her borrow her flower brooch, the most precious thing she owned. A single pearl formed each of the petals, set in gold, with a cluster of real ruby chips in the center. Tati gave her the brooch as an anniversary gift.

When the girls met at the metro station, they giggled to see each other so dressed up. Gabi had curled her hair and pulled it back with her mother's amber hair combs. Adriana told Gabi she looked exotic. Gabi complimented Adriana's elegant brooch.

Adriana kept checking her pocket to be sure the tickets were still there. *La Bohème, 10 November, 18:00.* She also checked for the paper that stated she had official permission to stay out past curfew. They walked to the opera house to meet Timo and his friends. Timo thought if they all walked down the street together, the group would be too large and they would draw attention. Whenever Timo exercised caution, Adriana knew she'd better heed it.

Adriana and Gabi arrived at the National Opera early. Excitement about seeing an opera had won over her nervousness about spending an evening with university students. A large banner bearing the name *La Bohème* hung suspended from each of the two outer arches along the front of the white building.

They waited to the side of the massive entrance door, centered under the middle arch. To try to keep warm in the chilly night air, the girls pulled their neck scarves tighter, hopped in place, and blew into their gloved hands. Their shivering continued, so they decided to keep moving. They stepped onto the lawn in front of the opera house to look at the massive sculpture of famous composer George Enescu, seated on his throne as though he ruled the opera. From that vantage point, they strained to check out each person who walked down the sidewalk from the direction of the dorms. Where were Timo and his friends?

Adriana kept looking at her watch. The minutes ticked by, and she started to worry.

"Timo gave me our tickets," Adriana said. "Should we just go in?"

"Will he get mad if we don't wait?"

"Maybe, but I don't want to miss anything either."

Gabi shrugged. "They could already be in there, wondering where *we* are."

Adriana didn't think being early sounded like her cousin's style, but she didn't want to be forced to stand out in the lobby until the first break, so the girls entered, showed their tickets and were handed their programs. When they found their seats, high up in the balcony, they could see that the other seats in their row sat empty.

They had time to read the program. Giacomo Puccini wrote *La Bohème*. Even though the story took place in Paris in 1830, the opera itself was in Italian.

Seconds before the curtain began to rise, Timo and his friends rushed in. Timo slid into the seat next to Adriana, followed by Simona and another girl, and then Marcu and Beni. Then the first notes sounded.

Adriana noticed a man in a black hat and coat leaning against the wall, watching them. A nagging thought in the back of her mind warned her to watch out for him, but soon she became so caught up in the story that she forgot.

She had never seen a set design so exquisite or heard music so superb. As far as Adriana could follow, Act I began with a group of young starving artists, the bohemians, living in an attic apartment in Paris. In the second act, one of the Bohemians, Rodolfo, falls in love with a seamstress, Mimi.

As Act II ended and the curtain went down, it was time for intermission.

Adriana looked for the man against the wall. He had gone, but she'd noticed other men, also in black coats, milling around, looking at the audience instead of the stage. She felt on edge but didn't have time to dwell on it.

"This is my favorite cousin, Adriana," Timo said to the girl Adriana hadn't met, putting his hand on Adriana's head. Then he turned to Adriana. "And this is Simona's roommate, Rodica."

Adriana smiled and touched Gabi's arm. "I'd like to introduce my friend, Gabi."

"Gabi, those two guys are Marcu and Beni. Simona here comes from Timişoara. We've known each other forever," Timo said. He draped his arm casually around Simona's shoulders.

Simona pushed against Timo's chest and laughed. Her short brown hair, cut in a mass of layers, combined with her smile to give the impression of playfulness.

Did Timo *like* this girl? Adriana had never seen her cousin act this comfortable with any other female. Out of the corner of her eye, she noticed Gabi raise her eyebrows. Gabi had picked up on the chemistry too.

Simona was cute, but Rodica was a beauty with her classic porcelain skin and dark features. Adriana felt suddenly conscious of how her best efforts to look sophisticated paled in comparison to Rodica.

As some of their group left to stretch their legs out in the lobby, Timo looked all around and then leaned in and whispered to Adriana, so softly she had to strain to hear.

"Sorry we were late," he said. "I heard something on Radio Free Europe, and I had to keep listening. Big things are happening, and

I mean big." He looked into Adriana's eyes. "Last night, people in Berlin—I can hardly believe this is true—jumped up on top of the wall that has separated East and West Berlin for all these years, the same wall where most everyone who tries to escape is killed—"

"Shhh. Not here."

"I'm not afraid." He paused. "They started tearing it down! It happened last night. Remember the date—9 November. That is the day the wall came down."

Adriana stared at him and mouthed the words, "The Berlin Wall?"

"They used chisels and hammers and their bare hands. They've still got a lot more of the wall to take down, but enough is gone that people have been flooding across it. They are leaving, and nobody is stopping them."

Adriana looked around her at the people seated in the opera. "I bet nobody else here knows this."

"Probably not."

"This is amazing!"

Just then, her new friends returned. Act III began shortly after.

Adriana sat there and tried to listen to the beautiful music and look at the exquisite set designs of Paris, but she felt as though she watched herself watching. Her mind was hundreds of miles east of Paris. Her mind was in Berlin.

She could tell that the rest of the opera was a tragedy. Rodolfo leaves Mimi, but after she gets some terrible illness, she returns to the attic and sings with Rodolfo about their past happiness. But it's too late; Mimi dies.

People all around Adriana dabbed their eyes or cried openly at the beauty of the music and the melancholy story. Tears collected in Adriana's eyes, but they weren't tears of sadness.

Hers were tears of sheer joy. The Berlin Wall was coming down!

CHAPTER TWENTY-FOUR

ALEX: HOPE

LEX WAS RUNNING ON sheer adrenaline. He'd met with Ofelia at the vacant pharmacy last night at midnight and received the most incredible news. He couldn't think of anything else. The Berlin Wall coming down fueled him. He did his duty as courier, passing the news on to the next links in the underground chain. When he returned to his flat, he couldn't sleep.

How could anyone who knew what was happening sleep for even a second?

When he arrived at class the next morning and saw Corina sitting at the opposite end of his row, quiet and withdrawn as she had been lately, he realized he hadn't thought of her once all night. His mind was full of possibilities of another kind. He felt an emotion so rare he struggled to identify it. Finally, Alex gave it a name: hope. He felt hopeful about the future. It had nothing to do with Corina, or any other girl for that matter.

Adriana squirmed in her seat and seemed as antsy as how he felt. At the first break, he pulled her aside and whispered, "Have you heard? You seem like you know."

She just nodded and squeezed his shoulder.

That afternoon, the class had to watch another propaganda movie about the evils of America and capitalism. Alex smiled to himself. He was certain the frequency of these films proved that the government was scared. Ofelia warned him that the more unsure the officials became, the more they would clamp down. She predicted that things would get worse before they got better.

The film ended with the glare of a bull's eye on the screen and rapid clacking as the end of the tape kept looping around. Liviu flipped the projector's switch off and strode to the front of the classroom.

Alex liked it better when Liviu sat at his big important desk in the back of the room. Even though he couldn't totally ignore his presence, he didn't have to look at him and he could pretend he wasn't there. But not now.

Alex could see how Adriana had gone a little overboard for Liviu. With his defined muscles and the dark stubble on his face, Liviu looked older than the rest of the guys in their class, and he probably was. Alex wouldn't be surprised if he had failed a grade or two. Like a cheap coat of whitewash sprayed on to cover scuff marks on a wall, Liviu's outer charms had soon worn away to show the hollowness inside.

"Comrade Professor Filip has asked me to address an important issue," Liviu began.

Professor Filip cleared her throat. She stood in the back of the classroom. "Professor Filip is enough," she said.

Liviu leveled his steely gaze on her. "Not comrade?"

"Too many words," she said. "Professor Filip will do."

"I see." Liviu raised his eyebrows and made a quick notation in the small notebook he always carried. He cleared his throat. "You will all report to the military training grounds at 7:30 sharp tomorrow and every Sunday for the rest of the month." Liviu paced in front of the class, first to the right and then to the left, with his hands clasped behind his back. "As you'll recall, at the first training of the Youth's Preparation for Defense of the Motherland, the officers and I organized you into platoons, with platoon leaders. Your success in defending the Motherland involves each person, each platoon, carrying their weight, working together like a fully functioning machine. If one platoon fails, you all fail. The students in the platoon led by Alexandru Oprea were evaluated at the last training exercise and deemed a sloppy mess. Because of that one platoon, you are *all* required to meet for regular training *every* Sunday from now until everyone gets it right."

Alex noticed a few people begin to grimace, but when Liviu caught their eyes, they swallowed any trace of an expression. "This will take the place of your study groups until you are notified otherwise," Liviu continued. Alex felt Liviu's eyes boring into his own. "You do not want to find out the consequences to being late or causing any other issue."

Why did Liviu always try to humiliate Alex? Last year, for the first time in Alex's life, he was initially excited when another guy had joined his row. Why did it have to be someone as cocky as Liviu?

Nobody liked the training exercises, but the worst part for Alex was missing their study group. He knew that whatever Professor Elisabeta Filip planned to impart to them was something far superior to the military techniques they'd learn. She'd already inspired them with things they needed now more than ever.

Gabi had encouraged Alex to just be himself around Corina and Adriana, and he'd expected to be able to test it out at tomorrow's study group, but now they wouldn't be meeting. He felt confident that he could act natural with Adriana, but it didn't seem like anything or anyone mattered to Corina these days, least of all Alex. She seemed completely withdrawn from her friends.

Alex raised his hand. "Mr. Negrescu," he said when Liviu acknowledged him. "Excuse me, but I thought the state was concerned that we grasp the engineering principles we've been learning.

Haven't we been told that the best way we can defeat the enemy is with our engineering know-how, with the strength of our minds? But you seem to indicate our physical strength may be more important. I'm confused. Could you explain the difference between yield strength and tensile strength to us?"

"Of course, but ..." Liviu seemed caught off balance. "The point is you need to be prepared to defend—"

"How does compressive strength fit in?"

Liviu started to open his mouth, then closed it.

"Isn't it true that ultimate strength shows the maximum stress we can sustain without breaking?"

"Oprea, a word. Outside." Liviu gestured toward the door.

Once they were both in the hallway, Liviu turned and hissed at Alex. "You better watch out. I know what you're trying to do, but you forget I'm the one in control here. I have been trained to become the most powerful leader I can be. And nobody—certainly not you, not by a long shot—can get in my way. I can just squish you like a—"

Alex held his hands up. "It was just an honest question."

"You'd better be on time tomorrow and ready to work. I'm watching you." With that, Liviu turned back into the classroom.

CHAPTER TWENTY-FIVE

ADRIANA: MISSING

After school let out, Adriana took her spot in the long line that twisted around the corner from the bread store. The gray sky threatened snow. It was certainly cold enough for it. Adriana reknotted her green scarf and burrowed her hands deep into her pockets, oblivious to the people in the queue in front of her. When someone touched her arm, she jumped.

It was Simona.

"*Buna ziua*," Simona said in her cheerful voice. "How are you?"

"*Bine.*"

"Did you like the opera last night?"

"Very much," Adriana said. "What did you think?"

"I loved it!" Simona said.

Adriana never spoke to people in the *pâine* line. In fact, she couldn't remember ever hearing anyone talk. She kept surveying her surroundings, checking for spies. After seeing those men at the opera, she couldn't be too careful.

Simona must have noticed. She leaned in. "Look, I'd love to get to know you better. When you come to visit Timotei next, you can stop by my dorm. Okay?"

Adriana nodded, but she also felt suddenly shy. "Can my friend Gabi come too?"

"Of course she can."

"Then I'd like to."

As Simona walked away, Adriana smiled. A college friend, all her own.

Adriana kept smiling as she walked to her flat. When she reached the top of the stairs, she saw Mrs. Petrescu open her door. A box of cigarettes leaned against her door frame. Mrs. Petrescu reached down and grabbed it so quickly, she probably thought Adriana didn't see it.

Adriana decided to go along. "Hello, Mrs. Petrescu. How are you today?"

"Good afternoon," she said and ducked behind her door.

Adriana wondered what she was being bribed to do. It must be something big.

Once she was safely inside her flat, Adriana removed her coat and shoes, placed the bread on the kitchen table, and walked to her bedroom.

Last evening, she'd arrived home pretty late for a school night and went straight to bed. Like all Romanians, Adriana had been trained to be careful with her clothes; she had so few outfits, she had to make them last. But last night was an exception. She was so tired, she barely got her fancy dress hung up. She opened her wardrobe to inspect it. The dress had slid to the edge of the hanger. She straightened it, then buttoned the bodice so it would stay put. She checked over the front for stains, then the back. Suddenly, she realized she hadn't seen Mama's brooch on the front.

She flipped the dress over. The pearl flower brooch with the ruby chips was not there! She checked the floor beneath the dress. Nothing. She felt panic rising in her throat. Adriana ran to the hallway to search her coat. Had the brooch caught on the lining? Surely it didn't fall off on the street somewhere.

Every place she searched, she came up empty. Her sense of dread grew.

Just then, the front door opened. It was her mother.

Of course. It had to be that Mama had taken her own brooch back. Why didn't she think of that before?

"Is something wrong, Adriana?" her mother asked, after they kissed.

"You took the brooch off my dress, right?" Adriana said. "I was worried—"

"The brooch? The one from Tati?" Mama compressed her lips. "I didn't touch it."

Adriana felt her eyes filling up.

"Adriana …"

"It's not there," she whispered.

Her mother strode into Adriana's room and pulled the dress out of the wardrobe, scanning it for the brooch. She sat down on Adriana's bed.

"Draga, let's be calm. Think. Where could it be?"

"I've looked everywhere here."

"Then you'll go back to the opera house. They have a lost and found. It has to be there." She paused. "If it fell off on the street …"

Adriana buried her head on her mother's shoulder. "I'm so sorry."

Mama sighed. "I know you didn't mean to do this, but you do need to learn to be more careful." Her voice constricted. "This is very special to me, especially now …"

Her mother got up and walked into her own room. She closed the door. She hadn't raised her voice; she didn't have to. Adriana couldn't have felt guiltier.

Adriana had to do something. She had an hour before curfew, so she grabbed her coat and scarf and ran down the stairs. She ran all the way to the opera house.

The crowd for that evening's show had already gone in, so she quickly entered the building and approached the woman at the ticket counter.

"Excuse me," she said. "Do you have a lost and found?"

"Da," the woman working there said.

Adriana described the brooch. The woman said she hadn't seen anything like that, but she looked through the box of items while Adriana waited. Not there.

Adriana's face started to crumple.

"Now, now," the woman said. She appeared motherly. "Don't cry. I'll send an usher up to check the area around your seat. Do you remember your seat number?"

They waited while the usher looked.

He started down the broad staircase, shaking his head.

"I'm sorry," the woman said. "It's not here."

"But maybe he didn't look hard enough—"

"It's not here." The woman pressed her lips together. Her tone had changed.

Adriana knew not to push it. She sighed and turned toward the door.

"When we clean up after the performance tonight, I'll have someone look again," the woman said.

"*Mulţumesc*," Adriana said, her face turned away so the woman wouldn't see the tears forming in her eyes.

Adriana walked home slowly. She'd failed.

When she entered the flat, she didn't hear any noise coming from her mother's room nor see any evidence that Mama had eaten. After her mother didn't answer when she rapped on the door, Adriana pushed the door open without making a sound. Her mother was asleep on her bed.

Probably for the best. Adriana didn't feel ready to face her right now.

She didn't feel like eating either, but she had bought some fresh bread earlier so she cut a few slices.

Adriana ate her meal alone. She could think of nothing but the missing brooch. *Please help me. Help me find it.* The words ran through her mind, but she didn't know whom she was addressing.

As upset as she felt, she couldn't let the magic water hour go by, so she collected water in all the tubs and cleaned up the dishes. Then she warmed a brick on the stovetop, wrapped it in a piece of flannel, and put it under her sheets, at the foot of her bed. She climbed into bed to read more of *Les Misérables.* She couldn't put it down.

True to what the bishop asked of him, Jean Valjean completely turns his life around. He becomes an honest man and builds a factory. Valjean is moved by the plight of one of his workers, Fantine, so poor she has to give her child, Cosette, to some terrible people to watch over her. Fantine is dying, so Valjean vows that he will take care of her child.

Valjean becomes so virtuous that when he hears of another man being arrested—a man who was thought to be the former convict Jean Valjean—he turns himself in. Because the bishop had given him such an unexpected gift of grace, one he couldn't possibly repay, he is able to do the same and pass on kindness to this stranger.

Adriana put her bookmark in and slipped the novel under her mattress. That's what she needed right now: a gift she didn't deserve. She'd been careless and lost the thing most precious to her mother in all the world. It was all her fault. If only she could find the brooch. She'd do anything.

CHAPTER TWENTY-SIX

GASLIGHT

AFTER THEIR MILITARY TRAINING exercises ended, Adriana invited Gabi to come with her to visit Timo.

As they walked to the metro, Gabi turned to face her. "Are you going to tell me what's wrong?"

Adriana didn't answer.

"After the opera, you told me the most fantastic news about the Berlin Wall coming down. How can you be in such a bad mood after news like that?"

Adriana sighed. "It's so terrible, I can't talk about it."

"Now who's being the dramatic one?" Gabi softened her tone and looked into Adriana's eyes. "You know you can tell me anything."

"I lost it," Adriana said. "I lost my mother's brooch."

Gabi sucked in her breath. "Did you check the lost and found?"

"Yes. They say they don't have it. But if someone found it, you know they'd keep it."

"Is that why you want to see Timotei?"

"Yes. I need to ask him if he saw it," Adriana said. "Hopefully he picked it up and is holding it for me. If that's not the case, maybe we can go ask Simona. Do you have time to come with me to both their dorm rooms?"

"Of course."

When the girls arrived at Timo's dorm, P-12, Adriana suddenly felt shy about entering it with Gabi. What if some of the boys were coming out of the shower wearing just a towel? The girls would be so embarrassed.

The girls stood outside until Adriana spotted a guy walking toward the door.

"Excuse me," she said. "Can you see if my cousin is in? And if he can come out?"

"Of course," he said. "But I need a name."

"I'm Adriana."

"I meant his name." He winked at her.

"Oh." She felt her face grow hot. "Timotei Grigorescu. Room 308."

The boy sprinted up the steps and into the lobby, his laughing eyes seared in her mind.

They didn't have to wait long. Before the boy Adriana sent in returned, someone came up behind her and grabbed her around the waist.

She jumped.

"I'm sorry." Timo stepped out from behind her. "I didn't mean to scare you, Green Eyes."

"I sent some guy in to look for you ..."

Timo shrugged. "It's okay. I'm sure he can use more exercise. Let's go over here," he said, shrugging toward the riverbank. "Is this your first time to the dorms, Gabi?"

Gabi nodded. "Does it show?"

Timo laughed.

"I lost Mama's brooch," Adriana blurted out before they reached the iron fence. Her voice quavered. "Tati gave it to her. She's really upset. Please tell me you have it."

Timo frowned. "Why would I ... no, I don't have it."

Adriana felt like crying. "I've looked everywhere. Went back to the opera house. Asked everyone. I saw spies lurking all around, but how could they have taken a pin off me without me feeling it? I think maybe I'm losing my mind."

"Why would you say that?" Timo asked gently.

"Every week, I lose something, or I'm certain it's in one place and then I find it in another."

"What kind of things?" he asked.

"Tati's picture in my room. Aunt Violeta's slipper basket. One night, I went to get our black tea bags—the only kind we ever use—and there were green tea bags where the black ones had been."

Timo blew out his breath. "You're not going crazy. Someone's trying to make you *think* you're cracking up." He grabbed her shoulders. "You're not."

Gabi and Adriana both looked at each other.

"How can you be so sure?" Adriana asked.

"You're a victim of what's called gaslighting," Timo said. "Have you heard of it?"

Both girls shook their heads.

"Gaslighting is another lovely technique our Securitate adopted from the East German Stasi. It's a kind of psychological harassment that the Stasi have perfected."

"What is it exactly?" Adriana asked.

"The concept is very simple, yet so effective. A spy breaks into peoples' flats and moves their furniture around, changes the time on a clock, removes pictures from the wall. Nobody suspects a spy of doing something that mundane, so the obvious answer is you're losing your mind."

"That's exactly what I've been thinking!" Adriana exclaimed. "I don't know why I didn't suspect the Securitate before. Of course it's them. It's always them." She exhaled relief. "This means I'm not going crazy!"

"Your mind jumped there because the Securitate spies are good at what they do. They have years of practice," Timo said. "Tapping phone lines, placing mysterious phone calls, installing bugs, making unnecessary deliveries—basically watching us all day, every day."

"But why? I don't get why moving pictures around is a spy strategy," Gabi said, frowning.

"They hope the subject will stop trusting themselves, feel defeated, and thereby, stop resisting. That they'll spill everything they know. And if it goes far enough, they're locked away with a mental breakdown."

Adriana's hands balled into fists. "I'll never let them do that to me."

"Of course you won't, Green Eyes. You're strong," Timo said. "You too, Gabi. At least, I assume my cousin doesn't associate with people who are weaklings." He smiled. "Besides, knowledge is power. Now that you know what's really going on, you can defy them." Timo gave Adriana a hug. "You *will* defy them."

"For now, the only thing I want to defy is the odds of me losing Mama's brooch forever." Adriana bit her lip. "You want to go up to Simona's with us? I ran into her yesterday, and she told me to stop by anytime. Maybe she knows where the brooch is."

Timo led the way to a building marked with a large P-23. They walked up uneven concrete steps and down a hallway so dark they had to squint to read the number on the door: 217.

When they knocked, Simona opened it. Her face broke out into a smile when she saw them.

"I can't stay long," Timo said. "I have some studying to do. But the girls have a question for you."

"Well, I hope you girls can stay to chat a bit," Simona said. She held her arms out for the girls' coats.

She invited Adriana and Gabi to sit on one of the beds. "This one belongs to Rodica, who you met. My bed's up there." She tapped the mattress above them. "Our other roommates live close enough to go home every Sunday."

While Gabi, Timo, and Simona chatted, Adriana surveyed the room. Three other sets of bunk beds lined the walls of the rectangular room. A small table, covered in a woven red cloth with a pitcher of black-eyed Susans and a hotplate holding a teapot, stood in the center of the room. Opposite the door was a window with a low bookcase below it. The girls had hung posters on the walls and curtains at the window, things she'd never expect to see in Timo's room. This room reminded Adriana of Professor Filip's *garsoniera*. Same compact size, but this one housed eight girls.

Simona carried three cups from the bookcase and lifted the teapot from the hotplate to pour them each a cup of tea. She sat down beside them on the same bed. Adriana picked up her spoon and stirred sugar into her tea. Timo stood and looked through the books on the shelves.

Adriana cleared her throat. "Simona, did you happen to see the brooch I wore at the opera?"

"Yes, it was beautiful."

"I mean … have you seen it *since* the opera?"

"You mean, it's missing?" Simona's eyes grew wide.

Adriana nodded.

"Sorry, I haven't seen it—"

"Can you ask Rodica?"

"Of course," Simona said. "But I doubt she has it."

For the second time today, Adriana felt like crying. That brooch meant the world to Mama.

Gabi caught Adriana's eye. She must have noticed how upset Adriana was, because she mercifully changed the subject. "How do you all manage with so many girls in your room?"

"Everyone is quiet and respectful. It works fine." Simona stirred her tea.

"Did you and Rodica know each other before you came to the university?" Gabi asked.

"No, but we get along like sisters." Simona blew on her tea. "We're assigned to dorms based on our degrees. All of us in P-23 are philosophy students." She nodded at Timotei. "You know Timotei and Marcu study history. The dorm next to us is for architecture students. Marcu told me he wishes he studied architecture."

"He never told me that," Timotei said.

"He says he loves buildings. Especially the old ones." She smiled. "So do I, actually."

"You must hate it that most of them got demolished," Adriana said.

Gabi raised her eyebrows at Adriana.

Simona nodded. "I do. Our wonderful systematization policy—"

"Philosophy sounds like an interesting field to study," Gabi said, changing the subject for the second time.

"It's logical." Simona shrugged. "Rational. To learn about knowledge, I mean. Why else go to a university?"

"Watch out!" Timo laughed. "Once you get Simona started …"

"Ever since I read that Socrates taught Plato, and Plato taught Aristotle, I've wanted to learn about philosophy," Simona said. "Can you imagine being in those classes? Ideas being freely exchanged from such great minds. That's what I wished college would be like."

"I guess that didn't work out," Timo muttered.

Gabi gaped at him.

"Did you girls say the other night you'll study engineering?" Simona asked.

Adriana nodded. "We're in the Science and Math High School."

"And we graduate this year," Gabi added.

"Do you know where you'll be assigned?" Simona asked.

"Not yet," Gabi said. "We don't even know whether it'll be chemical or aeronautical or mechanical … there are so many."

"I wish we had a say in it," Adriana said.

Simona nodded and took a deep breath. She looked at Timo. "They need to understand how it works at the university."

"What she means is, you'll never have a say," Timo said. "Nobody does."

Adriana watched Gabi's eyes widen. She couldn't wait to debrief with Gabi about how brave—or was it stupid—Simona and Timo were to say such things in front of someone they'd just met.

"Sometimes I think our professor hasn't even heard about the ancient philosophers. He just lectures us about the recent ones, the ones who impact our daily lives. Like Marx and Engels." Simona rolled her eyes. "But we can't *discuss* their ideas, much less ever disagree." She took a big sip of her tea and reached for her notebook.

"Okay, this is where I need to leave," Timo said. "This is too much education for me. I have my own studying to do."

He leaned down and kissed Adriana goodbye, then Simona, but he just waved to Gabi, then turned to leave.

"Do you want to hear what my professor said yesterday?" Simona asked.

Adriana and Gabi nodded. As Simona flipped through her notebook, she said, "Professor Voicu was practically foaming at the mouth, talking about his hero, Lenin. It's like he's worried something's about to happen and he has to cram Lenin's philosophy—that God cannot possibly exist and anyone who thinks he does is stupid or on drugs—into our brains before it's too late." She continued rifling through the pages. "Here it is. Lenin said, 'There is nothing more abominable than religion.' But Socrates said if you don't examine your life, it's not worth living. I think," Simona leaned in and whispered, "religion helps us examine our lives."

Adriana cleared her throat. She whispered, "Should you talk about … that?"

"Sorry. I just don't like small talk about small things. Especially after Professor Voicu got me riled up."

Adriana saw Gabi scan the ceiling, as though looking for microphones.

Simona lowered her voice. "Have you girls ever thought about these things? About God?"

"Not really," Adriana said, and stirred her tea again. "I mean, a little. But then I just keep thinking it's not very believable—"

"How can you explain the beauty of the mountains? The complexity of how our bodies work? How we all seem to know right from wrong—whether we admit it or do anything about it." Simona paused. "Where's that come from if not from God?"

Adriana looked around. "Aren't you afraid you'll get caught?"

"If I do, I do. It's natural to be curious, isn't it? To ask questions. To not believe everything you've been taught." Simona thought a moment. "Here's a question for you. This will help you examine your life and what you believe. You don't have to answer, just think about it. Alright?"

"Okay," Adriana said.

"Has there ever been a time in your life—maybe something happened—and you started to think that *maybe*, just maybe, our government is wrong and there is a God after all?"

Both girls remained silent, but Adriana noticed Gabi's eyes light up.

"You might think of a big dramatic thing, like someone you love nearly died, or maybe they did die. Or it might be something little, something that moved you, like watching a beautiful flower push through a crack in the sidewalk," Simona said. "Just think about it."

"We will," Gabi answered for both.

"But for now, we need to get going. We have to get home before curfew," Adriana said.

The girls stood to put on their coats.

"How long exactly have you known Timo?" Adriana asked Simona as she tucked the edges of her green scarf inside her coat. Gabi had her hand on the doorknob.

"Oh, we started school together in first grade. My family's flat is right above his."

"He seems to be sweet on you."

"Timotei?" Simona laughed. "No. I mean, I love Timotei. I shouldn't laugh ..."

Gabi looked at Adriana as though to ask, *Can we go now?* "Thanks for the tea," Gabi said to Simona.

"Please come visit again," Simona said.

Gabi lowered her voice and spoke directly in Simona's ear, but Adriana heard what she said. "I believe too."

Adriana watched Simona clasp Gabi's hand and smile. Gabi had mentioned her faith to Adriana but it wasn't something they really discussed.

The girls exited Simona's dorm and walked outside. Soft snowflakes filled the sky. A light layer clung to the ground.

"That was intense," Adriana said.

"I never knew philosophy students were so serious."

Adriana rolled her eyes. "Especially Simona. She seemed so light-hearted."

Gabi cleared her throat. "That question she asked us—about God—if you ever want to talk about it, I'm—"

Just then, the sound of someone running up behind them ended their conversation.

Adriana froze. She turned. It was just Timo.

"You've got to stop doing that," Adriana said. "Can't you just approach people like a normal person?"

"Sorry."

"You're not the only one. Simona scared me too," Adriana said.

"What'd she do?"

"After you left, she went on for a while about her professor and ..." Adriana looked both ways and then whispered, "Lenin."

"Oh," Timo laughed. "Simona told me her professor's getting to her. If she gets worked up, watch out. Look, I've known her all my life. She's fine. Don't worry about it."

"Don't *worry?* It feels like everyone's on edge ... I mean, more than usual."

"They are. All the loyal comrades are," Timo said. "Something unbelievable happened when the Berlin Wall came down. For the first time, the faithful Party members are scared. And that's a good thing."

"But we still shouldn't talk about it. What if someone overhears? And right after you told us about gaslighting—"

"Look, I didn't mean to upset you. I bet the brooch will be there when you get home."

Timo leaned down and gave Adriana a kiss on both cheeks. She wanted to, but she wasn't sure she could believe him.

Gabi offered to walk home with Adriana, even though their apartments were in opposite directions from the river. When they arrived at Adriana's building, Gabi insisted on coming upstairs. Adriana had been so jittery all day, she must have worried Gabi.

Mrs. Petrescu met them at the top of the stairs.

"Adriana, come in here please," she said. She looked at Gabi as though she wasn't sure about her. "Your friend too."

Adriana shot Gabi a look, hoping Gabi could read her mind. *This is strange.*

The girls followed Mrs. Petrescu inside her flat. They stood by the door with its giant peephole. Adriana noticed Mrs. Petrescu's stool, where she sat and watched people and recorded the comings and goings, as all building informers did.

Mrs. Petrescu motioned to them to step in farther, away from the door. The three of them huddled in the kitchen.

Mrs. Petrescu had something wrapped in a handkerchief. She placed it in Adriana's palm.

"I was ordered to do this, to take something that is precious to your family," she whispered. "But I can't live with myself until I make it right. I heard your mama say this was a gift from your father."

Adriana's eyes got big. She opened the handkerchief. Her mother's flower brooch sat inside.

She spontaneously threw her arms around Mrs. Petrescu. The lady seemed caught off guard, but after a moment, her stern visage melted and she smiled.

Mrs. Petrescu leaned down to whisper again. "You and your mama have already suffered for years. It was enough to lose your father and then for you to be taken in for questioning last spring. Why make me take something so precious? They're just a bunch of bullies."

Adriana still held Mrs. Petrescu's arm.

"They gave me chocolates and cigarettes for taking this. I don't smoke, but I do love chocolate. But when I tried to eat it, it tasted bitter. I couldn't swallow it. It came back up. I knew it was wrong."

"Thank you," Adriana said, her voice thick with emotion.

"It's our secret," Mrs. Petrescu said, looking at Gabi with her eyebrows raised.

"I promise. I won't say a word," Gabi said.

"Here." Mrs. Petrescu reached for an opened chocolate bar on the counter. "Take this. I think you'll be able to enjoy this more than I could."

"*Mulțumesc*," Adriana said as the girls walked out of her flat.

In the hallway, Adriana turned to Gabi. "Want to come in and share this?"

"I've never said no to chocolate before," Gabi said. "Sure."

Once inside, Adriana broke the bar into three pieces, then called for her mother to come join them. She hid the brooch underneath her mother's napkin.

Mama was the picture of politeness, as always. She greeted Gabi and didn't say or do anything that could possibly be questioned. But Adriana could feel the tension in the air. Things were obviously not resolved between her and her mother. Not yet.

Adriana tried to contain her smile while her mother sat down. With one flick of her wrist, Mama opened her napkin and spread it on her lap. The brooch rolled out onto the table.

Mama caught her breath. Then she stood and pressed Adriana against her.

Gabi put her chocolate square in her mouth and left.

CHAPTER TWENTY-SEVEN

ALEX: DOMINOES

O N THE THIRD SUNDAY of their now weekly military exercises, Alex tromped to the training grounds, so exhausted he could barely focus. Piles of snow, black from car exhaust, lined the sidewalk. How would he be able to handle a whole day of rigorous training? Besides school and being a platoon leader, every few nights this November, he'd been awakened and summoned for his courier job. He didn't want to add up the number of nights he'd gone without sleep altogether.

Things had definitely been heating up across the Soviet Bloc. Of course, you'd never find a newspaper article about what was happening or hear it on the TV news. If people knew about recent events, they had an unspoken pact to keep quiet about it. Alex didn't know who to trust, who he could talk to about the news, who would be happy, or who would be upset.

Alex enjoyed having earned a level of trust as a courier so that he was now informed of what the messages he delivered had to say. He could barely keep up with all the changes.

As he stood at the corner of Grozavești and Independenței, waiting for the traffic light to turn, he started ticking off some of the victories on his fingers.

The Berlin Wall was now a part of history. East Germans had successfully torn it down and streamed past the old checkpoints and through No Man's Land into West Berlin. The very next day, 10 November, the Bulgarians staged a coup and removed their dictator. One week after that, the Velvet Revolution, so-named because it was soft and peaceful, began in Czechoslovakia, marking the fiftieth anniversary of a deadly student demonstration against the Nazis. It ended after just one week—on 24 November—when the Communist leaders resigned.

The light changed and Alex crossed, thinking about how the dominoes that were set in motion had picked up speed. First Poland had toppled, then a couple months later, Hungary followed suit. This month, three more countries had fallen. Altogether, five countries total from the Eastern Bloc had shaken off their oppression.

He should be thrilled, and he had been, but that had all changed two days ago. He'd thought nothing could stop the momentum now, convinced that Romania and Ceaușescu would be the next domino to fall.

But, on 24 November, the same day that Czechoslovakia became free, Romania became less free. Alex's dreams, so buoyant before, had received a reality check. Sure, he felt discouraged, but he hadn't lost hope altogether. Didn't he expect change would come harder here?

Ofelia was right. Ceaușescu and his cronies in Romania must be terrified. So terrified, in fact, that they set up a hasty so-called election and called for a meeting of the Communist Party's XIV Congress. As a socialist republic, not a democracy, it was laughable to say the Romanian people voted in this or any election. There was never more than one candidate or one party. The results always came out the same: Ceaușescu won.

With this latest sham election, Ceaușescu successfully locked in his dictatorship to another five-year term. More than that, he sent a message to anyone thinking of rebelling that they might as well give up. Ceauşescu would always win. He would never peacefully leave power.

Five more years of hell. Unless it wasn't peaceful.

The newspaper *Scînteia,* The Spark, the official voice of the Communist Party, boldly proclaimed the news: *Ceauşescu Re-elected 24 November.* The next domino in Eastern Europe, poised to fall, had been propped up just in time. Alex's classmates probably had no idea how close Ceauşescu's evil regime came to capsizing.

But Alex knew.

As he walked, he spotted the training ground ahead. Liviu, taller than most, stood out from the crowd. Alex knew the youth brigade fell under the Patriotic Guards, the civilian arm of defense supervised by Communist Party officials, but the actual tactical training was conducted by the army. Liviu was a figurehead. He merely strutted along the sidelines, flexed his muscles, and used his obnoxious whistle. Alex noticed how tough Liviu acted when he yelled insults at his fellow students and then how quickly he transformed himself into a yes-man whenever the officers approached.

Alex enjoyed annoying Liviu. Alex may be quiet, but he had a strong will and was smarter than Liviu. He wouldn't permit Liviu to best him.

He'd now arrived at the Youth's Preparation for Defense of the Motherland. Alex reported in and got his classmates lined up in their platoon for the day's inspection. He merely glanced at Adriana and Gabi. No chatting allowed. Corina avoided his gaze.

Drill Sergeant Popescu stepped up in front of the group. "I have an announcement," he said, in a voice loud enough he never needed a megaphone. "You have improved enough that we will revert to the original schedule: meeting every other week."

Alex took note. That proved the government felt confident of their renewed control.

"Today you will learn combat skills. You will be trained to handle small arms, use demolition, and fire grenades. Every citizen—including students—must be combat-ready," Popescu barked.

With that, the government's paranoia showed. Maybe they didn't feel as secure as Alex imagined. Why would they need to be combat-ready unless the authorities feared an attack?

As they stood in formation, another officer stood up to demonstrate the day's exercises.

Last Sunday, even with Liviu watching him like a vulture hovering overhead, Alex had survived the shooting drills without incident, much better than Corina had fared. When she'd fired her rifle, she fell over backwards from the recoil. Liviu made her run laps as punishment, then shoot the rifle again. Both Gabi and Adriana had to restrain Alex from punching Liviu for that.

"Oprea, pay attention!" Liviu yelled, his face so close that Alex could feel Liviu's saliva hit his cheek.

"Yes, sir, Negrescu, sir!" Alex yelled back. He stuck his foot out, just a little bit, but it was enough.

When Liviu pivoted to march down the next line, he tripped and started to fall forward on his face, but he whipped his hands out in time to catch his fall. He quickly straightened up and calmly brushed the dirt from his palms. Alex could see blood already filling the scrape marks.

Liviu whipped around and shoved Alex to the ground. "I've warned you, Oprea!" he barked. "Give me one hundred push-ups. Now!"

Liviu planted his foot firmly in the middle of Alex's back as Alex struggled to do the push-ups.

Drill Sergeant Popescu came over to see what had happened. Alex braced himself for more serious consequences. Instead, Popescu got close to Liviu's face.

"Negrescu, remove your foot now. You are a *student*, and don't you forget it," he said. "I'm aware Captain Zugravescu trained you in his little school and that you are his pet. I know he has big plans for you. But believe me, he doesn't know you like I do. You will never live up to his expectations."

Alex tried to suppress his smile as Liviu walked away.

While Alex continued with his push-ups, the other students had to run, climb a wall, crawl under a wire fence, and shoot at a bull's eye at the end. If they didn't hit their target perfectly, and sometimes even if they did, the officers would make them go back and start again.

By the end, everyone was doubled over, breathing hard, coated in dirt. The other students limped home, but Alex had to stay to finish the exercises.

Liviu loomed over him, silent and glaring, as he finished—running, climbing, crawling, and shooting—giving his all to the regime.

Would anything ever change? Once again, Alex had decided to take a risk and entertain hope, just to see it defeated. It was life as usual in Romania. Hope had let him down.

CHAPTER TWENTY-EIGHT

ADRIANA: LIBERTY, EQUALITY, BROTHERHOOD

December 1989

T HE ONLY GOOD THING about Ceaușescu being re-elected
was that the weekly military training returned to an ev-
ery-other-week schedule. Adriana would take any victory
she could get. She welcomed the return of their study groups. This
afternoon, the first Sunday in December, they were to meet at Professor Filip's *garsoniera* for the second time.

Before the election, when she encountered fellow Romanians
on the street, she could tell the difference between the ones who
had heard the news about freedom coming to their neighbors in
the Eastern Bloc and those who hadn't. The ones who knew had a
sparkle in their eyes and held their heads a little higher. But their
short-lived days of hopefulness had come crashing to an abrupt
end. Now, post-election, everyone she saw assumed the default
submissive pose that characterized Romanians. They just shuffled
along, heads lowered, eyes cast downward.

She didn't have the energy to get out of bed this morning. Seeing the fresh snow that fell overnight—which didn't look very deep,

but still, it was snow—and remembering Mama would be working her extra shift at the factory, Adriana decided to read more of *Les Misérables*. The action had picked up and she expected to finish before long. Victor Hugo's story, a saga really, had covered fifteen years. The action now encompassed the Paris Uprising of 1832, the same time period as the opera she saw, *La Bohème*.

In the story, young people, mostly college students, are the ones who carry their ideals into battle. They erect barricades all over the streets of Paris. Their rallying cry is *Liberté, Égalité, Fraternité:* Liberty, Equality, Brotherhood. These young people, some Adriana's age, vow to fight to the death for such abstract principles.

Adriana put her bookmark in her novel and closed it. She had to mull that over.

Of course, she wanted freedom, but she didn't know if she wanted it badly enough to give her life for it. Sure, she hated living in a world where she always had to be careful what she said, where she went, even what she thought. Even with all the novels she'd read, she had trouble imagining what liberty would look and feel like. She wouldn't know how to live without sneaking around in secret. How would she handle being allowed to make her own choices?

And equality? Karl Marx and his socialist principles were supposed to be all about equality. He claimed the working proletariat class was equal to the privileged bourgeoisie class; in fact, he wanted to do away with the class system altogether. And yet, the Communist Party members lived much better than the workers. What was equal about that? The workers were the ones who kept everything running, not because they wanted to, but because they were forced to.

The one concept of the three Adriana had the hardest time grasping was brotherhood. She had a sisterhood with Gabi, her sister-friend. But to share a brotherhood—a personhood—with all Romanians, that felt too much like being a comrade and subjecting everyone and everything to the good of the state. She longed to be an individual—to be herself—and she didn't want to lose that to a lofty ideal like brotherhood.

Adriana sighed. This novel gave her so much to ponder. She thought about Mrs. Petrescu's decision to take a risk and defy her orders by returning Mama's brooch. The timing seemed curious. It happened after Adriana had been so upset when she thought she'd been careless and lost the brooch. After she cried out for help—to whom she didn't even know. In terms of world events, the missing brooch didn't rank up there very high, but it did as far as things that mattered to Adriana.

She thought about Simona's question. *Do you think that maybe there is a God after all?* Simona said the answer could be something dramatic or something small.

As soon as Simona had asked it, Adriana knew her answer was dramatic. When her father lay dying and she overheard him pray, she wondered if God might really exist. Tati, a lifelong atheist and believer in the Communist idea that God is a fable made up by superstitious old women, must have had a change of heart in his final breaths. Why, if there wasn't some truth to it?

Adriana slid her book under the mattress and rose from her bed. She knew someone else who'd been silently crying out for help, and she'd chosen to walk away and give up on their friendship. If Jean Valjean could change, so could she. She had enough time before their study group started to do something about it. She'd at least take the first step.

When Corina answered her door, Adriana could tell she'd been crying.

"What's wrong?" she asked, knowing that the polite thing would be to ignore what she clearly saw. But the whole purpose of this visit was to stop pretending there wasn't a problem.

Corina wiped her eyes with the back of her hand. "Nothing."

"I don't believe you," Adriana said softly. "I can tell something's bothering you."

The door opened wider. Adriana followed Corina into the living room.

"We can talk until study group," she said. "My father's out."

Adriana perched uncomfortably on the sofa beside Corina. She cleared her throat. "Look, I ... I know we haven't always ... what I'm trying to say is, I'm sorry for how I've treated you. I haven't always been a friend to you, but I want to."

Corina's eyes filled up. She nodded. "I've always felt jealous of you."

Adriana put her hand on Corina's arm. "You've seemed different lately—"

"I am different." Corina sighed.

"Do you want to talk about it?"

Corina shook her head. "Not really." She closed her eyes for a second. "But I think you might understand. What I'm about to tell you, I haven't mentioned to a soul. Can I trust you not to tell?"

"Of course."

"I found out some news about my mother."

Adriana waited for her to continue.

"Apparently, my mother was Hungarian," Corina whispered. "She was targeted because of it and taken in for questioning and ... she never came back."

Adriana forced her expression to remain deadpan, as though she heard news like this every day. "That's how she died?"

"Yes."

"Didn't you say it was a car accident?"

"That's what my father told me."

Adriana let that hang in the air between them a moment before tiptoeing around it.

"So you just found out?"

"Yes."

A dozen questions sprang to Adriana's mind, but she ignored them all. "I'm so sorry, Corina. I know what's it like to lose a parent to this regime."

"I thought you would." Corina paused. "My father told me so I'd be extra careful of who I associate with."

Adriana raised her eyebrows. "I don't understand."

"So I wouldn't be harassed. Being half-Hungarian."

"I didn't realize."

"That's because you're not Hungarian." Corina sighed. "This is all new to me too."

Adriana had been leaning forward, on the edge of the sofa, but now she leaned back and released the breath she didn't know she'd been holding. She remembered seeing Corina perk up—a temporary spark came to her eyes—when she told her and Gabi about Hungary being free. She must have felt proud.

Corina looked up at the clock on the wall. "We need to leave."

"Before we go, I don't understand why you and Alex ... you know."

Corina picked up her book bag and started toward the hallway where she donned her coat. "I just have too much to sort through. It's not fair to him. Besides ..."

Adriana followed Corina. "Besides what?"

"He probably wouldn't want to be my boyfriend. If he knew."

Adriana bent to slip on her shoes. "That you're Hungarian?"

Corina nodded. "Half-Hungarian, but still."

"He's not like that, Corina," Adriana said softly. "Are you saying you didn't tell him?"

Corina shook her head. "Look, it'll never work out," she said. "You should be with Alex anyway. You two were always meant to be together. Not him and me."

When they arrived at Professor Filip's, they found Alex inside. Adriana noticed Corina look down when they walked past him, then take the seat farthest away from him.

"Where's Gabi?" Adriana asked.

Alex shrugged.

"Let's get started without her," their professor said. "It's been a while."

The three students opened their notebooks.

"Today we're going to discuss the responsibility every engineer, every citizen for that matter, has to Romania."

Adriana had been thumbing through her notebook, looking for a blank page, but at those words, her head shot up. She never would have expected this kind of talk from Professor Filip.

Nobody spoke.

"Come on. I know you must have ideas. What's your role? Your moral responsibility?"

Alex cleared his throat. "Scientists investigate. We need to investigate things for ourselves. Discover the truth on our own. Not take someone else's word for it."

"Good." Professor Filip nodded. "How do you do that?"

"Use your mind. Your common sense," Adriana said.

"How does using your common sense help you become a better citizen?" Professor Filip asked.

"We listen to what people say, notice what we see," Corina said. "We ask ourselves: is it logical?" She cleared her throat. "Even … to look inside at how we feel. What do we *feel* is true?"

Adriana noticed Alex studying Corina as she said those words.

"Say you watch one of the films we show in class," Professor Filip said. "The film says that Americans want to start a war with us, and if they do, we'll surely beat them. What about that?"

"Why do they want to fight us?" Alex smirked. "Besides, if they did, they're bigger." He whispered, "We're the ones who'll lose."

"We need to notice what's happening," Adriana said. "Notice how the things that go on don't always match the words we hear from the top."

"Excellent," Professor Filip said. "Don't believe everything you hear. You must evaluate. What do you believe is true and right? You are young adults, and you have your own minds."

Adriana smiled. Young adults. Most people considered anyone still in high school to be a child.

"There may come a time for another step, which none of you has mentioned: to stand up for what you determine is right. To use your voices to speak out." Professor Filip rose to her feet and made a fist with her right hand. "Stand up on your own two legs. Come on, stand up with me."

The three students stood. Adriana felt her pulse quicken.

"I know many people are disillusioned right now. It seemed that things might be thawing. And now they've stopped. But don't give up!" She slapped her fist into her left palm. "Our country needs you. Romania will suffer if you don't stand up and speak up."

As Professor Filip finished speaking, her door opened. Gabi entered, white as a sheet. She didn't remove her snowy boots but just stood in the doorway.

"What's wrong?" her teacher asked.

"Something happened to a friend of ours," Gabi said. "Is it alright … can Adriana come with me?"

Adriana stared at Gabi. She suddenly felt cold and afraid.

"Who?" Adriana asked.

"Uri."

CHAPTER TWENTY-NINE

GABI: GOODBYE

ONCE GABI AND ADRI were safely outside, where no ears could overhear, Adri said, "Tell me what happened."

"Nobody's seen Uri for a week. He could be sick, or he got lost wandering, or …"

Adri shivered. "In this cold and snow?"

Gabi nodded. "A man who works with Uri came to our apartment," Gabi dropped her voice to a whisper, "in the middle of our church service. Papa and the man talked for quite a while. The man said he knew of Papa from things Uri had told him, and he thought Papa might be able to help. He'd overheard talk about a so-called accident that happened to several of the workers at the palace. He grew more and more worried as the days passed, so he went to Uri's flat. No answer, so he asked Uri's neighbor. She hadn't seen Uri all week either. She kept Uri's spare key, so she let the man inside his flat. The man said he could tell Uri hadn't been there for some time. It looked like he'd left for work in a hurry and expected to come home any minute. His dirty coffee cup was in the sink where he'd left it, and there was dust on everything." Gabi paused. "Adri, Uri never came home from work. A week ago. And you remember what he told us?"

Emotion choked Adri's voice. "That the workers who build Ceaușescu's palace could go missing at any moment, never to be seen or heard from again. Especially if they work on the underground floors like he does."

Gabi shivered. "Uri's friend said 20,000 people have worked on the palace so far."

"That many?" Adri stopped walking. "I mean, I knew it had over a thousand rooms but still—"

Gabi nodded. "And that's not even the most amazing number. He said that 3,000 of them are missing, probably more."

Adri was silent for a moment, her brow furrowed.

Gabi knew it was a lot to process.

Adri put her hand on Gabi's arm. "But Uri's more paranoid about the Iron Guard—"

"Yes, but Adri, he has a right to be paranoid, even if his mind mixes up the past and present. We have to be realistic about what's happening. Ever since that earthquake back in the seventies, somebody's been working on that monstrosity twenty-four hours a day, all these years. Those workers have seen things. The powers that be can't risk them telling anyone."

"I don't care about the palace or politics," Adri said. "Just Uri."

"I know. In my gut, I feel like he's …"

"We don't know that."

"No, but we'll know soon. Papa went with the man to talk to someone who might have more information. We're to meet Papa outside Uri's, at the cemetery."

The girls boarded the metro and rode it in silence, then walked in silence through the snowy streets. When they arrived at the cemetery, they opened the iron gate and walked to the double grave where Uri's parents lay. Gabi brushed the snow off the tombstone with her gloved hands, then wiped her hands on her coat.

"If the news is bad, just remember what Uri told us," Gabi said.

"That he's lived a long life?"

Gabi nodded.

"He said he's ready," Adri said. "The thing is, I'm not."

As Adri said that, Gabi saw her father approach from the back of Uri's building and make his way toward them. He didn't walk hunched over as though it was bad news, but then, she'd never seen her father walk like that. She didn't know what to expect, so she braced herself for the worst.

"*Buna seara*, Adriana. Hello, Princess," Papa said as he bent to kiss Gabi.

The girls waited for him to continue.

"I'm going to pretend to give you some money," Papa said. "In case anyone watches." He opened his wallet and pulled out a couple of lei.

As he pressed them into Gabi's hands, he looked into her eyes. His were full of compassion. Gabi knew what he had to say.

"I'm sorry, girls."

Adri looked down at her boots.

Papa continued, "Uri told me many times that it was a miracle he lived through the war. He said he was on borrowed time, and now that he was so old—"

"But he wasn't too old to us," Gabi said. Her eyes started to fill up.

Papa reached out to comfort her.

Gabi blinked the tears away. "Will he be buried—?"

"There isn't a body."

"So maybe he's not really—"

"He is," Papa said.

"How do you know?"

Papa cleared his throat. "I spoke with a man who witnessed it."

"But he might have revived—"

"Gabi, stop," Papa said. "I didn't want to tell you the details." He inhaled deeply. "Uri was burned to death. It wasn't an accident; he was clearly murdered."

Gabi felt like the wind had been knocked out of her lungs.

"His neighbor will let us in his apartment to gather his valuables," Papa said. "Come with me, girls."

The three entered Uri's building and walked upstairs with heavy steps. An elderly woman stood at the top, peering over the railing and twisting the edge of her apron in her hands. She didn't say a word; she just unlocked Uri's door and then stepped aside.

"Thank you, ma'am," Papa said. As he put a hand on the neighbor's shoulder, Gabi noticed the lady's eyes were wet. She must have loved Uri too. How could anyone help but love Uri?

They looked through the tiny flat, starting with the bare living room. Papa took a framed photograph from the coffee table. He looked at it and smiled, then passed it to the girls. "His wedding day."

A much-younger Uri, dressed in a plain black suit and having his head covered with a yarmulke, smiled at the camera. He stood behind a lovely woman, seated and wearing a modest white dress. She had kind eyes and looked happy, exactly how Gabi pictured Uri's wife, Deborah.

Next, they entered his bedroom. The quilt had been pulled up over the bed. Papa opened the wardrobe. It was nearly empty of clothing. Uri lived very simply.

Gabi noticed a drawer in his nightstand and opened it. A letter sat on the top of a few other papers, which Papa gathered and put in the inside pocket of his overcoat. The letter was addressed, *To My Angels*.

"I think this is for you," Papa said. He handed the letter to Gabi.

Gabi grabbed it and started to read it silently.

Adri tugged on her sleeve. "What's it say?"

Gabi read it aloud.

To My Angels, Grațiela and Andrea,

Gabi laughed. "He never could remember our names," she said to her father. "Adri and I stopped correcting him a long time ago."

I am not a rich man, but the good Lord has seen fit to bless me with treasures in other ways. The hand of God saved my life many times. He has always used unremarkable and unexpected people to help me. My life has spanned some terrible times where I have seen the ugliest hatred and blackness that can reside in the hearts of people, and yet, God has seen fit to let me glimpse the most beautiful goodness and love too. I am a man wealthy in friends and rich in blessings. I tried to live with justice, mercy, and humility, as the Holy Scriptures say. I believe I did my work as excellently as possible. I have no regrets. I am satisfied.

At this point in my life, I never expected to make new friends. Then I met two angels who took an interest in my life and my stories. These angels volunteered to take care of the final resting places of my people. They showed compassion to anonymous people long dead, who did not have family to care for their graves.

When it is time for my days on earth to end, I ask that whoever finds this letter will respect my wishes. My dearest wife Deborah preceded me in death and we had no children to leave things with. I do not have much as far as worldly goods, but I do have my wife's diamond ring (my gift to her on our wedding day) and her emerald necklace (her inheritance from her grandmother). They are hidden in the sugar bowl in my kitchen. Not a very sophisticated hiding place, but it has served me well all these years. One is for Graţiela and one is for Andrea. You girls can choose; I am not good at that sort of thing.

And so, I leave you girls, my angels, in peace. Thank you for bringing joy to an old man. I pray you will have a long life, full of grace and blessings. I hope you enjoy freedom, as I never could. Now that I look back on the entirety of my life's journey, I feel that I was free, on the inside, where it really counts. And that is what I want for you most of all.

Remember to look up! Find your help in the Lord.

I go to the eternal home prepared long ago for me.

Shalom!
Uri Goldmann

As the girls started to cry, Papa pulled Gabi to one shoulder and Adri to the other.

"He loved you both," Papa whispered. "Let's look for that sugar bowl."

They walked into the kitchen. Gabi noticed the coffee cup sitting in the sink. Four cannisters lined the counter.

Adri opened the lid of the second largest. "This is the one my mother uses for sugar," she said. She peered in. "It's just sugar in here."

Papa opened the drawer and took out a wooden spoon. "We'll look a little harder." He lightly punched at the sugar with the spoon, then slid it along the edges of the cannister. Gabi could tell by his expression that he found something.

Gingerly, he lifted a small plastic bag out of the cannister. He wiped sugar crystals off the bag and placed it on the square table.

Both girls crowded closer as Papa opened the bag. A diamond ring and a necklace with a small green stone rolled onto the surface.

Adri stared at the jewelry, as though she'd never seen anything so lovely before.

But Gabi barely peeked at it. She looked away. How could she care about something so material when her friend had died?

"Is that an emerald?" Adri asked.

Gabi shrugged. "That's what his letter said."

"You girls must choose," Papa said.

"I can't," Gabi said. "What do you want, Adri?"

Adri bit her lip. Gabi hoped that meant she was thinking about the emerald. "I can't choose. You knew him first. And best. You decide."

Gabi wanted the diamond ring, but how could she say that?

"Take the diamond ring, Gabi. It probably felt more personal to Uri than the necklace. Uri chose that diamond for his bride." Adri smiled. "Besides, I'm partial to emeralds."

Gabi slid the ring onto her finger. It was too big so she moved it to her middle finger. "Thank you, Adri. This will always remind me of our friend."

CHAPTER THIRTY

ADRIANA: FREEDOM

THE CITY AWOKE TO a magical scene the following Sunday, transformed and glistening. The snow that had started furiously while they were in school the day before had quickly covered over the remnants of last week's snow. After coming down so hard that the white sky and white ground blended into one large white canvas, Professor Filip had received word that the Youth's Preparation for Defense of the Motherland had been cancelled for today, but the military exercises would be held next Sunday, no matter the weather. Snow in December was not unusual, but this amount would make outdoor drills difficult, if not impossible. Mama had not been as lucky. Factory workers still had to work today to exceed their quotas, snow or no snow.

Adriana gazed out the window, seeing soft white drifts that sparkled like coarse sugar crystals and feeling the promise of a day by herself to finish her novel and think. Her thoughts, jumbled and mixed up in her brain, needed to be sorted and examined.

She pulled her copy of *Les Misérables* out from under her mattress and read the last few chapters. Adriana identified with Cosette, being raised by someone who tries so hard to protect her that she gets squelched.

Jean Valjean hides Cosette away from the world in a convent, but the world still gets in. She's young; she meets Marius, and they fall in love. But Eponine is also in love with him. Marius leads the doomed uprising in the streets and when a bullet comes toward him, Eponine sacrifices her life to save him. Cosette and Marius end up together.

Adriana closed her book. The story gave her a lot to mull over.

Valjean's life was transformed because of the bishop, so much so that in the end, he takes the very gifts he received—grace and forgiveness—and passes them on to Javert, his archenemy. He has a chance to kill him, but he frees him instead. In the end, everyone dies except Cosette and Marius, even Valjean. Not even the uprising survives.

The recent uprisings throughout the Soviet Bloc all ended with the people gaining their freedom. They succeeded without bloodshed, but the people didn't know that when they started. They were willing to stand up for what they believed in, to fight if it came to that, and even to give their lives.

Adriana sighed. It looked like freedom had passed her country by. There were only a handful of people who had been brave enough to take their chances and speak the truth. But now, even those people were too beaten down to lift their heads. Her hopes had floated to heights devoid of reality. Maybe she'd been living too much of her life in this make-believe world of fiction.

She threw her book down on the bed.

She might as well face it. Nobody was going to fight here. Romania would never be free. She felt defeated. And sad. And angry.

Uri's death stabbed her in the heart all over again. Dear Uri. What did he mean about being free on the inside, where he said it counts?

She had an idea of someone who might be able to help her understand that. She bundled up in her boots, coat, scarf, and gloves, and ventured outside.

The brisk air slapped her in the face. At least the snow had stopped coming down, but it was deep enough to make the walking slow-going. She tromped through piles of it, powdery on the top and crunchy underneath, to the tram stop. The blinding whiteness made Bucharest look clean and new. Pure even.

What a joke. Bucharest could never be pure.

Adriana climbed down from the tram at Grozavești. She trudged along the trodden path to the girls' dorm. The drifts rose high along the edges of the sidewalk.

When she rapped on Simona's door, Simona answered right away.

"*Buna*, Adriana," she said. "Come in." She opened the door wide and kissed Adriana's cheeks in greeting.

Adriana's face and lips were so cold she could barely move.

"Are you frozen?" Simona asked.

"Yes." Adriana shivered.

"Would you like some tea?"

"Yes, *mulțumesc*." Adriana stepped out of her snowy boots and hung her coat on the hook. No matter how cold she was, Adriana had been taught to always remove her outerwear so she'd feel the difference when she went outside.

"Sorry our heater doesn't work," Simona said.

"Nobody's heater works," Adriana said.

Simona patted Rodica's bed for Adriana to sit down and put the teakettle on the burner. "We'll get you warmed up with some nice hot tea."

"Where are your roommates?"

"Rodica went to the library—in this weather," Simona said. "And the other girls are at their homes."

Adriana was glad to see that they were alone. The teapot's whistle sounded. Simona poured hot water in Adriana's mug and handed it to her.

"Is something wrong?" Simona said. "You look troubled."

"No," Adriana said. "I just have something to ask you."

"Go on." Simona smiled.

"I want to ask you about freedom. Someone important to me wrote something about being free on the inside." Adriana paused. "I know you think about things—important philosophical things—and I just thought you might have something to say."

"Freedom is about your heart. Your mind. It's not about your circumstances," Simona said. "You can be free in prison. You can be free—"

"Here in Romania?"

Simona nodded.

"I know my thoughts are my own, and I can let my mind soar. But when I do that, I'm still here. Still being watched. Nothing has changed, not really."

Simona looked straight into Adriana's eyes with an intensity Adriana had rarely felt. It was uncomfortable. "I think your friend was talking about freedom that comes from God."

"I was taught there is no God—we all were—but now I'm not sure—and I want to know ..."

"You want to know what I think." Simona said this as a statement more than a question.

"Yes."

Simona ran her fingers through her short layers. "I think God exists. In fact, I feel certain of it."

Adriana took another sip.

"Tell me," Simona said. "Do you know anything about Jesus?"

"My grandmother believes in him," Adriana said. "And so does my friend—you know, Gabi, who you met—and her parents."

"Have they told you much about him?" Simona asked.

"My grandmother told me about the day he was born, the first Christmas," Adriana said. "She told it like it means something to her. But she's an old lady, and everyone knows they believe superstitions and fables."

"Do you think she's crazy?"

"Well, no—"

"You might think I'm crazy, but it's okay." Simona paused. "A few years ago, I became curious about what truth is. I mean, is there anything we can fully trust to be true? So, I asked my bunica all this because she seemed so wise and ... content with life. She said that first I needed to settle the issue of whether I believed there even was a God. She said she'd pray that God would let me know if he's real. And he did."

"How?"

"Well, he didn't say anything out loud." Simona laughed. "I started to feel his love for me. It was *real*, and it made me feel free. On the inside."

Adriana let Simona's words settle into the space between them. She put her empty mug down. "Thanks for the tea, but I think I better go now."

Simona gave Adriana a hug. "Anytime you want to talk, I'm here."

As she walked home, Adriana thought about freedom. She longed for freedom to come to her country. But whatever happened, she wanted to be free on the inside. Like Uii was. Like Simona.

CHAPTER THIRTY-ONE

GHOSTS

W HEN ADRIANA STEPPED OUTSIDE, she saw that flurries had begun afresh, so she hurried home, trying to beat the new snow. Once inside her door, she stomped snow off her boots, thankful to be home. It was still early enough that she could do some more reading.

She heated her brick to warm up her bed and made herself another tea.

After that intense conversation, she longed to burrow into the latest novel she'd borrowed from Aunt Violeta's secret room. Now that she'd finished *Les Misérables,* she was eager to start this new one. When did she ever have the luxury of reading two novels in one day?

She fluffed up her pillows, leaned back, and opened the cover of *A Christmas Carol* by Charles Dickens. After reading such a long novel last time, she was glad this one was skinny. Aunt Violeta told her Dickens was a British author from the 1800s. She'd promised Adriana would love it.

Marley was dead, to begin with. There is no doubt whatso-
ever about that. The register of his burial was signed by the cler-
gyman, the clerk, the undertaker, and the chief mourner. Scrooge
signed it...
Old Marley was dead as a door-nail.

The opening chapter drew her into the story immediately. Marley's ghost wakes up Ebeneezer Scrooge late one night. Marley says he is doing penance, wandering the world without rest while he drags a heavy chain created by his life of swindling people. Marley warns his old business partner that he still has a chance to escape that pitiful fate. He tells Scrooge that three more spirits will appear to him that night.

Intrigued already, Adriana couldn't put the novel down. The first ghost that Marley promised, the Ghost of Christmas Past, takes Scrooge on a journey through his life, highlighting the worst things he'd ever done.

Adriana thought about that. If a ghost came to haunt not just a person, but a country, her country, he'd uncover a lot of wrongs. Oppression. Brainwashing. Terror. What would happen if the ghosts of all the people sacrificed to a ruthless regime cried out? So many unknown people whose lives had been taken. And a few she knew: her father, Alex's father, Corina's mother, and now Uri. She shivered to think about it.

As she reflected, she heard a knock on the door. She looked at her watch. Mama should be home any minute. She wondered who this could be. She stuffed her book under the mattress and hurried to the front door.

When Adriana looked through the peephole, she saw Mrs. Petrescu. She opened the door.

"You have company," the lady said, and stepped aside.

Mrs. Petrescu's tall frame dwarfed Adriana's petite grandmother standing behind her, holding a satchel. Adriana squealed and threw her arms around Bunica.

"Thank you for your hospitality, Luminița," Bunica said to Mrs. Petrescu.

"Not a problem," Mrs. Petrescu said. "I enjoyed it."

"I'll be sure to visit Iulia," Bunica whispered. "Now mind you, I won't be back that way for a couple of weeks."

Mrs. Petrescu nodded to Bunica and grasped her hand.

Adriana hooked her arm around her grandmother's and led her into the flat and took her bag.

"So you're staying a couple of weeks?"

"Yes, I haven't come for a proper visit in a while." Bunica said. "If your mother won't have me, I'll ask Violeta to put me up."

"Of course, Mama will love to have you with us." Adriana squeezed her grandmother's arm. "When you were talking to Mrs. Petrescu, what did you mean … hospitality?" Adriana asked. "And who's Iulia?"

"When I arrived, nobody was home. Luminița—Mrs. Petrescu—invited me inside her flat," Bunica said. "We had a lovely chat and then she fixed me lunch and, well, I guess I lost track of the time."

"With Mrs. *Petrescu*?"

"She's a good woman, draga. Not what you think," Bunica said. "Iulia is her younger sister. She's handicapped. She lives with their mother, who's getting older, in Brașov and … well, I offered to check in on them."

Adriana just stared. She'd lived beside Mrs. Petrescu her whole life, but she knew nothing about any of this. She'd never even heard her first name. How was her grandmother able to pull such information out of people?

"When do you expect your mother home?" Bunica asked.

"Soon."

"I worry about her long hours," she said.

"Me too. So why are you here?" Adriana said, then suddenly felt embarrassed. "I didn't mean that how it sounded. I'm thrilled you're here. Always. But you don't usually come in the winter and especially in a snowstorm—"

"Let's just say I had an important message to deliver. And it wasn't snowing hard when I left."

"A message? For Mama?"

Bunica shook her head.

Adriana's hands flew to her mouth. Once in Armonia, she'd confronted Bunica on why she traveled so frequently and at a moment's notice. Bunica had admitted that Adriana's suspicions were correct. Her grandmother—her *grandmother*!—was a courier for the Resistance, delivering covert messages.

Adriana got Bunica settled onto the sofa to wait for Mama while she heated up the kettle for more tea.

When she returned with two warm cups, Adriana whispered, "Why do they still bother with the messages? After the election, isn't it all hopeless now?"

Bunica sat up, with a glimmer in her eye. "No, draga. Things always get worse before they get better. The darkest part of the night is just before the sun comes up."

Adriana leaned forward. "Can you tell me the message?"

"I'm not supposed to," Bunica said. "But I don't see what it'll hurt this time." She looked toward the radio. "May I?"

Adriana nodded.

Bunica clicked on the radio and she still lowered her voice. "My message is for the churches. The ones in hiding."

Adriana thought of Gabi's father's underground church. "What is it?"

"To be careful," Bunica said. "They're cracking down on Christians."

"Haven't they always?"

"They've stepped it up recently. Someone in Oradea was caught delivering a small book torn out of the Bible—called Philippians— to an underground church. The man was beaten to death by the

Securitate, and all the people in the church were taken into custody." Bunica took a sip of her tea. "This week, they're rounding up
pastors all over the country. Sending them off who knows where."

"I have to tell Gabi."

"No need," Bunica said. "I delivered the message to her father
Constantin personally when I arrived. That was my first stop. But
I'm also concerned about Mihai. I think everyone—not just Chris-
tians, but radicals and dissidents—needs to be on alert."

"Uncle Mihai's not home," Adriana said. "And Aunt Violeta's
doing inventory."

"I guessed as much," Bunica said. "I stopped there already."

"Uncle Mihai's at work. I can go tell him."

Bunica started to protest, but Adriana wouldn't hear any of it.

"I can do this. I *want* to do this." She fluffed up the pillow on
the sofa. "You've had a long trip, Bunica. Just stay here and make
yourself comfortable. Tell Mama I'll be back soon."

CHAPTER THIRTY-TWO

FEAR

ADRIANA MOVED AS FAST as she could through the snow as she made her way to Uncle Mihai's office. She had to outrun her mounting fear. If Bunica was worried about Mihai, then she should be too. Radicals, dissidents, Christians—what match were they against the well-oiled machine of Communist Romania?

The flurries of snow had increased in size and ferocity. Thankfully the city kept the showy part of downtown shoveled. Her feet slid out from under her on an icy patch outside the National Library and she careened into a powdery drift. As she picked herself up and brushed the snow off, she wondered if Timotei was inside the library, doing more research.

She circled the grand Atheneum and headed for the back entrance. As she tugged on the old door, she spotted Captain Zugravescu, in his military uniform, standing outside the spy hangout, the Athenee Palace Hotel, talking it up with two men dressed in black overcoats and black hats. Zugravescu had his back partially turned to her, and the men facing her didn't look her way. They seemed engrossed in their conversation.

Once inside, Adriana found her way along the narrow hallways in the dim light, hoping she could remember all the turns and stairways in the bowels of the concert hall's backstage. When she reached the last door, Uncle Mihai's office, she heard muffled voices, not nearly loud or clear enough to pick out the words.

She knocked lightly on the door. Immediately, she heard movement in the room. She probably frightened them. "Uncle Mihai," she called, knowing his colleagues wouldn't be frightened of a girl.

Uncle Mihai opened the door. "Scumpita, what are you doing—"

"Bunica came to visit," Adriana nodded and lifted her eyebrows, hoping he'd sense that she had more to say about it than just that.

He ushered her inside. "Come in."

Two people sat in the chairs in front of his desk.

"Please meet my niece." Mihai turned to Adriana. "It's best we don't share names, but these friends are part of the symphony." He touched the woman on the shoulder and said, "Pianist," and the man, "Cellist."

"Nice to meet you." Adriana nodded.

"Does Bunica need me for something?"

"She brought a message for you," Adriana said.

"What is it?" Mihai asked.

Adriana balked. She looked at the two strangers seated at the desk.

"You can speak. My friends are safe."

She stood on her tiptoes and cupped her hands around her tall uncle's ear. "Be especially careful right now. They're cracking down."

Uncle Mihai let out a deep, loud laugh.

Adriana didn't expect that reaction. She looked at her uncle, her eyes wide. What if someone heard?

"It's okay. It's my office. I can laugh if I want." Mihai turned to the others. "We need to watch out. They're coming for us."

Then he strode to his desk and pressed on the wall panel. "Follow me. I want you to repeat that."

The panel swung toward him. He leaned in and said, "We have an important announcement to make."

"Another one? Nadia Comenici defecting wasn't enough?" a voice coming from inside asked.

Adriana looked up at her uncle.

"It's true. Our star gymnast fled across the border to Hungary on 27 November. She left with a group of others, on foot and at night. Nadia claimed she felt like a prisoner here."

"Don't we all?" another voice asked.

Mihai took Adriana's hand. "Come on inside."

When Adriana's eyes adjusted to the darkness, she counted six people in the secret office, two women and four men. As Adriana scanned the small room, her gaze came to rest on the famous opera singer, Carmen Ștefan, whose face was plastered on posters all over the city. Adriana looked at her uncle and widened her eyes.

"These are my friends. Fellow artists," he said. "I can tell you recognize Carmen. We also have two painters and three writers here."

One of the men cleared his throat. "Can I assume our new member has been thoroughly vetted?"

Mihai smiled. "Thoroughly. She believes the same things we do. She's suffered already."

Carmen held out her hand to Adriana. Her eyes were full of compassion.

"My mother-in-law just brought me a message." He turned to Adriana. "Would you care to repeat the message?"

Adriana stared at him. She wanted to refuse, but all eyes were on her and she didn't want them to see how nervous she felt. "Be especially careful right now. They're cracking down."

Several of the people in the room covered their mouths with their hands and chuckled.

Mihai smiled. "There you have it. We need to be careful. They're coming for us."

Adriana didn't see what was so funny. The message made her heart pound faster and her head constrict.

Carmen must have noticed her confusion because she looked into Adriana's eyes. "We laugh because there's nothing new about that. The current government has always feared us: the *inteligenția*, the ones they call dissidents."

"But I still don't understand …"

"We're known for sowing only discord," the other woman said. "I like to think I make beauty."

"Every problem in the country, if they ever acknowledge problems do exist, they blame us," Mihai said. "Usually, we had nothing to do with it. But that's changing. We refuse to be silenced anymore. It's gone too far, too long. We're ready to take our chances." He looked each person in the eyes. "They need to start fearing us."

"Even if they kill our bodies, our words—our dissent—will live on forever," one of the men said.

Adriana's eyes welled up with tears. She'd longed to know that her fellow Romanians hadn't given up, that they refused to continue going through life as though they were comatose and letting the powers that be wipe their feet on them.

But still. This hit close to home. Too close.

Her mind went to how she'd suffered. The pain of her father's murder, always fresh, still stabbed her heart so badly at times she didn't think she could breathe. Her own long, scary night spent all alone in interrogation. The fear she felt when Uncle Mihai was arrested and held in jail for months. She couldn't take more of that. It had been enough.

Maybe Mihai was willing to take his chances, but she wasn't willing for him to. If these artists had no fear, she had enough of it to go around.

Uncle Mihai raised both of his hands, palms out, to silence the room. He took Adriana's hands in his and looked into her eyes. "Scumpita, I'll be careful. We all will. We do take this seriously, believe me. We're just talking big, but don't worry. None of us want to be martyrs for the cause. We just want to be free."

Adriana nodded and squeezed his hand.

"Now you go home and tell Bunica not to worry about me."

When Adriana made it to the back door and stepped outside, she noticed the sky had darkened substantially. The sun had sunk quite a bit in the short time she'd been inside. She looked down at her watch.

As she did, someone behind her grabbed her other arm. She gasped and wriggled around to try to see. It was Liviu.

"What were you doing in the Atheneum?" Liviu said. "On a day when you were supposed to be at the training?"

Adriana knitted her eyebrows together. She could act tough even though she felt the opposite. "Did they forget to tell you? It was cancelled …"

"Don't get smart with me, if you know what's good for you."

Liviu's tone sounded sinister. Maybe all the talk about being martyrs for the cause made her extra jumpy. Or maybe she did need to be afraid of this guy she usually ridiculed.

"My uncle works here. I went to tell him my grandmother's in town." She shook his hand off her arm. "Of course, you know everything, or at least you think you do, don't you? Who doesn't know the concertmaster's office is here? And you probably know he works all the time."

"I think I'll pay Mihai Zaharia a visit. Since I'm here."

"Since you're here? Don't you come here all the time?" Adriana pointed to the Athenee Palace. "Or at least, there?"

"Are you spying on me?"

"No," she said, shaking her head. "Everyone knows your people like it there."

He grabbed her arm again, even harder this time, and looked at her with an icy stare. "If I were you, I'd watch how I speak. You may be young, but you're far from innocent. You have a record. Have you forgotten?"

"You know I was innocent." Adriana wriggled out of his grasp and rubbed her arm. It hurt. "You made yourself a laughingstock when you tried to set me up. A failure in judgment—isn't that what it was called? What did I ever do to you? Why do you hate me and my family so much?"

Liviu didn't respond. He yanked the door open that she'd just come through, leaving her standing there with her heart pounding.

She followed him in and projected her voice. "So you're here to see my Uncle Mihai? He'll be so glad to—"

Liviu shoved her back out the door. "I know what you're trying to do. It's too late."

The door clicked shut in her face.

Maybe Liviu had figured it out, but all that mattered was whether Uncle Mihai heard her. She had to trust that Mihai and his friends remained hidden in the secret office, and that their hiding place was enough.

CHAPTER THIRTY-THREE

TIMOTEI: WAKE UP!

Sunday, 17 December

TIMOTEI AND MARCU SLIPPED through the darkness into the back door of the vacant restaurant at Piața Unirii. Timotei had called for an urgent, late-night meeting of Students for a Free Romania. He wondered who had received the word and how many would come.

When they walked through the stripped-bare kitchen into the former chef's office, his question was answered. Timotei noticed Serghei, Claudia, and a handful of others had beaten them there. He watched Beni file in silently and cram into the small room. He looked for Simona; she wasn't there.

Just then, Serghei stood up. He pushed his wire-rimmed glasses up his nose. "Timotei has some news for us. Tell us what you've heard," he said, gesturing to Timotei to stand beside him.

Timotei began. "Most of you know we've been picking up chatter on Radio Free Europe all week. We knew something big was going down, and we heard it might involve Christian pastors, but I hadn't been able to reach my friends in Timișoara to verify anything. Today, my local sources intercepted the first broadcasts over the short-wave—originating in Hungary." He paused for dramatic effect. "It's started, friends. Here in Romania, it's started."

Murmurs rippled through the gathering. Serghei paced and raked his fingers through his unruly hair. Timotei caught Marcu's eyes. They glistened.

"Two days ago," Timotei continued, "on 15 December, the authorities tried to force another pastor into exile. This pastor is an outspoken ethnic Hungarian who lives in my hometown, Timişoara. His name is László Tőkés. Random people in Timişoara—Romanians and Hungarians united for once—made a human chain around his building. They couldn't keep the police from capturing Tőkés and sending him away, and many of the protestors were beaten and arrested in the process. But here's the thing. Now the people had a specific cause to rally around. They were angry. More and more people joined them, and they all marched as a group around the city."

"How are you sure of this?" Serghei asked.

"Heard it with my own ears over the broadcast from Radio Free Europe. Besides, my friend in Timişoara, Vasile, verified it. He's been with the protestors from the start. He said that both nights, people have remained with the group, outside in the open *piaţa* all through the night."

"What changed?" Beni asked. "Other pastors have been taken—"

"I've heard of Tőkés. Isn't he the one who gave that interview on Hungarian TV?" Claudia asked.

"He had the courage to criticize the systematization policy of demolishing whole villages and large parts of our cities," Serghei said. "On television." He pounded his fist into his palm. "The kind of courage we all need."

"He did do that. But nobody can say for sure why this time is different. I have my own ideas," Timotei said.

"Like what?" Marcu asked.

"Vasile said people in Timişoara claim there's something more going on that they can't explain. That someone—something—bigger than us is in charge," Timotei said. He noticed puzzled expressions on the faces looking back at him.

Perfect timing for Simona to pick that exact moment to burst into the room, out of breath. Her hair looked messier than usual, the layers sticking out in every possible direction, as though she'd just been caught up in a ferocious windstorm.

Timotei turned to her. "We were talking about what's happening in Timișoara. Maybe you can tell them what you told me."

"Did Timotei tell you it started when they tried to evict Tőkés?" Several of the students nodded.

"My parents …" Simona paused, "my parents are Christians."

Serghei had a stunned expression on his face.

"They've been meeting in secret, like us, for years now," Simona continued. "They tell me that when Tőkés was taken, the word spread rapidly from cell to cell of underground churches all over the city. As soon as each cell got the word, the people huddled together in their darkened flats all over Timișoara. Forty-eight hours later, they have not left their cells."

She paused. Nobody breathed; everyone present hung on her words.

"These groups of believers are praying around the clock, without stopping to sleep. They pray for freedom for Tőkés, but more importantly, for freedom for our country." Simona stopped for a breath. "Look, we always say we need to recruit more help. They are recruiting the biggest ally they can think of. They are asking God to give us victory. That has to count for something."

Timotei watched his group of *inteligenția* react. Marcu looked uncertain, just as Timotei felt. Claudia seemed to scoff at Simona's words. Beni closed his eyes and looked down at his hands, listening intently.

But Serghei laughed. "Come on, Simona. I'm all for freedom of religion, but can you honestly say you believe that superstitious religious stuff?"

"I do," she said, softly but confidently.

Beni raised his eyes, looking straight at Serghei. "Why not?" His voice grew louder. "Why's it so hard to believe what she's saying is true?"

Simona smiled at him.

Timotei didn't know Beni very well. He was usually so quiet and soft-spoken. Beni, the medical student who lived at home with his parents, had never been so heated.

"Timotei?" Serghei asked.

"I ... I don't know what to think," Timotei said. "It's true, we were all raised to believe that talk about God is pure myth. But think a moment. Who told us that? The government? What have they ever said to us that we can trust?"

"Yes, the government lies to us. But that doesn't mean Marx's ideas about religion were lies. Use your common sense, man! We need to act like the intelligent people we are," Serghei said. "Not like a bunch of superstitious old women."

"Look, shouldn't we just focus on the task at hand?" Marcu said. "Our freedom. That's why we're gathered here. Let's not get caught up arguing about these side issues. We don't need to settle the religion debate right now. *After* we're victorious, we'll have all the time in the world to decide whether we believe in God or not. Just imagine, maybe we'll even be able to debate it in public." Marcu rose out of his seat. "We have to win first."

Serghei stroked his goatee with his index finger and paused. A moment later, he said, "Good point. Let's return to the relevant news of the day. Timotei, do you have more facts for us?"

"As I said, the events with Tőkés occurred two days ago. Since then, the crowd moved to Opera Square. They estimate the size of the crowd has now swollen to thousands. People started shouting *Jos Comunismul*. Down with Communism, indeed! Someone burned a portrait of Ceaușescu in the open square. As the people rioted and chanted, the army moved in with their armored trucks, firing tear gas and water cannons at first." Timotei's throat tightened. "But soon they brought in live ammunition. Tanks and helicopters. People have been killed."

Silence greeted him. The mood hung heavy in the room.

Timotei cleared his throat. "People in Timişoara—my home—have given their lives for us to be free. We can't let them down. We must take up their cause!"

"Yes!" said Marcu.

"In the crowd at Opera Square, someone started singing—singing!—*Deşteapta-te Romane*, and then a flood of voices joined in," Timotei said. "You all know of the song, right?"

"*Wake up, Romanians*," Marcu said. "Written during the 1848 Revolution."

"Marcu, is there anything you don't know about history?" Simona smiled.

Marcu flushed crimson. "I'm not sure about that, but I do know this song served as a national anthem of sorts. The Communists banned it when they took over at the end of World War II. The lyrics of *Deşteapta-te Romane* are especially offensive to the government."

"Wake up!" Serghei said, pounding his fist in his palm. "That is my charge for each of us. We must wake up our countrymen."

Timotei spoke up. "But only tell those you suspect are on our side. Spread the word, but don't just shout it from the street corners. We still need to be careful. I don't want any of you sacrificed—" Timotei's voice caught. "We need to be ready. This movement *will* come here. I just know it. We can't let those lives—the lives of the patriots—be lost in vain."

"I know another student group. I'll tell them," Beni said.

"I can spread the word to my classmates, my neighbors in the dorms," Marcu said.

"Simona, can you find other cells of believers here in Bucharest?" Timotei asked.

Simona nodded. "I'll try."

"One of my architecture professors," Claudia said. "I'm pretty sure he's one of us."

"Good!" Serghei said. "Let's meet back here, tomorrow night, same time. We'll share intel and count who we've awakened. Invite more students to our meeting. And we'll keep meeting every night until this is finished."

Timotei raised both hands and formed the sign of V for Victory with his fingers. "Go and spread the word, but please … be careful."

Monday, 18 December

Timotei couldn't sleep more than an hour or two on Sunday night. The next day, he didn't go to class. Neither did Marcu.

Most Romanians awakened the morning of 18 December to a normal Monday, business as usual, not having any idea what had been happening at their western border for the last three days. But slowly and without any media help, the word started to get out.

Early in the morning, Timotei waited outside Mihai's flat to tell him the news. Mihai promised to spread the word among his large group of freedom-loving friends.

Next on Timotei's mental checklist was Adriana. He waited outside her flat around the time she should be leaving for school. When she walked out the door of her apartment block, Timotei caught her by the arm. She jumped and put her hand over her mouth, probably to muffle a scream.

"Timo!" she hissed at him, "I told you to stop scaring me."

"I didn't mean to scare you," he said. "I have some news that is going to make your day. Actually, it'll make your year."

She raised her eyebrows and threw her hands up, as if to say, *I'm waiting.*

"Revolution has started in Romania. In Timişoara actually."

Adriana's mouth sprung open. "What did you say?"

"It's started, Green Eyes. People have been protesting around the clock—shouting 'Down with Communism' and sleeping outside in Opera Square—since 15 December. And the army has been shooting them. And killing some." He paused to let his words sink in. "Look, I'll give you more details later. But for now, pass the word to your professor, and your courier friend, and your study group friends. Anyone else you know who will be happy to hear this news."

Her eyes filled with tears. "I'm sorry, I'm just … I can't really believe this. I mean, we've wanted this for so long."

"I know." Timotei said and gave her a big hug. "I want you to come to the student meeting with me tonight—"

"I can't tonight."

"How about tomorrow night? We're meeting every night now. You haven't been since that first one you crashed."

"I will," she said. "And I promise to tell my friends."

"Ask them to spread the word too," Timotei said. "And now I must run."

He kissed his cousin goodbye.

Later that day, Timotei walked downtown to the Telephone Palace, where everyone who didn't have a telephone—a large percentage of the population—went to place their calls. Entering a large room rimmed with wooden telephone booths, he approached the desk where a woman clerk handed him a number. Timotei sat on one of the benches for over an hour until his number was called.

He entered the vacant booth the clerk indicated and dialed the new number he'd memorized from Vasile. The person who answered the phone said that Vasile was down at Opera Square. She asked if she could help. Timotei knew that this number was secure; it rang in the flat in Timișoara where Resistance workers listened to the short-wave radio. He also knew that people in the phone booths next to him may be listening to him. He decided to take a chance.

He whispered into the receiver. "What's the latest news?"

"Voice of America radio has joined the conversation along with Radio Free Europe," she said. "The crowd is still strong, even though the army from Bucharest came and started firing. The body count is piling up, but everybody refuses to leave. They say they will stand until the end."

Timotei delivered this most recent update to the Students for a Free Romania at their meeting that evening. All reports confirmed everything he'd already heard.

Each member reported back with names of people and groups they'd awakened. Marcu added up the total number of people they'd told. There was a groundswell of people. And it kept growing.

CHAPTER THIRTY-FOUR

ADRIANA: GET READY

ADRIANA PRACTICALLY RAN ALL the way to school. Yesterday, her life was the same old routine. But today, everything changed the moment her cousin met her outside her flat. Timo gave her a mission for today, the most important one of her life so far. She'd been entrusted with a message, one she wanted to believe but couldn't quite wrap her mind around yet.

Drill Sergeant Popescu had been tougher than usual at military training yesterday. She'd attributed it to him trying to catch up since the exercises had been cancelled the week before due to the snowstorm. Now she knew better. He must've received the same word she now carried. Words of hope for her; words of panic for the government.

She arrived in her classroom before any of the other students and paced. She willed her professor to get there early so she could pass on Timo's news. When the door opened, the first person to walk in wasn't Professor Filip, but the next best person: the other person Timo had specifically named.

"Alex!" Adriana grabbed his arm and whispered in his ear. "Have you heard?"

Alex shook his head.

"People have been gathered in Timişoara for three days now. They're protesting in the city center, shouting 'Down with Communism.' And some are being killed, Alex, but they won't go home."

Alex didn't move, as though he was in shock.

"Alex, did you hear me?" Adriana shook his shoulder.

As she did that, Professor Filip entered the room.

"Alex, Adriana," she said. "You're here bright and early—"

Adriana rushed to her side and repeated her whispered message.

Professor Filip's eyes grew large. "Come to my flat after school. Tell Gabi and Corina. We'll have an impromptu study group—"

Just then, Liviu entered. "An unscheduled study group?"

Professor Filip cleared her throat. "Why, yes. We never finished our discussion from last time, so we're continuing tonight."

"What were you discussing?"

"Liviu, I don't answer to you. Don't forget who's the professor and who's the assistant here." She turned her back on him and strode to the front of the classroom, setting her books on her desk with a thump.

During their lunch break, Adriana had been able to whisper the news to Gabi and Corina. Thanks to Mrs. Goga watching Teodor, all three girls were free to walk straight to their professor's flat after school. Professor Filip told them to go ahead; she said she'd be right behind them, after she recorded some grades in her ledger. Alex would arrive last. He told Adriana he had to deliver the message to his contact first.

The girls talked about the incredible happenings in Timişoara in hushed voices, all the way to Professor Filip's street. They didn't have to wait long on Strada Ana Davila before they spotted their professor rounding the corner and waving at them.

"Come on up," she said as she bounded up the front steps.

They followed her into her *garsoniera*. Professor Filip beamed her brilliant smile at them. She hadn't been able to suppress her joy all day.

"I want to hear details," she said. "Everything you know about …" she lowered her voice, "Timişoara." She held up one finger and walked over to her radio to click it on. "But first, take off your coats and shoes and get comfortable while I make us a big pot of tea."

Several minutes later, they were all settled on the sofa with cups of tea in their hands and a floral plate of sweet crackers sitting in the middle of the coffee table.

"Now," Professor Filip said. "What do you know?"

"My conversation with my cousin was really rushed," Adriana whispered. "I don't know much. Just what I already told you."

"I have learned that it started on 15 December outside a Hungarian pastor's flat and moved to Opera Square." Professor Filip said. "Thousands of people gathered and chanted *Jos Comunismul.* The army started shooting, tanks rolled in, helicopters, everything. Three days now and the people still refuse to leave."

"Such courage," Corina said softly, shaking her head.

"What can we do?" Gabi asked. "I want to help, but we're so far away."

"We need to be ready," Professor Filip said. "These things have a way of spreading. We're in the capital. If this is going to stick, it must come here."

"How do we get ready?" Corina asked.

"That's what I've been thinking about all day," Professor Filip said.

Adriana spoke up. "My cousin said to tell everyone we know who we're certain will be glad to hear this news. He says it needs to spread, or else how will people know what's happening?"

"My parents. I'll tell them," Gabi said. "And they can tell their … friends."

"Good," Professor Filip said. "And I'll spread the news among my colleagues who are on our side." She stood and paced. "But we need more. We're on the verge of something spectacular. We need a plan of action. A system to contact each other if the action moves here from Timișoara—"

"Don't you mean when?" Adriana asked.

She smiled. "You're right. *When*." She cleared her throat. "What we need is a code word—"

As she said that, the door swung open without anyone knocking first. Alex entered, breathless.

"Alex, what's wrong?" Professor Filip asked.

"I was followed here," he whispered. "Quick, pull your notebooks out and make it a real study—"

Liviu burst through the door.

"Professor Filip," he said, "So this is where you live." His eyes surveyed the one-room flat. "Very cozy."

"Liviu!" Professor Filip stood up. "What are you doing here?"

"Since I monitor two of the study groups, it seemed fitting that I find out what my *esteemed*," his lip curled when he said that word, "mentor is teaching that is so important it required an extra meeting."

"We had such a robust discussion about thermodynamics last time, we had to table it for later. Since you're here, Liviu, maybe you could explain the four principal laws of thermodynamics to us."

Instead of answering, Liviu marched over to the sofa and grabbed Corina's notebook. Adriana peeked at what Corina had jotted on the page.

Zeroth law of thermodynamics. If two systems each in thermal equilibrium with a third system, also in thermal equilibrium with each other …

Liviu dropped her notebook as though it was hot.

"I know there's more going on here," he said. "And I'm going to uncover it and report you. You'll never teach again. And the rest of you—" he looked each student in the eyes, one at a time, "The rest of you will not be allowed to graduate."

He stood there with a smug expression on his face.

Nobody moved.

Professor Filip walked to the door. "I suppose we will have to postpone our discussion of the zeroth law until the next scheduled study group." She held the door open. "I will see you all in class tomorrow morning."

Adriana wanted to stay. But she and her friends had no choice but to follow Liviu out the door and down the steps. They walked silently to the Eroilor metro station where they climbed aboard their respective trains. Alex, Gabi, and Corina took the first train. Adriana watched them leave. She saw Alex tilt his head in the direction of her apartment. As she waited on the platform with Liviu, she hoped she understood Alex's signal correctly.

She and Liviu rode to her station without speaking. Thankfully, Liviu remained on the train when Adriana disembarked.

After dinner that evening, during the water hour, Adriana washed the dishes while her mother took a bath. Bunica sat on the sofa, knitting. She looked up when a knock sounded at the door and raised an eyebrow at Adriana.

Adriana knew who it was before she answered.

"Alex! You're out after curfew," she whispered after she ushered him inside.

She noticed he wore all dark colors, as though he regularly crept around the city after dark.

"I won't be long. Just tell your cousin something. Tell him the word is spread." He smiled a broad smile. "People know, and they're getting ready."

CHAPTER THIRTY-FIVE

TIMISOARA

Tuesday, 19 December

WHEN ADRIANA EXITED HER building's lobby on her way to school the next day, Timo stepped out from the shadow he'd taken cover in.

"How'd it go?" he asked.

She jumped. "Will you quit lurking?"

"Sorry," he said. "I skipped class again. I just … I'm too focused on bigger things to sit in a classroom right now." He looked at her. "So, how'd it go?"

"Good. They all know. Alex, Professor Filip, Gabi, Corina. And they're spreading the word." She bit her lip. "Should I tell Mama?"

"Your call," he said. "I think she's safe. But she was a loyal Party member for many years."

"I told Bunica. I'll let her decide," Adriana said. "What about Mihai?"

"He's passing the word. I'm going to see him now." Timo paused. "Be careful. And be strong. I'll be back tonight to take you to the meeting." He kissed her on both cheeks and departed through the park.

Later that evening, Adriana and Timo walked stealthily along the streets until they reached the vacant restaurant. They silently entered the space where the secret student society was meeting for the third time that week to share news of Timișoara. Enough new students had joined the group in the last two days that Timo said their numbers had tripled. Some students sat in the few chairs scattered about, others sat cross-legged on the floor, and the rest stood. All were dressed in dark colors from head to foot.

Adriana felt out of place with so many university students. This was her first meeting since that one she barged in on. She decided to just observe; she was too intimidated to speak.

When enough people had arrived, Serghei stood and motioned to Timo to join him. "Timotei will give us the latest report from Radio Free Europe," Serghei told the group.

"The crowd at Opera Square continues to grow. Someone estimated 100,000 people now," Timo said.

Serghei whistled.

Timo said, "The rallying cry changed from *Down with Communism* to *We Are the People—*"

Simona spoke up. "Not just that, but they also started chanting *Exista Dumnezeu!*" She practically jumped out of her seat. "Imagine: God exists! Out in the open like that." Simona's voice rose with her excitement. "My parents told me a pastor, Petru Dugulescu, jumped up on the balcony of the Opera House and led the crowd to recite the Lord's Prayer. After all these years of suppression, the Bible was quoted out-loud by thousands. I mean … whatever you do or don't believe, you must admit that's amazing."

Adriana watched Simona as she spoke. So passionate. Simona always brought the subject around to God. Adriana noticed other students' eyes filling up.

"I don't know what to think about this," Claudia said.

"Look, in the other countries, it was all about politics," Marcu said. "The old system had failed and a new system took its place. Peaceably. It feels different here."

"We're getting ahead of ourselves," Serghei said. "We haven't won anything yet. Until we do, the world won't even know what's going on in Timişoara and all those lives will have been sacrificed for nothing."

"Still, Marcu's right," Beni said. "It *is* different here. It's not peaceable. As you just said, people have *already* been killed for this. The death toll keeps climbing. And God exists? We haven't heard words like these chanted in any of the other countries."

"Let's table that discussion," Serghei said. "We're gathering facts right now, not speculation."

"The mayor of Timişoara declared martial law," Timo reported. "He went on television to say he did it to combat the vandalism of a *few* hooligans. And he sent his officials to the factories to make people resume work." He smirked. "I guess that's what we'll read in the newspapers: vandalism and hooligans. They had to come up with some story to try to explain away what's happening."

"The word has gotten to other cities in Romania. I know people who've said they're organizing themselves. They're ready for action," Marcu said.

"Where?" Beni asked.

"Cluj and Braşov that I know of," Marcu said. "Probably other cities too."

"Some people have cut the Communist symbol out of the center of the Romanian flag," Simona said. "They've been waving that new flag all over Timişoara."

Adriana smiled. If only she had a flag, she'd rip the center out of it and hang it high above the city.

"Our intel is really stepping up," Timo reported. "Other short-wave reports say that Ceaușescu left yesterday, on 18 December, for Iran, where he was given a red-carpet welcome—"

"Iran? Why Iran?" asked Claudia.

"I have an idea," Marcu spoke up. "Romania is a big trading partner of Iran. I've heard talk that Ceaușescu wants to buy one million barrels of oil from them. That's probably why."

Simona smiled at him. "How do you know all this stuff, Marcu?"

Marcu shrugged. Adriana also noticed a smile play on his lips as his face reddened.

"Well, I don't know the politics like Marcu here, but I can tell you one thing," Timo said. "Apparently, Ceaușescu feels confident enough that he left the job of quelling this revolt to his wife and his lackies. First Lady Elena sent her people to Timișoara to resolve the situation. The spokespeople in Timișoara demanded that Ceaușescu resign—"

Claudia cheered, "Yes!"

The volume level in the restaurant kept growing. Adriana felt uncomfortable, but as she looked at the faces of the students around her, they didn't seem to mind anymore. The courage of the people from Timișoara had emboldened them.

"Our Supreme Leader's going to be in for a big surprise when he returns," Marcu said.

Serghei spoke up. "Good, good. Any other facts to report?"

"Another thing, the government sent in miners and facto-ry workers from Oltenia by train to Timișoara," Timo reported. "These guys owe their allegiance to Ceaușescu and they'll do any-thing he says. The factory bosses handed out wooden clubs as they boarded the train. They told them to kill the hooligans. Said they're devastating Timișoara."

"I heard a lot of the miners didn't believe that," Simona said.

"We can only hope," Timo said.

"No, really. Listen." Simona became animated again. "I heard that some of these miners have ended up joining the protests."

"Simona, where do you get your information?" Serghei asked.

"My parents' good friend told them. He overheard one miner say that he and his buddies realized it was all a big lie. He said the hooligans weren't ruining Timişoara but he knew who was."

"It's happening." Claudia looked at the group, her eyes moist. "It's finally our turn."

"My parents reported something else," Simona said. "Some of the Christians—the ones who've been praying around the clock, hidden away in secret—they've said they're too weary to keep praying. They can't continue anymore."

"I think that's the least of our worries," Serghei said. "So what if they stop praying? We need people to come out of their hiding places and join the fight. That's what matters most."

"How can you say that, Serghei?" Simona's eyes flashed at him. "Maybe this is all happening *because* they're praying. Maybe that is the most important part."

"Look, you can believe anything you want, no matter how far-fetched," Serghei snickered. "If we become free, then religion will also be free for Romanians. But I want to know about *real* things, objective ways we can influence the outcome. We can't do anything about people being too tired to pray in Timişoara, now can we?"

"I wonder. Do people in the West even know what's happening here?" Beni asked. "Don't all Westerners believe in God? When they find out, I bet they'll join us in praying."

"Or maybe the West will finally send troops over." Serghei clenched his jaw. "Isn't that the fairy tale our grandparents expected, after World War II ended and the Communists took over? They never came to help … and look what happened to us."

"That sounds personal to you," Timo said.

"It was. It *is* personal," Sergei said. He removed his glasses and rubbed his hand over his face. When he put his glasses back on, his voice hissed with venom. "You want to know *how* personal? My grandfather was sent to the gulag in Pitești in the early fifties. They tortured him and tried to reeducate him. But they ended up killing him instead."

Adriana closed her eyes.

"Then my father took a stand once, just a small act of rebellion. He refused to join the Party. His bosses said he wouldn't be promoted, but instead, he lost his job. And our home." Serghei's voice cracked. "My father took his own life." He paused. "All at the hands of the Communists. So yes, it is personal."

The group went silent. Adriana studied Serghei's face, partially obscured by his flat brown worker's cap. His eyes blazed behind his wire frames. The first time she met Serghei, he seemed intense, but that was nothing compared to the anger she sensed now. She knew they called him Serghei the Bear; the name fit.

After a few moments, Serghei spoke again, his voice more subdued. "Look, not just my family, but thousands upon thousands have suffered here. We need this revolution to be victorious. And we won't wait for help to come from someplace else. Not from some fictional God, who's never come to our rescue before." He looked at Simona. "Not from other countries. We need to be ready—each of us. Ready to die." Serghei pounded his fist into his hand. "Freedom is worth the cost. And more than freedom. We must avenge what they've done. We should wipe the Commies off the face of the earth."

A few students murmured their assent, but most sat in shocked silence.

"No, Serghei," Beni said softly. "Not vengeance. Justice."

"How do you suggest we get rid of the 'Commies,' Serghei?" Marcu asked. "We have no weapons. Besides, violence never solves anything. It just leads to more violence."

"We can rise above, and we must." Timo commanded the group's attention. "Let's not stoop to their level."

Adriana inhaled a steadying breath and exhaled it as she looked around the room. "I think," she began, her voice tremulous. As she thought about what she wanted to say, her voice grew stronger. "We rise above by refusing to cower. We stand on our legs and use our voices. And we do this because we are right." She paused a moment. "Not because we are powerful."

"Amen!" Simona said.

Marcu yelled, "Freedom! Freedom to Romania!"

Every person in the room stood. Timo looked at Adriana with eyes full of pride.

CHAPTER THIRTY-SIX

ALEX: THE WINTER OF DISCONTENT

Wednesday, 20 December

ALEX COULD HARDLY BELIEVE the words Adriana had told him—was that only Monday? When he met Ofelia at the empty *farmacie* that evening and she confirmed it, it began to feel more real. The event he'd been waiting for—and risking his life for every time he delivered intel for the Resistance—was starting to come true.

Alex suspected that Liviu knew about Timişoara. He seemed to patrol the aisles of their classroom more vigilantly today, scrutinizing each student, one at a time, as he walked back and forth. When he reached Alex's desk, Liviu stared at him with an expression so icy Alex shivered.

Liviu walked to the front of the room and, with his back to the class, he talked to the professor in a low voice. Then he turned on his heel and stomped out.

Professor Filip called Alex to her desk.

"Negrescu has filed a report with the principal. He claims he caught you cheating today."

"But we didn't have an exa—"

"Don't be impertinent. We take cheating seriously in my classroom," Professor Filip continued, in a loud voice. "You are being suspended. Effective immediately."

Alex stood still. He knew he gaped, but he couldn't help it.

"You must take this note home." She tore a piece of paper out of her notebook, scribbled something on it, folded it, and handed it to Alex.

I hereby suspend Alexandru Oprea from school.

Professor Elisabeta Filip

20 December 1989

"Now go!" she said, with a faint smile on her lips as she searched Alex's eyes.

As Alex walked out, he could see Adriana's questioning expression. Corina looked down.

Corina still ignored him, pretending not to care. Who was he kidding? It had been going on long enough, he had to face the fact that she probably wasn't pretending.

He bolted out of the classroom and hurried toward the outside door. He opened the folded paper and read the words the professor had written at the bottom.

Gradina Botanica, 17:00.

He was glad to be suspended. The time sitting at his desk after he learned what was happening elsewhere in his country had been painful. Alex felt so antsy. He walked home to see if his mother had answered the phone. If someone had called to say they dialed a wrong number, he could go to the drop-off spot immediately. He hoped his source would call. He longed to find out more.

Wherever he went today, whatever he did, he just had to do something.

As the hours dragged on, Alex knew no more than he did yesterday. He longed for details. People on the street were either fantastic actors, or the news hadn't funneled down to them yet.

Finally, the time arrived to meet Professor Filip at the benches hidden away inside the botanical garden. He got there first. A few minutes later, Adriana and Gabi appeared.

"Alex," Adriana said, "classes are cancelled indefinitely! All over the city."

"Are you kidding?" he asked, as Corina ran up behind them, out of breath.

"It's true!" Gabi said.

Before they could talk more, Professor Filip arrived, picking her way carefully down the path in the twilight, wearing her impractical heels. She'd slung her book bag over her shoulder.

"I'm sorry about the suspension, Alex. I had to—" she began.

"I'm glad," Alex said. "No offense, but there are more important things right now than school."

Professor Filip nodded. "My colleagues and I have outlined some information to pass on to all the student cells, in case the protest progresses to Bucharest." She cleared her throat. "Every time you go outside, dress as warmly as you can and don't wear silly shoes. Like mine," she said, thrusting her foot out for inspection. "You never know how long it'll be before you can go home. Also, eat well. Eat everything on your plate whenever you get the chance. You'll need fuel."

"So you expect " Corina said.

"I don't know what to expect. Expect the unexpected. That's my motto," Professor Filip said.

"I heard in Timişoara they've stayed outside all night long," Adriana said.

"My point exactly." Professor Filip cleared her throat again. "Whether you tell your parents what's happening and whether you go or not is up to you. But before you leave your flat, please tell them you love them. You never know."

"Am I missing something?" Alex asked. "Go where?"

"Before I dismissed the class, I told them that Ceauşescu has called for a spontaneous rally tomorrow morning. He will give a speech from his usual spot—the balcony of the Central Committee headquarters in Palace Square. He gave the mandate to cancel all classes. Every student, every citizen, is encouraged to attend. I completely understand if you decide to stay home and watch the address on television, but if you go, I think you'll see history being made. And if you do go, please be attentive. You don't know who to trust. Securitate agents may pose as people who seem sympathetic to the cause, to get you talking and then trap you in what you say."

Alex noticed the somber expression on the girls' faces.

"We may need to assemble before the speech, maybe even tonight. So I've devised a code. If any of you calls anyone else in our study group or sees them and says the phrase: *It's winter and I'm discontent,* then you'll know to move."

"But where?" Alex asked. "Where do we move?"

"The minute you receive a call with that code—tonight or early in the morning— report immediately to the first floor of the History Department in University Square. All the various student cells around the city will gather there and wait for further directions. And if you don't receive a phone call with that code, you are to report there as soon as the rally ends."

The students nodded.

"Another thing," Professor Filip said, her throat tightening. "It may turn violent, like it did in Timişoara. I can't keep you from being out in the middle of it. But I don't want anything … I care about you." Her voice caught.

Corina's eyes filled up. "We care about you too."

Adriana nodded, the picture of seriousness. Corina looked as white as the snow drifted beside the path. Gabi had an expression of excitement in her eyes.

"Before we split up for now, I want to leave you with something. I chose the code phrase because it won't raise any alarms. Who isn't discontent in winter? 'Now is the winter of our discontent' is a famous line from *The Tragedy of King Richard III* by William Shakespeare."

Alex noticed Adriana nod her head and smile.

"King Richard is ruthless. He kills anyone who stands in his way. This goes on for years and the people have taken enough," Professor Filip said. "The night before a big invasion, Richard has a dream. The ghosts of all the people he's killed appear and curse him. The next day, he is killed." She paused. "This is our winter. And we are discontent."

"Yes!" Alex pumped his fist in the air.

Professor Filip smiled at the students gathered around her. "Remember, you stand up with your voice. With your courage. Violence is never the solution." She inhaled a deep breath. "Now go. It's our time. Be strong, but please, be careful."

Alex was the first to leave. As he rounded the corner by the lily pond, he heard footsteps. The garden was usually vacant in the winter. He turned and caught a glimpse of a guy wearing a long black overcoat and jumping over the iron railing in the back. He'd recognize that coat anywhere. It was Liviu's.

What had Liviu heard? Alex considered turning around to tell the others, but the plans were already set in motion. All the student cells were being mobilized. There was no going back now.

Later that night, Alex's phone rang, but it wasn't one of the girls with the code.

"I'm sorry to disturb you," the caller said. ""May I speak to Aurel?"

"You've dialed the wrong number," Alex said and hung up.

Alex was already dressed in dark colors. He slinked out the door and made his way to the abandoned pharmacy on Strada Aurel Vlaicu. He noticed more soldiers than usual patrolling the streets, so after waiting for his route to become clear, it took him quite a while longer than normal to get there.

He shimmied through the broken window, catching the shoulder of his dark brown wool jacket on a jagged pane of glass. He heard it rip and saw the fabric flap open.

When he entered, he found Ofelia pacing inside.

She exhaled when she saw him. "There you are!"

"What's happening now—"

"Did you hear Ceaușescu on the news tonight?"

Alex nodded. "Yes. He called the events in Timișoara an external aggression on Romania's sovereignty caused by hooligans."

"Exactly. That means the government is aware that word of what's happening in Timișoara is being spread and they want to get ahead of it." Ofelia paused. "Ceaușescu just returned today from a couple days in Iran and this was his first order of business."

"Iran?"

"Yes, strange as that seems," Ofelia said. "Here's the message for you to deliver. When Ceaușescu addresses the crowd tomorrow morning in Palace Square, everyone who's sympathetic to our cause *must* be there." She grabbed Alex's shoulders and looked him in the eyes. "Now go and disperse the news, to your contacts and beyond."

"Does this mean …"

Ofelia smiled. "Tomorrow's the day we've been waiting for in Bucharest. We could be free soon."

Alex pumped his fist and left.

The sun rose the following morning and streaked the winter sky in shades of pink and violet. To all appearances, it was just another day. Alex knew differently.

None of his classmates had called to say *It's winter and I'm discontent.* He couldn't stay home any longer waiting for the telephone to ring. He had to be there to watch history unfold.

His mother snored on the sofa, no doubt sleeping off the vodka she'd consumed the night before. His dark brown jacket sat folded on the coffee table beside her. His mother had sewn the rip together with white thread, using large sloppy stitches. She must have done it during the few hours he slept. Usually, she wouldn't even notice anything that Alex needed.

He looked at her with new eyes and, for the first time in a long while, he saw more than a drunk. He saw a mother. *His* mother.

He gently poked her shoulder until she grunted.

"Mama, wake up. I have something to tell you."

She pushed herself up on her elbows. "This better be good—"

"Ceaușescu's giving a speech downtown. I'm going."

She shrugged. "Why did you wake me up to tell me—"

"I'm going to protest."

Mama sat straight up. "What are you saying?"

"There's a chance this will turn violent. I don't know. But I'm doing this for my country. For my father. For his memory. I need to defend his good name."

"No, Alex. I don't want—"

"But Mama, I can't stay home and let other people be the ones who stand up for my freedom. I must go. Please try to understand."

She nodded, as her eyes started to fill. "You are your father's son, alright."

Alex leaned down and kissed his mother. "I love you."

She patted the side of his face.

"Thank you for mending my coat, Mama."

"Come back to me, son."

CHAPTER THIRTY-SEVEN

ADRIANA: IT'S STARTED!

Thursday, 21 December

A DRIANA SAT ON THE sofa next to Bunica as though transfixed by the television. Her grandmother gripped her hand so tightly that her fingers ached. They waited for Ceauşescu's speech to come on TV. Adriana bounced her knee, willing the phone to ring, willing the person on the other end to say the words that would call her to action. *It's winter and I'm discontent.*

But the telephone didn't ring and she couldn't wait any longer.

"Bunica," she said, letting go of her grandmother's hand. "I have to go. Please explain to Mama."

"I know you do." Bunica kissed her on both cheeks. "May God go with you, draga. Stay safe."

Adriana grabbed her warm layers and sped out the door and down the stairs. As she ran along side streets toward Palace Square, she noticed it didn't feel all that cold outside.

When she arrived at Palace Square, the crowd was already beginning to swell. Buses had driven up in single file and lined the *piaţa*. Each bus unloaded scores of workers, red Socialist Party of Romania flags clutched in their hands. She wondered if they even knew what this was all about. She was certain they'd been threatened. Why else would they come?

Adriana made her way to the side of the square nearest the History Department, in case she had to make a quick getaway. The first person she recognized was Alex. He waved at her and she ran toward him.

"Alex, I'm glad you're here," she said. "Have you seen any of the others?"

"Not yet. Liviu's up front near Securitate headquarters. See him standing beside Captain Zugravescu?" he said, pointing.

"What's been happening so far?"

"Party members have filled up their usual spots in the front rows. They're waving their flags high."

Adriana noticed both the red Party flag and Romania's tri-color flag. Some held large black-and-white posters with images of Ceaușescu on them; others held posters of his wife, Elena. Red horizontal banners, large enough to be held by six or seven people across, read *Long Live the Communist Party* or *Long Live Comrade Nicolae Ceaușescu*.

They overheard a couple men talking in hushed tones nearby.

"My boss tried to force me to stand in the front and look like I support him. Told me they'd put me in prison if I refused," one of them said. His voice rose. "But why would I be afraid of that? Haven't we been imprisoned our whole lives?"

"Hush now," his friend said. "Be careful."

"I'm tired of careful," the first guy said. "I don't care who hears me anymore."

Even though Adriana kind of expected the speech to be boring—just like all the other speeches she'd endured throughout her life—she felt the tension in the air and suspected this one may end very differently than all the others.

As the time for the speech drew near, Adriana looked around. The crowd seemed to fill every meter of the huge *piața*.

At that moment, both Ceaușescus walked out onto the balcony of the Central Committee, flanked by several men in long black coats. Bucharest's mayor introduced Supreme Commander Nicolae Ceaușescu and Deputy Prime Minister Elena Ceaușescu. The president took the microphone, and Elena took her usual spot by his side.

Ceaușescu greeted his comrades, friends, and citizens of the capital of Socialist Romania. He thanked those who organized what he called "this great and popular gathering."

People clapped in perfect sync, as though they were robots.

Just then, about one minute into his speech, the sound of voices began in the back of the crowd and rolled over the people like a wave. At first Adriana wasn't sure what they were yelling, but as the chant moved her way, she heard it clearly: *Ti-mi-șoar-a!*

Adriana heard popping sounds next, followed by screams of terror coming from the crowd.

Alex craned his neck to see what was happening. "I think that's gunfire," he said.

Adriana grabbed his arm.

Elena's voice was picked up by the microphone. "Someone is shooting!"

Ceaușescu looked all around. "What is it? Is it an earthquake?"

For once, Adriana thought, *Elena is right*. Someone was shooting. Regular people did not have guns; only the army and Securitate had weapons.

Ceaușescu kept shouting into the microphone, "Hallo! Comrades, hallo! Hallo! Comrades!"

Elena shouted to the crowd, "Silence! Sit down! Keep calm!" When the crowd didn't obey, she yelled, "Silence! What's the matter with you, comrades? This is a provocation."

Adriana was glad to be present as history was happening. She needed to witness the defiance with her own eyes, to feel the palpable electricity in the crowd, to hear the words being chanted, even to smell the gunfire.

After a few moments, when the chaos subsided enough, Ceaușescu resumed his speech, as though nothing had happened. "I want to stress again that we must demonstrate strength and unity, using all of our power and force for the sake of Romania's independence, integrity, and sovereignty."

The workers in the front of the crowd applauded wildly, led by Elena the cheerleader. The Party faithful yelled, "Long live Ceaușescu!" keeping time with their claps.

Ceaușescu told the crowd he'd made an important decision that day, as if one decision would fix all the problems. Salaries would be raised from 2,000 lei to 2,200 lei each month. Adriana scoffed. That would only give people enough money to buy a few extra loaves of bread per month. Big deal.

Even though Ceaușescu appeared out of touch with the reality that was unfolding before him today, he didn't try to pretend that nothing had happened in Timișoara. He blamed the fascist agitators from other countries for stirring up the hooligans there. But once he said the name of that city, something changed. He had uttered the magic word that woke the people from a long, forty-plus year sleep.

Words rose from the back of the crowd again, like soft music building to a crescendo. *Ti-mi-șoar-a!* This time, the people seemed emboldened. The words grew louder, stronger.

Ceaușescu appeared disoriented.

More people joined in. Adriana and Alex added their voices. It seemed that everyone was chanting. *Ti-mi-șoar-a!*

Adriana's pulse raced as people started to jeer and whistle and yell insults at the dictator. Ceaușescu looked confused, as though what he thought he heard couldn't possibly be true. It seemed his delusion—that his people actually adored him—won out. In the next minute, Adriana—close enough to see his face—read his expression as basking in their praise.

Some people defiantly yelled with loud voices, *Down with Ceaușescu. Down with the dictator. Down with the tyrant. Death to the criminal!*

Now it seemed Ceaușescu understood. Adriana saw a shocked expression on his face. He raised his right hand, as though to demand silence. Ceaușescu's bodyguards quickly scrambled to cover him and Elena, pushing them back inside the building.

Alex looked at his watch. "It's only been seven minutes since Ceaușescu resumed his speech."

Another noise swept in from the edges of the gathering. It sounded like fireworks to Adriana, but she knew better now. It was gunfire.

Shrieks ricocheted around the *piața*. Someone grabbed a bullhorn and shouted, "The Securitate are firing on us."

The mob erupted in chaos. People ran away from the Central Committee building, screaming. Many tripped and fell, causing others to fall on top of them.

Someone else took control of the bullhorn and yelled, "The revolution is upon us!"

A cheer rose from the crowd as people ducked and ran to take cover from the shots fired. Thousands of panicked people fled in every direction. Mass chaos reigned.

Adriana watched in amazement. She and Alex stood there, frozen in place, bumped into from every side. The city was in turmoil. Some citizens screamed in terror. With her own eyes, Adriana witnessed the Securitate shooting wildly into the crowd. She watched people flee to dodge the bullets.

Then Alex's flight instinct must have kicked in. "Come with me!" he yelled to Adriana. He grabbed her arm and started to run for shelter, pulling her with him. They sprinted toward their meeting place in the History Department.

With the mob and confusion, it seemed to take forever to make their way through the mass of humanity and past armored military trucks now clogging the streets. Adriana heard gunfire in the distance, followed by intermittent screams. The square was strewn with trampled-on signs, broken glass, and discarded posters.

As they neared University Square, Adriana heard rumbling.

"The tanks are coming!" someone shouted.

Just before they reached the side door of the History Department, which faced Boulevard Nicolae Balcescu, Adriana spotted a row of army tanks rolling down the boulevard, headed their way. "Look!" she cried out to Alex.

Revolutionaries had started to line up in the street, defiantly facing the tanks. They stood several rows deep, in front of the exhibition hall called the Dalles Room. As the tanks kept coming, the people didn't budge. They stared down the tanks, blocking them from continuing forward.

It was a stand-off. Nobody moved.

Adriana noticed a flat worker's cap on one of the guys in the front row. Serghei! Serghei and a group of thirty or so people stood united against the army. The guy beside Serghei got down on his knees and, with outstretched arms, offered flowers to the troops in the front tank.

Adriana and Alex dashed for safety. They ran inside the door of the History Department. The first people they saw inside were Professor Filip and Gabi.

"Where's Corina?" Alex asked.

"Corina isn't here yet." Professor Filip said. "Alex, I need you to construct barricades. Gabi, show Adriana around."

Gabi pointed out Dr. Luca Tomeci, a young professor who taught at the Medical Department. He'd quickly taken charge and set up a temporary triage unit inside the history building.

Professors who taught languages, chemistry, art, economics—all the disciplines—commanded the various stations. Luckily, several of them also taught medicine. They rallied the students who'd assembled to assign them tasks.

Some students volunteered for the risky job of surveying the *piața* outside and carrying in any wounded they found. Volunteers had lined up desks to lay the wounded on and taken doors off their hinges to serve as stretchers.

Others took their stations at the outer doors. Their assignment was to look over each injured person as they came in and determine where they should go. The ones who were badly hurt and needed aid immediately in order to survive would be cared for first, on the ground floor in the room nearest the door—Room 101. They called that the Urgent Room. The ones who could wait for help would be carried down the hall to Room 106. The trek upstairs to Room 201 was reserved for the ones beyond help.

Dr. Tomeci ordered some of the students to go outside and bring back whatever they could find that might help them. "We need medical supplies and clean cloths to make bandages. We also need to fashion more stretchers. There's no time to ask permission. Just take what you need. Whatever it is," he said. "And if you find anything—anything at all—that will help us protect ourselves, bring it back here."

Students broke wooden legs from the desk chairs to carry with them as clubs. They ran out of the building and along the street. Adriana and Gabi joined them. They watched as one group smashed pharmacy windows, grabbing bandages, rubbing alcohol, any medical supplies that could help tend to the wounds.

It was pandemonium.

Adriana and Gabi split off with a group that entered the un-locked doors of a nearby restaurant, filling their arms with stacks of white linen tablecloths and bottles of fizzy water. Once they returned, Gabi got busy ripping the linen fabric for the improvised bandages.

Dr. Tomeci and Professor Filip inspected the loot.

Someone carried in a tri-color Romanian flag they took from a flagpole. Professor Filip handed Adriana a knife and pointed to the

Communist symbol in the center: an idyllic country scene encircled by wheat and topped with a red star. "Cut that out like they've done to the flags in Timișoara," she said. "And then you let it fly high so everyone can see it."

When Adriana finished cutting, she ran upstairs to the second-floor window to hang the new flag.

From the window, she could see that the army tanks had moved forward on Boulevard Nicolae Balcescu. Mere meters now separated the rows of tanks from the rows of revolutionaries facing them. The people stood fearlessly, defiantly, as though daring the tanks to shoot.

Then she heard the first volleys burst out. The entire front row of revolutionaries fell.

Serghei the Bear had fallen. Adriana didn't know Serghei well, but she knew him. As horrible as the scene through the window, she couldn't look away.

The tanks continued to fire. With each additional burst, more people toppled. Then the tanks began to roll forward, headed toward Palace Square. The revolutionaries left standing jumped out of the way. The tanks rolled right over the dead or wounded bodies, crushing them flat.

Adriana threw up in her mouth. She bent over, with her hands on her thighs and took several deep breaths, trying to clear the image from her mind. What had she just witnessed?

As she continued to breathe, she knew she had to do something. This was war. The people needed a visual symbol.

I have to hang this flag.

She leaned out of the window and attached the flag to the pole. It waved proudly over University Square.

Then Adriana hurried down the stairs and outside. A small group of students stood near the doorway.

"Did you see the line of tanks?" she heard someone say.

"They killed those students in cold blood!" another voice said.

"This is just like Tiananmen Square." Adriana recognized the person who spoke. It was Claudia from Timo's group.

Adriana thought of the failed revolution that took the lives of students in Beijing last June, just six months earlier. "Those students in China were so brave. Just like these people."

Claudia turned to look at her. "You're the one from the meeting," she said. "Timotei's cousin. I liked what you said the other evening. Those were some powerful words."

Adriana nodded. "Thanks."

"Those Chinese students and what they suffered should be an inspiration for us," Claudia said. "I'm going to paint the words 'Tiananmen Square' on the wall. Maybe it'll give our people courage. You want to help?"

"I do," Adriana said. A couple others also agreed.

Claudia led the way to the Architecture Department, just behind the history one. She broke the glass in the door, reached in to turn the handle, and led the group down the hall until they reached a storage room. They ransacked the place, grabbing cans of paint and brushes.

They opened their cans and started slopping paint on the outside wall of the Architecture Department. In the center of University Square in Bucharest, Claudia painted the words: *Piața Tiananmen II.*

Someone else wrote simply, *Down with Communism.*

A guy squatting beside Adriana painted, *Rise up off your knees and stand on your own two legs.*

Adriana thought of the words Timotei quoted when he first told her about Timișoara. She grabbed a brush and wrote *Deșteapta-te Romane.* Beneath it, Adriana painted out the words to the first verse.

> *Wake up, Romanians, from the sleep of death*
> *Into which you have been sunk by the barbarian tyrants.*
> *Now or never, make a new fate for yourself*
> *To which even your cruel enemies will bow.*

CHAPTER THIRTY-EIGHT

ALEX: TO THE BARRICADES!

UNIVERSITY STUDENT TOOK ALEX by the arm. "Come with me. We need help putting up barricades."

Alex hurried back out to the streets, following the stranger who stuck out his hand and grinned.

"I'm Beni," he said. "First-year medical student. I'm a member of the Students for a Free Romania."

Alex reached over to shake his hand. "I'm Alex. Still in high school. I also want a free Romania."

"This is a day we will never forget, Alex," Beni said.

In front of the Dunarea restaurant on Calea Victoriei, a couple of blocks from the fighting, several students had already started amassing trash cans, bicycle racks, chairs, a kiosk with papers advertising items for sale thumbtacked over it.

A female student came running up, carrying a small table. She threw it on the pile. "How's this?"

"Pretty good, Simona," Beni said. "For a girl."

Simona laughed and punched him in the arm. Alex noticed she wore a long pullover, a thick neck scarf, and a fleecy cap, but no coat.

"You might get cold later," Alex said. "Here, take my jacket." He slid out of his jacket and handed it to her.

"*Mulţumesc*," she said.

The chef of the Dunarea restaurant stood in his opened door-way. "Take whatever you need," he said. "Freedom to Romania!"

Several guys, all appearing to be college age, hauled every piece of furniture not nailed down out of the Dunarea. The chef said they should confiscate anything they could get their hands on to block the tanks from rolling into the square.

"We're going to build the largest barricade right here," Beni said. "We'll call it Barricade Central. It'll be the command center."

Adrenaline coursed through Alex's veins, taking any small remnants of fear along with it. He was ready to do battle. Anything to set his country free.

After they piled the restaurant tables and chairs on the growing heap, Alex followed Beni and two new members of the Students for a Free Romania, Adam and Nelu, to the smaller street along the side of the restaurant. A blue Dacia was parked there. Nelu opened the unlocked door, put the car in neutral, and they pushed it to Barricade Central. Several others joined them to successfully hoist the front of the Dacia up, leaning it against their makeshift barricade.

Suddenly, Alex heard a volley of shots, much louder than the gunfire he'd heard earlier.

"The tanks are coming!" someone yelled.

As soon as the Dacia was in place, they saw a tank approach, its large gun rotating as it rolled. All they could do was take cover. Alex crawled on his elbows toward the doorway of the Dunarea restaurant. For the first time, Alex was glad for his training in defending the Motherland. It was helping him defend himself *from* the Motherland.

The tank aimed straight for the barricade. At that moment, Alex heard Beni cry out and saw that he was trapped under the Dacia's back bumper.

"Quick! We have to pull Beni out," Alex yelled to the others.

Adam, Nelu, and the others each grabbed part of the Dacia and lifted it a few centimeters. It was enough for Alex to slide Beni out to safety in the doorway of the Dunarea.

As soon as Beni was free, everyone ran and ducked out of the path of the tank. As Nelu tried to fling himself out of the tank's course, the armored vehicle rolled right over the Dacia, completely crushing the car. A soldier's head popped up from the hatch on top of the tank. He sent out a volley of bullets, aimed directly at Nelu. It looked like flames leaving the gun. The bullets ripped through Nelu's neck. Alex watched, helpless, while the scene before him unfolded in slow motion.

The expression etched on Nelu's face before he toppled to the ground was one of disbelief.

"No! No!" Alex heard someone yell before he realized it was him.

Adam ran to kneel beside Nelu. Blood spurted up from Nelu's mouth. Adam put his fingers into the gaping hole in the side of Nelu's neck as Beni pumped his chest.

Beni wouldn't stop pumping. Blood just trickled from Nelu's mouth now. Adam placed his fingers on Nelu's wrist.

"It's over," he said. "He's gone." He gently pulled Beni off Nelu.

Beni collapsed in a pile.

Alex felt numb. He picked up Nelu's lifeless arms as Adam lifted his legs. Together, they carried Nelu to the building for triage. Alex didn't think about what he had to do; he just did it, as though he were sleepwalking

Alex and Adam walked into the History Department, Nelu suspended between them. Beni, bloodied and limping, followed.

Dr. Tomeci sprinted toward them. He took charge of Nelu. He checked for a pulse. He shook his head.

Beni bent forward and put his head in his hands. "It's my fault. He helped save me—"

Dr. Tomeci laid his hand on Beni's shoulder. "It's not your fault, son," he said softly.

Beni lifted his face, contorted in pain. Dr. Tomeci opened his arms for Beni to step in. Alex saw Beni's body heave with sobs.

Others carried Nelu's body to the room for those who no longer needed help.

The cost of this revolution felt real now.

Alex took off down the stairs and ran back onto the street. He leaned against the side of the building and vomited.

Now he was really angry.

CHAPTER THIRTY-NINE

ADRIANA: MARIUS

AFTER ADRIANA HAD FINISHED painting the words to rally people to action, she returned to triage. More victims had arrived, and Adriana was glad people more qualified than her were lined up, ready to help.

She watched Gabi hold a young man's hand and smile at him as Dr. Tomeci extracted a bullet. Adriana was proud of her best friend. Gabi's ready smile could infuse even the sickest patient with courage. She naturally loved people, and it showed. With Gabi's dramatic flair, Adriana had always thought she should be an actress. But seeing her compassion shine today, she changed her mind. Gabi would make a fantastic nurse.

Dr. Tomeci had mostly been treating students who weren't severely wounded. When Adriana walked past the Beyond Help room, she saw a sheet being pulled over a body.

She asked Professor Filip's permission to go out to Palace Square to see what was happening now. "Of course. You don't need to ask my permission, although I appreciate knowing where you are," she said.

"Have you seen Alex or Corina?"

"Corina's not here, but Alex brought in that guy." Professor Filip motioned toward the body with the sheet over it. "Looked like he took it pretty hard."

Adriana let the weight of reality hang in the air a moment. People were dying all around them. She wondered if Alex knew the guy he brought in. She and her friends were seeing things they never wanted to see.

She walked outside and headed toward the *piața*, hugging the buildings. When she reached the edge of it, the sight that met her eyes shocked her. Although many people had dispersed, a crowd still remained. She also saw soldiers, Securitate officers, and officers wearing the uniform of anti-terrorist squads. Military trucks and tanks moved around the *piața*. Shots were being fired from the rooftops of buildings down into the crowd. She watched a soldier club a man repeatedly until his face was bloody. Firefighters opened up their water hoses and sprayed people, knocking them down with their powerful streams.

As she stood on the sidelines, mesmerized and unable to tear herself away, Adriana saw both the worst in people and also the best. An old lady, about Bunica's age, doled out several loaves of bread to the soldiers.

When the lady walked past Adriana, her *punga* now empty of bread, Adriana had to stop her.

"Why did you do that? Why did you show kindness to the enemy?" Adriana asked.

"I wanted to remind them who they are," the lady said. "They are Romanians, the same as me. I gave them our daily bread. It was an offering of peace."

"What did they say?"

"They said *mulțumesc*." She smiled. "One of them looked just like my grandson. He had tears in his eyes when he took the bread from my hand."

In the madness, Adriana spotted Liviu with a rifle strapped to his back, talking to a group of soldiers who'd just randomly fired on unarmed citizens. He turned to climb inside an army tank. Liviu's eyes fell on her as he started to close the hatch. He stopped and just stared at her for a moment, as though he had something to tell her. Whatever it was, she didn't want to hear.

She couldn't take any more of this insanity. She had to go home.

When Adriana arrived at her flat, the first person she saw was her mother. Mama's expression showed how worried she'd been.

"What a relief!" Mama first smothered her in a hug and then berated her for leaving. "What were you thinking?"

"I had to go, and I'm going back," Adriana said. "It's terrible out there, but I'm just here … Honestly, I don't know why I came back. I needed a break from it all."

Arm in arm, Mama guided Adriana into the living room, where she saw Aunt Violeta, Bunica, and Mrs. Petrescu. Adriana collapsed on the sofa, next to Aunt Violeta. She never expected to see Mrs. Petrescu in her flat.

She must have stared at her, because Mrs. Petrescu twisted the hem of her blouse in her hands. "I couldn't stay home alone. I had to wait with someone—"

"With friends," Bunica said.

"Where's Uncle Mihai?" Adriana asked.

"He's at the Atheneum," Violeta said, "helping anyway he can. Just like you."

"We're not hearing anything on the news, as you'd expect," Bunica said. "This morning, after the commentator said the crowd was about 100,000 people, we heard some noise and then Ceaușescu asked if it was an earthquake. Then the television broadcast suddenly went off the air. The screen turned black."

"Tell us what's happening out there," Mama said.

Adriana filled them in on what she knew. "I guess I lost it after I saw ... innocent people. They're killing people who are just standing there."

Her mother's expression looked stricken.

"Mama, my job is to tend to the wounded. So I'm safe. I just want to catch my breath before I go back."

"I insist you stay long enough to eat something." Mama rose to stir the soup that had been simmering, but before she did, Adriana saw her choke back tears.

"Just give me some bread, Mama," Adriana said. "I'll eat it as I go."

"Tell us what you need," Violeta said.

"We'll need lots of bandages before it's all over," Adriana said.

"I can rip up my sheets," Mrs. Petrescu said, and left to get started.

Adriana went into her bedroom. She pulled her door closed and leaned against it. Her thoughts turned to her friend Uri and the horror he'd lived through. He found freedom on the inside, but during his long life, he never saw his country being free.

She fumbled in her drawer for the necklace Uri left for her. She wanted to wear it close. She wanted to touch the small emerald as she worked in triage, to remind her that her friend—her mentor—longed for her and Gabi to experience freedom.

Mama pushed open her door as Adriana fixed the clasp on the necklace.

"I need to tell you something before you go back," Mama said.

"What?"

"I was wrong."

Adriana gave her a puzzled look.

"We were wrong—your father and I—to follow the Party so blindly. At first, it sounded good. Everyone being equal. All citizens being workers, eliminating the bourgeoisie altogether. They told us change would be difficult and we just needed to bear with it." Mama took a breath. "So we did."

"Mama, I know all that—"

"I have to say it. Your father and I both saw … inconsistencies. But by then, we knew the consequences of voicing our own opinions. So we stuffed it and kept going." She wiped her eyes with her hand. "Right or wrong, we went along. We did it for you, or so we convinced ourselves. All that mattered to us was keeping you safe, and we did that by not causing trouble." Mama cupped Adriana's face in her hand. "I wish we'd been stronger. Like you."

Adriana nodded.

"We all did whatever we could to survive," Mama continued. "You must understand."

"I do. I think I do," Adriana said. She wanted to tell her mother it was alright, but she just couldn't deal with her confession right now. "But if you'll excuse me, I need to make some phone calls before I go back."

She tried Corina first. No answer. Where could she be? Adriana hadn't seen her all day.

When she dialed Gabi's number, her mother answered on the first ring.

"It's Adriana. I wanted you to know Gabi's fine," she said. She heard Mrs. Martinescu exhale a long breath. "You'd be so proud. She's a perfect nurse."

"And how are you?"

"I'm holding up. I just took a short break, but I'm going back."

Adriana heard Teodor in the background. Mrs. Martinescu must have made a funny face, because Teodor, now eight months old, exploded in baby laughter. He had no idea what was going on.

Mrs. Martinescu said, "Tell Gabi we're here. Her father's in the *piața* somewhere." She cleared her voice. "Tell her we love her. And you too, Adriana." Then she spoke louder. "And we've been praying constantly. If you children can do what you're doing, we can pray. Out loud, without fear. Without the shades drawn. I refuse to hide any longer."

Adriana took the back streets to the history building, picking her way carefully over the carnage, sidestepping the splotches of red on the cobblestones. In the distance, she could see smoke rising over the city.

She bent low, below window level, as she walked so close to the buildings that her arm scraped against them. She cautiously looked both ways whenever she reached the end of a building, then raced to the next one for cover.

When she arrived at the History Department, she could see how much had changed. Students and professors carted victims up and down the stairs on homemade gurneys. The wounded filled the hallway, their blood smeared on the floor. Dr. Tomeci, Professor Filip, and the other professors looked exhausted as they kept barking orders on where to take people.

Professor Filip caught Adriana's eye. "Go to Room 106, the Waiting Room. The ones who aren't hurt as badly. I'm afraid we've neglected them."

Relieved to avoid watching people die, Adriana entered the room. The bandages Mrs. Petrescu had cut were in her pocket.

She looked at the patients. They were all so young, probably university students.

She made the rounds, wrapping their wounds, talking to each one, seeing what she could do to help ease their pain.

One guy kept trying to leave. "I can't stay here and let other people die on the street for me," he said. He sat up in the bed and swung his legs around. He put one leg down and then looked at the other, probably for the first time. It was drenched in blood. He tried to put his weight on it, and then he fell back, passed out in pain.

As Adriana asked what she could do, there was only one thing her patients kept repeating: "What happened to my friends? Can you find them?"

Adriana promised she'd try to find out. She repeated the names to herself, then backed out and walked down to the Urgent Room. She had to go see if these friends were among the people who would die if they didn't get help.

When Adriana entered, she saw Gabi standing over one of the patients, a girl, talking gently to her. Gabi held her hand and stroked her hair. As Adriana watched, a deep rattling breath escaped from the girl. It sounded just like Tati did at the end. She watched Gabi, her dearest friend, close the girl's eyes with the back of her hand. A slow tear started its path from Gabi's eye to her chin.

Adriana walked up and hugged Gabi. She didn't say anything. There was no need.

Gabi spoke in a hoarse voice. "Her name was Mihaela. She told me she was studying languages. She had ten bullet holes." She wiped her face. "How could Romanians do that to Romanians, Adri? I don't understand this. These students, they never had a chance."

Just then, Professor Filip called out to Adriana. "Can you find out what's happening at the barricade? Find Alex. Corina's out there too. See what they need."

Adriana squeezed Gabi's arm. "Keep strong," she said as she turned and ran out of the building. Anything to get out of this place.

Twilight had started to descend when Adriana headed for Barricade Central in search of Alex. She hadn't thought of it before, but today, 21 December, was the winter solstice. The shortest day of the year.

On the way to the Dunarea restaurant, Adriana noticed more people had slashed the Communist symbol out of flags. The new flags—three stripes with an empty center—proudly waved from statues and flagpoles and windowsills, calling people to be courageous and to stand up.

Confusion and chaos were everywhere. Blood ran freely in the street. Some people remained in the square; more were huddled against buildings. Adriana wasn't prepared for what real battle was like. How were the people still there with no means to fight back?

When she reached the barricade, she found Alex behind it, leaning against the tall hodgepodge pile of junk.

She'd thought of Alex as Marius from *Les Misérables*. How perfect that he was at the barricades, just like Marius.

"I'm so glad to see you!" she cried.

Alex grabbed her hands. "How is it where you are?"

"We're surviving. Professor Filip wanted to know what you need."

"We need people. We have to guard this barricade. We hear it's one of the last ones standing," Alex said. "We need people to haul the wounded out."

"Tell me what you've been seeing."

"People being shot. Clubbed to death. Stabbed. Crushed by water jets. Run over by tanks." Alex wiped his face with his sleeve. "They're shooting from buildings all around the *piața*. From the upper windows."

"Do you have anything to fight with?" Adriana asked.

"I have this." Alex picked up a crowbar next to him. "We have this pile of rocks here. I have my fists, all that hand-to-hand combat we learned. I'll use whatever I can."

"Have we made headway?"

"Who knows? We're still standing. That's something," he said. "Look, the next shift is arriving any minute. Can you stay here with me until they come?"

"Anything," Adriana said.

"When they come, I'm going back out there. To the *piața*," Alex said.

"I'll go with you."

"No, please. Aren't you needed in triage?" Alex asked.

"But I feel so helpless there."

"I'm staying out all night," Alex said. "I refuse to go home until this is over."

"Alex, I'll stay out with you."

He cupped his hand against the side of her face. "No, Adriana. You're too important to me. I won't be able to live with myself if something happens to you."

Before Adriana could respond, her cousin Timo and his friend Marcu sprinted to the barricade. Adriana hugged Timo.

"Hi, Green Eyes," Timo said. "I've brought your replacement, Alex."

Marcu ducked behind the barricade and carved out space to settle in for his shift.

"What's the latest report?" Alex said.

"The army continues to press down. They've shot so many people, nobody can count," Timo said. "But more people keep coming."

"I just saw a guy from my classes," Marcu said. "He said that liberty won't be brought to us on a silver platter. That we will win it with our blood. He said they can't kill all of us." Marcu squeezed his eyes closed. "Those were the last words he ever said."

Alex stood up. "I'm ready to get back out there."

"Come with me, then," Timo said. He turned to Adriana. "I saw Mihai. He's pulling the wounded off the streets into the Atheneum."

"Please be careful," Adriana said. "Both of you."

Alex leaned down and kissed her. He kissed her on each cheek as everyone did, but as his lips moved from her left cheek to her right cheek, they brushed against her mouth—quickly—as though it was an accident. Or was it? Alex tenderly held her gaze longer than usual.

Before she could say anything, Alex and Timo darted off down the street.

In the midst of all the violence and destruction, Adriana couldn't help but smile. Ever since she read *Les Misérables*, she wondered if she and Alex would end up like Marius and Cosette sometime in the future. Now she knew. Alex did love her after all. She'd been right all along.

Lives were being snuffed out all over the streets of Bucharest. She had no guarantees that Alex would be safe. What if she lost him? Now, after waiting so long to know he felt the same way she did. The thought made her stomach clench in fear.

As Adriana crept back toward triage, out of the corner of her eye, she spotted Corina, standing near the restaurant and staring toward the barricade. When Adriana looked her way, Corina turned and hurried away. Did Corina see the kiss?

Adriana called out to Corina. She didn't want to hurt her. She wanted to explain, to soften the story of what Corina saw. She didn't want Corina to find out this way.

Adriana chased after Corina, calling her name. She watched Corina dart past the safety of the building on the end, straight toward the open square, where the fighting was. Just like poor Eponine, still in love with Marius, in *Les Misérables*.

She froze as she had another thought, one that made her feel sick. A bullet meant for Marius would have killed him if not for Eponine.

She had to stop Corina. She chased Corina into Palace Square, but she soon lost her in the crowd and the mayhem.

But she was needed at her post in triage, in the Waiting Room, so Adriana returned.

CHAPTER FORTY

TIMOTEI: SIMONA

TIMOTEI CIRCLED BACK TO Barricade Central and stayed there with Marcu. They planned to defend it until Romania secured their freedom. Timotei hadn't lost hope that the people would be victorious.

Marcu and Timotei talked for hours, about things that mattered a great deal and things that didn't. They listed their favorite places they'd been, described their favorite foods in detail, talked of what they wanted to see change in their world. They talked about Serghei's death.

"It hasn't hit me yet about Serghei. I just feel kind of numb about it. One thing I know, he was ready to die for this cause. He almost expected it," Timotei said.

"Serghei the Bear," Marcu said. "Our fearless leader to the end."

"Dying for this cause would've been an honor for him," Timotei said.

The two friends let that thought linger between them. They sat in comfortable silence.

Then Marcu cleared his throat. "You know, I've been afraid to tell you something," he said, "mostly because I thought you might not like it. At first, I thought you liked her, then I thought you'd be over-protective of her."

Timotei was already smiling before Marcu spilled it. He knew what was coming but he wanted to hear it from Marcu's own lips.

"I like Simona."

Timotei laughed. "Of course you do! It's so obvious, brother."

"So you don't mind?"

"Mind?" Timotei squeezed Marcu's shoulder. "I'm delighted. As long as you know what you're getting yourself into. She's a fireball. Simona does not have an off switch. Whatever she puts her heart to, she gives it all she's got."

Marcu smiled. "That's what I like about her." His face took on a serious expression. "If we make it out of this, I'm going to tell her how I feel."

"*If* we make it out of this? We're going to win," Timotei said. "I know we'll win. Simona knows it too."

"You're right, of course," Marcu said. "I do believe freedom is coming to Romania. I just … I don't know. After Serghei, I just have a bad feeling. There will be more losses before it gets here."

About midnight, government forces tore down the last standing barricade the students had constructed, Barricade Central in front of the Dunarea restaurant. Timotei and Marcu were forced to flee. The full moon spilled light onto their path as they ran for cover.

Someone yelled the news that Ceaușescu had declared martial law. The military was now officially in control. Anyone caught outside after dark could be arrested.

That news made the ever-shrinking number of protestors who remained even more determined to stay outside.

Timotei and Marcu moved out into Palace Square, hugging the buildings while they scoped out the scene before them. They moved cautiously, seeking cover as they ran. Shots continued to be fired sporadically.

The first person Timotei spotted that he knew was Alex. He and Marcu invited Alex to come with them in search of their other friends.

As they looked for them, Alex motioned to the others to duck. He pointed out a guy patrolling the square. "That's my classmate, Liviu," he said. "He's in training to be Securitate. Watch out for him."

Marcu spotted Simona, Beni, and Claudia huddled behind a burned-out Dacia.

Simona called to them. "There's room here. Come join us."

The three guys squeezed in close to the others to stay warm.

Simona looked at Alex. "This jacket's keeping me toasty. Do you want it back?"

"No, I'm fine," Alex said.

"*Mulţumesc*," Simona said. "At least you can snuggle here next to me."

Timotei nudged Marcu. "You should have offered," he whispered. "You let a high school guy be more gallant than you."

Marcu grimaced.

"This weather's a miracle," Simona said, her eyes shining. "Think about it. When is it ever this warm in December in Bucharest? We're outside all night, and nobody's freezing to death."

"Good, because there are enough other ways for us to die," Timotei said.

For the next couple of hours, the group packed in tightly together, camping out in the open square in winter, along with scores of other young people. If anyone dozed, it was just for a few minutes. Who could sleep on a night like this?

While it was still dark out, Timotei left with Marcu to see what was happening elsewhere. They promised to return when they could.

The two roommates sprinted across the square and took refuge in a recessed doorway of a building pocked with bullet holes. They could see fire on the rooftops of nearby buildings. It looked like the

National Library was on fire. The smoke caught in their throats and stung their eyes.

"Did you sleep at all?" Timotei asked.

"No. How could I?" Marcu wiped his face with his hand. "Watching Simona cozy up with that kid."

"Alex is not a threat to you. Just put him out of your mind," Timotei said.

As they spoke, Timotei noticed the sound of the bullets had ceased. "Do you hear that?"

"I don't hear anything," Marcu said.

"Exactly."

Marcu returned to report back to their friends behind the burned-out Dacia. Minutes after he took off, Timotei spotted Simona walking close to the building where he hid. In the dark, with her fleecy cap hiding her curls, at first glance he thought Simona was a boy.

"Here," he shouted, waving his arms from the doorway.

"There you are," Simona said.

"You just missed Marcu," Timotei said. "You know, the guy's crazy about you. He talks about you all the time."

"Really? I kind of like him too." Simona laughed. "I hope you didn't tell him too many stories from our childhood."

"I only remember good things, you know that." Timotei's voice became serious. "You know I've always admired you, Simona, but never more than now."

He heard a chuckle. "You're making me blush. What's got into you? Let's go back out to Palace Square. It seems like the army has pulled back. Before too long, the sun will rise and we'll be able to see something."

Simona cautiously crept along the wall of the corner building. She knelt beside the building and slowly leaned her head out to look.

Timotei crouched beside her, safe behind the wall. "What do you see?" he whispered.

"All clear," Simona said. She took a step out from the building. Then she turned and stretched out her hand to Timotei. "Follow m—"

Before the word escaped, a barrage of bullets erupted, coming from a nearby roof. Simona screamed and collapsed to her knees. The bullets pierced Simona's back.

Timotei watched his friend's body crumple to the ground. He grabbed her under her arms and dragged her back, away from the guns.

Blood drenched Simona's chest and back.

"Simona!" Timotei shouted. "Stay with me, Simona. You hang on!"

Simona's lips moved but she had no strength to project her voice. Timotei leaned his head down to listen.

"Don't worry about me," Simona said. "We are going to win this fight. I know it. God will see us through."

"I can't—"

"Promise me. Tell my parents I love them," Simona whispered, just before she lost consciousness.

Timotei cradled Simona in his arms and began to scream uncontrollably. His arms still encircled Simona when Marcu came running.

"Simona!" Marcu cried. "Hold on. You are a fighter. I can't lose you now." He lifted Simona across his broad shoulders.

He ran with her to the doctor.

Timotei remained, unable to move from the spot where he had held his friend. He vowed to make sure what Simona suffered would not be in vain.

CHAPTER FORTY-ONE

ADRIANA: THE PRICE

A S THE HOURS WORE on, so had the number of wounded and the amount of blood.

More and more people, mostly university students, had already died and needed to be transferred from Beyond Help to the room next door, newly turned into a morgue. The bodies would stay there until they could be transported to the Medical Department's official morgue in Cotroceni, near Professor Filip's flat.

Adriana tried to help out downstairs in triage, where the patients had a chance to pull through.

At one point, Adriana witnessed Professor Filip break down in exhaustion and tears. Dr. Tomeci wrapped his arms around her to comfort her. Interesting. Other professors had broken down momentarily before wiping their faces and soldiering on, but she didn't notice Dr. Tomeci comforting them.

The only person Adriana hadn't seen collapse was Gabi. Gabi remained strong, cheerful to the victims, never balking from the most horrendous of wounds. Adriana watched Gabi soothe a patient whose shattered arm hung loosely from the rest of his body.

"Anyone you want me to get a message to?" Gabi asked him.

"My mama," he said. "Tell my mama I did it. I stood on my own legs—"

Those were the last words he spoke. Gabi gently closed his eyelids with the back of her hand and continued to cradle him in her arms.

Adriana slumped to the floor, against the wall of the triage area, and rubbed the tiredness from her eyes. "Gabi," she said, looking at her friend. "How are you doing this? How do you keep going?"

Gabi took a moment to answer. "The last thing Uri told me was to look up when things get bad. I can't explain it, but I think somehow God is giving me strength."

Adriana nodded and closed her eyes briefly. When she opened her eyes again, she saw Timotei's friend Marcu carry in someone on his shoulders.

"This is urgent! Please, we need help," Marcu cried. "Help us!"

Dr. Tomeci and a couple others ran to lift the victim and lay him gently on his stomach on a stretcher. He was unconscious. He wore a fleecy cap and a dark brown jacket. The back of his jacket was soaked in blood.

Adriana knew that jacket. The shoulder of the jacket had been mended by hand with large, white stiches. She'd recognize it anywhere.

It belonged to Alex.

She felt frantic. She jumped to her feet.

Professor Filip sprinted over. "Is this—?"

Adriana could do nothing but nod.

Gabi looked up. "Adri …"

Adriana took a deep breath to steady herself. This couldn't be happening. Not tonight. Not when she finally felt the promise of a relationship with Alex.

Gabi rose to stand next to Adriana, her arm bracing her friend's back, her fingers tightly gripping Adriana's shoulder.

Gabi watched as one of the other helpers flipped the guy over. Adriana couldn't look. She had her face pressed up against Gabi's shoulder.

"Adri, it's … it's not …"

Adriana raised her eyes.

It wasn't Alex. It was a girl. Adriana let her breath out, relieved, but then inhaled quickly when she realized she knew her. It was Timotei's friend. *Her* friend.

It was Simona.

Dr. Tomeci stood over Simona and checked her pulse. He laid her on her side and felt her wounds in her back and chest. "Two bullets entered her back and one exited her chest. One of the bullets may be lodged in her heart. She appears to have internal bleeding." He looked at Marcu. "There's nothing we can do for her. She's losing too much blood. We can't operate here, and we can't get her to a hospital in time." He put a hand on Marcu's shoulder. "I'm sorry."

"No!" Marcu cried.

As Dr. Tomeci stroked Simona's hair, she started to wake up. Dr. Tomeci held her hand. "We're going to do all we can to make you comfortable."

He turned to Marcu. "Take her to the room upstairs."

Adriana stared at him. "You mean—"

He spoke softly, "She's not long for this world."

Dr. Tomeci approached Adriana and laid a hand on her shoulder. "Do you know her?"

"Yes, I …"

"Go, be with her. Don't leave her alone."

Adriana followed Marcu into the Beyond Help room.

Marcu gently laid Simona on a makeshift cot and leaned over her, crying. "I love you, Simona. I never told you, but I do. Everyone loves you." His voice broke. "I don't know what I'm going to do without your light, your smile." He brushed Simona's curls out of her face and leaned down and kissed her. Then he stepped away, put his face in his hands, and sobbed.

Adriana took Simona's hands in hers and pressed her lips to Simona's ears. "Thank you for our talks. For being Timo's friend. For—"

"It's true! It's really true!" Simona said, strength fading from her voice. She had a faraway gaze in her eyes. She lifted her right hand, reaching up toward a place only she could see. "I'm coming!"

A rattling exhale escaped her throat, then her arm dropped heavily beside her.

"She's gone," Adriana said to Marcu.

He nodded and stumbled out of the room.

Adriana didn't have any tears left to cry for Simona. Friendly, outspoken, passionate Simona. Simona who loved truth. Simona, her cousin's dear friend.

She gently pulled Alex's jacket off Simona's body and crossed Simona's hands over her chest. She hugged the jacket to her body.

Adriana hadn't realized Professor Filip entered the room until she touched Adriana's arm. Professor Filip spoke tenderly. "We need you to help take care of the people we can save. Just take a few minutes to catch your breath and then report back at triage. Please."

Adriana folded Alex's jacket and handed it to her professor. Then she walked down the stairs and stepped outside. The night air, cool but not cold, revived her. She had no idea what time it was. She walked aimlessly, stunned.

She listened to the gunfire, intermittent and distant now, such a strange and foreign noise. She fingered the emerald necklace Uri left her. *Look up*, he liked to say. She looked up.

The cloudless sky felt oddly peaceful, dotted with silvery stars and a luminous moon. Adriana had seen death tonight for the first time since watching her father die. She couldn't feel any emotion yet about Simona's death; she couldn't feel anything at all.

Who did they think they were? What grandiose things did they—a disorganized bunch of students—think they could accomplish? They were kids, armed with nothing more than their idealistic dreams and no shortage of courage. They didn't have anything real, like weapons. Only abstract things, like hope.

Was it worth the price they had paid already for this hope of freedom? If they won, yes. But if not …

Adriana remembered the book she read, *To Kill a Mockingbird*. Atticus Finch said that courage is when you know you can't win, but you try anyway, and you never give up trying.

Many of her countrymen had that kind of courage. They were willing to pay the price, and she needed to do her best to take care of them. She drew a deep breath to steady herself and turned to walk back into the History Department.

Suddenly, she heard someone call her name. The voice seemed to come from the nearby alley. She cautiously walked toward it. It was Liviu, lurking in the shadows.

"Listen up," Liviu whispered. "I have to warn you about something."

"Warn me?" Adriana asked.

"Before all this started, the Securitate was ordered to search out the various subversive groups and haul them into headquarters. Zugravescu was about to drag in your uncle's group of dissidents. My task was to bring your study group in for questioning. Each of you had or has a troublemaker for a parent, so it would be easy for Zugravescu to find some reason to keep you all at headquarters. Then he was going to arrange some sort of 'accident' for you and your uncle. He ordered me to help." Liviu looked into her eyes. "Adriana, he's planning to kill you."

Adriana took a step backward.

"Your whole family's been on the Securitate's hit list for some time now. I just want you to know … I can't do that. I won't." Liviu paused. "Look, if anyone finds out I'm talking to you—"

"So why are you?" She studied Liviu's face.

"You know I grew up in a school that groomed future Securitate officers; my parents didn't raise me. I learned to follow orders, to never question anything. It's been my life. It's all I know." He looked down at his feet. When he spoke, his voice cracked. "But if all these people—these regular Romanians—are courageous enough to stand up and risk their lives, well, there must be a reason." He paused. "I think … it's possible I've been on the wrong side. I can't …" His eyes pleaded with Adriana. "Just be careful."

Adriana looked at Liviu, her former enemy, and nodded. "Thank you for telling me."

Liviu held no power over her anymore. She pitied him, but she no longer hated him.

She walked back to triage, unable to process all she'd seen and heard this night. Liviu's confession. Death and bravery and heartache. As soon as she reached the top step and opened the outer door, she encountered the chaos and screams all over again. People rushed past her, carrying victims in on stretchers.

After another hour of trying to help where she could, Adriana saw people bring the mangled body of a girl into the building. The girl was bloody and unconscious. Adriana looked closer.

It was Corina.

Adriana screamed. Dr. Tomeci came running. He looked Corina over quickly and said she had been shot multiple times, mostly in her knee. Blood gushed from her knee like a fountain. Her shattered bones stuck out from the flesh of her leg. Adriana took Corina's limp hand in hers for a moment before Dr. Tomeci told the stretcher bearers to take Corina to the Urgent Room.

He turned to Adriana. "I know you want to go with your friend, but we need you here right now, to help with triage."

Adriana couldn't control her tears.

"Don't worry. We'll take good care of her," he said.

Adriana stumbled down the hall.

Corina could be dying.

Alex was still missing. For all she knew, he might be dead.

Simona *was* dead.

As Adriana shuffled in a daze, words kept replaying in her mind: *God, if you're here, if it's true you exist, show me. We need help here. Please help us.*

CHAPTER FORTY-TWO

MERCY

I N THE MIDDLE OF the night, about 3:00, the fighting stopped, at least for the time being. Only a trickle of wounded were being carried in. Professor Filip ordered Adriana to rest.

"Follow me, Adri," Gabi said. "I'll get you settled."

Gabi led her down the hall, where the helpers had spread rugs and cloths on the floor of Room 208. A few others were already sleeping when Adriana laid down beside them.

"Are you going to rest, Gabi?" Adriana asked.

Gabi shook her head. "Not yet."

Adriana tried to sleep, but she only managed to doze fitfully, a few minutes at a time, awakened by a nightmare that didn't end when she opened her eyes. She rose and crept out into the hallway.

At the foot of the stairs, she found Gabi, still with the critical patients.

"Where's Corina?"

Gabi's face contorted in pain. "They took her ... her body," she said. "She's at the Medical Department building."

"You mean ..."

Gabi nodded and reached for Adriana. The girls held each other. Corina hadn't survived.

Adriana couldn't take any more of this. She ran out of the building.

In the dark, all was quiet. The streets seemed to be finally empty. Although the moon cast its glow, Adriana couldn't see well. Those who survived the night had probably fled and the wounded—and most of the dead—had been carted away.

She ran a couple of blocks into Old Town, away from where the fighting had been, where she stumbled onto a bench. She felt nauseous. Adriana doubled over with her head between her knees.

She thought about all she'd lost. Corina. Simona. Maybe Alex.

Adriana's life, her world, was being ripped apart, and she was powerless to do anything about it. In that moment, she felt lower than she'd ever been. She had nowhere to look but up. She had nothing to lose. She could no longer manage on her own.

She touched the necklace from Uri. *Find your help in the Lord*, he'd written in that last letter to her and Gabi.

For months now, she'd been observing Bunica, Gabi, Uri, Simona. She'd heard her own father cry out to God as he lay dying. They all said the same thing: God loved her and he wouldn't let her down. She needed someone she could count on right now. She might as well trust in this God that she'd been taught didn't exist.

Adriana had never really prayed before, but as she sat on the bench, the next words spilled out from her heart. *God, I want to believe. Help me to believe.*

Nothing happened. She didn't feel any magic. Her world was still in chaos. Her friends were still dead. And yet.

Adriana didn't know what *and yet* could mean; she couldn't think beyond this moment, but she felt curiously calm. In a way she couldn't explain, she felt God's love.

She didn't know how long she sat there. Adriana's whole history with Corina ran through her mind like a movie in fast motion. In the beginning, she didn't appreciate Corina. She'd give anything to have those years back, to rewrite the story of her life. She just hadn't understood Corina, hadn't given her a chance to prove that her sweet optimism was genuine, never an act. Maybe Adriana had been jealous of Corina all along. Corina was so pretty and all the boys noticed her. But now, now that it was too late, she could see things clearly.

How could she have been so blind? Corina liked *her*. Adriana was the one Corina told the truth to about her mother being Hungarian. Adriana was the one Corina confided in about why she had to break up with Alex. No wonder Alex had loved Corina.

This wasn't how she wanted to win Alex. That is, *if* he was still alive. She didn't want him by default.

In a daze, Adriana ran the rest of the way to Cotroceni. The sky was beginning to lighten. With all the commotion, the trams and metros were running sporadically at best. Even though it took a while to run, it felt good to move and the night air rejuvenated her. Adriana couldn't waste another minute by standing in line waiting for transportation.

When Adriana arrived at the Medical Department, out of breath, she burst through the door and stumbled down the hallway, right into Dr. Tomeci.

"Your friend—I think his name's Alex—is here," he said. "One of those rooms down there." He pointed down the hall.

Adriana could feel the blood drain from her face. No! Not Alex too.

She walked down the hallway and started peeking into the various classrooms. She walked into one with several bodies covered in sheets. She put her hand on one of the sheets, about to pull it back, when she realized she couldn't do it. Her hand shook and she thought she might faint.

At that moment, she heard voices coming from the room next door. She'd heard one of the voices before. Many times. She didn't dare hope …

Adriana hurried to the doorway to look. It was him! She saw Alex, and he wasn't lying on a slab. He was alive!

Alex was bent over one of the bodies while two male medical professors hovered nearby. He smoothed the hair back on the forehead and leaned down to touch his lips against the body's lips. "I love you," he said. "You have to get better. I … I can't live without you."

Corina? She was alive too?

"You have to step away now," said one of the professors. "Let us do our jobs."

Alex lifted the hand, *Corina's* hand, and held it as they lifted her onto a gurney.

A sob caught in Adriana's throat. She ran to Corina as the doctors started to wheel her away.

"It's Adriana," she cried. "Please, please get well. You're strong. You're a fighter. Come back to us."

She stood there, watching the men run with the gurney, pushing open the swinging doors marked Surgery.

Alex barely acknowledged her presence. He stood with his face in his hands.

Adriana approached him, gently. "Oh, Alex."

He looked up and smiled faintly. A smile that didn't reach his eyes.

"I'm so glad you're here," Adriana said. "I was … scared for you. And I thought Corina was …"

"Everyone did. They were taking her here, to the morgue, when she moved. Her lips moved. She said '*Help me.*'"

"Did they say what—?"

"Her leg is in fragments, so they're trying to put it back together now. *If* she lives, they're not sure she'll ever walk again." Alex wiped his eyes. "She'd passed out. She nearly bled out. Nobody could find a pulse, so they just assumed—"

"Do you know how it happened?"

"She lunged in front of a barrage of bullets meant for a couple guys." He took a deep breath and then let it go. "She's a hero."

"I'm so sorry." Adriana rested her hand on Alex's back. He didn't seem to notice. She decided to give him some privacy, so she stepped outside.

The sun was beginning to rise as she wandered, not sure where she was headed, and found herself at the gates of *Gradina Botanica* nearby. She staggered down a path until she stumbled upon the bench where her study group used to meet with Professor Filip. Those meetings felt so long ago.

Sinking onto the bench, Adriana's head dropped into her hands.

God, you must be real! My friends—both of them!—are alive. Thank you. I do believe. Please don't let Corina die.

She cried tears of exhaustion.

After a while, everything became clear. How could she have missed it all this time? All along, she'd had it wrong. Alex *did* love Corina.

Corina was the Cosette in their story. Corina and Alex belonged together, like Cosette and Marius. Alex and Adriana were friends, good friends since childhood, but only friends. She'd always felt close to him. They understood each other and had an easy camaraderie. Just because they became closer when her father died didn't mean they were meant for each other. Alex loved Corina for all the ways she was different from him.

Sure, Adriana had gotten her hopes up with Alex and held on to those hopes for so long, she knew it would take time to get over him, to get over the *possibility* of a relationship with him. The fact was Adriana had never been his girlfriend, yet it still stung to see that he preferred Corina in that way. But Adriana realized, maybe too late, that she already had what she really wanted from Alex—all she'd ever wanted: a good lifelong friend.

CHAPTER FORTY-THREE

TIMOTEI: STILL STANDING

Friday, 22 December

AS DAWN BROKE ON 22 December, Timotei looked out on Palace Square from his solitary hiding place behind an overturned car. Pink early morning rays streaked the sky. The square was nearly empty now, except for the spent bullets and debris and pools of blood. A small number of people still slept on the ground ... or were they dead?

Most of the people had gone home after the gunfire ceased at 3:00 in the morning. Timotei hoped they'd return, but he didn't know what to think. Maybe being safe in their own beds would make them see the events of yesterday differently. Maybe they'd realize how unlikely victory would be, how high the cost had already been. Perhaps some of the revolutionaries had already given up. It sure looked like the government had the upper hand.

But Timotei knew what his countrymen and women were made of. Many of them had real courage. Yes, it looked impossible for them to win, but that hadn't stopped them yet. Many refused to give up. If they could do it, Timotei resolved to stay until the end, whatever and whenever that would be. Win or lose, he'd see this through.

He needed to check what had happened while it was dark. He skirted the outer edges of the open square, noticing where the army was positioned, where the revolutionaries waited. The army held its ground, ready to strike, but a small number of students remained scattered along the edges of the square, in plain sight, defenseless.

Timotei spotted Marcu and Beni huddled in the doorway of a building along the sidelines and shouldered his way between them.

By the time the sun had fully risen, Timotei saw that more bedraggled people had already started to gather. They came in defiance of martial law and the new law that no groups larger than five people could gather. Both laws had been imposed last night and broadcast continuously.

"Do you see this?" Marcu asked. "Simona would've called this another miracle. People are coming to the *piața* again!"

People started to walk past them. Timotei overheard some saying they were going to give blood.

"Did you hear?" he heard another man say. "Ceaușescu is going to speak again at 10:00."

"Why? Doesn't he get it?" asked a woman walking beside him.

"He'll probably declare victory. And mete out the punishment for everyone who rebelled."

The word began to spread that Ceaușescu planned to give a second speech that morning, and he'd called on all the Party faithful to come listen and applaud. Workers from the factories had already started arriving, but they seemed subdued today. Nobody came waving flags or holding posters of the Ceaușescus today. From what Timotei could overhear, many of the workers gathering sided with the protesters, not the government.

Timotei could see that fire had destroyed much of his beloved National Library, its façade pocked with bullet holes. Helicopters flew overhead and dropped manifestos, further littering the square. Timotei picked up one of the papers.

"Listen to this," Timotei said to Marcu. "They're instructing us not to fall victim to the latest diversion attempts." Timotei laughed. "So that's what they call this? Not a revolution, but a diversion attempt."

Marcu grabbed the paper and read it. "It says to go home instead and enjoy our Christmas feast."

A lady nearby overhead. "Christmas feast, hah! When have we ever been allowed to celebrate Christmas?"

Another joined in. "Besides, we don't have any food!"

"And no money to buy food," someone else said. "Some feast!"

"Does Elena think she's Marie Antoinette? *Let them eat cake?*"

People laughed.

Soon after sunrise, periodic gunfire resumed. The Securitate and the army continued following orders. They continued to shoot protestors.

Timotei watched a guy run to join his friend. The friend asked, "Why'd you come back?"

"How could I not? I figured if I don't do this, maybe others won't either, and then what will happen?"

"Same here," the friend said. "I couldn't live with myself if I wasn't willing to sacrifice. I mean, look at all the people who've already done that."

An old lady approached one of the tanks with a handful of flowers. As she extended her simple offering of peace to the men inside the tank, a sniper on the roof aimed his rifle at her.

"Run!" someone from the crowd yelled to her.

"He won't shoot at me. I'm his fellow Romanian," she said. The words had barely left her mouth before the soldier fired and the woman crumpled to the ground.

Timotei's eyes filled up. A wave of nausea swept over him.

Just before the time for the speech to start, Timotei saw his cousin picking her way through the swelling crowd.

"Adriana!" he called. "Come over here!"

CHAPTER FORTY-FOUR

ADRIANA: VICTORY

AT 10:00 IN THE morning, minutes after Adriana had slid into place beside Timo and Marcu, Nicolae and Elena Ceaușescu stepped onto the balcony of the Central Committee building. A row of bodyguards and Securitate officers stood behind them, including Captain Zugravescu. As Nicolae Ceaușescu approached the microphone, the crowd responded with boos and jeers.

They began chanting again, a cacophony of noise rising from the crowd and adding to the commotion. As they did yesterday, people yelled *Down with Communism* or *Down with the dictator* or *Down with Ceaușescu*. But today, Adriana heard a new chorus join in. Only a few voices shouted the refrain at first, but as the chant echoed through the crowd, it gained momentum. Soon Adriana could make out the words. *Exista Dumnezeu! Exista Dumnezeu!* Simona's words. *God exists!*

The more the various chants were repeated, the more the crowd came to life, infused with strength. They were energized. The people were a force to be reckoned with, no longer beaten down, but now emboldened, unwilling to give up.

Ceaușescu stood at the microphone and helplessly called for order.

Instead of order, the most amazing thing happened next. With no warning, columns of army tanks, the ones who had been firing on their own people for the last twenty-four hours, turned, of one accord. The guns on all the tanks pivoted. They aimed at the striped brick building—Securitate Headquarters—between the library and the building where Ceauşescu stood. The tanks unleashed their firepower, raining bullets on the headquarters and on any Securitate officers in the way.

"Do you see this?" Timo asked.

Adriana nodded, unable to speak.

People began chanting, *The army is with us. The army is on our side.*

Adriana was witnessing another of the miracles Simona talked about.

The army had switched sides.

Securitate snipers lining the rooftops answered the volleys of bullets that flew from the tanks' guns. Tanks and armored trucks began rolling toward the Central Committee building with crowds swarming alongside them.

Bodyguards quickly ushered the Ceauşescus inside the building. Rioters swarmed the terrace of the building and tried to follow them in. Zugravescu and other Securitate officers pushed them back.

Everything was chaotic and frightening, yet Adriana felt frozen in place. Timo pulled her down to a squatting position. They ran, bent over, for the nearest wall, hoping to find some cover. It didn't look like any place was safe from the bullets.

Adriana felt helpless to do anything but watch the madness and confusion. People screamed and ran in all directions.

A girl about Adriana's age fell near her. As the girl gasped for breath, Adriana reached over and held her hand.

"You're not alone," Adriana said. "We're here with you."

"I'm not afraid to die," the girl said. "They lied to us. God does exist!" She smiled. Her face looked radiant. "I can see him." Then she took her last breath.

Time seemed to take a huge breath and hold it, caught in this moment, this day. Adriana didn't know how long she and Timo and Marcu crouched there, as though their feet were encased in cement blocks.

She heard mixed messages from the crowd.

"Nicolae and Elena fled through their tunnels, like scared rabbits hiding in their warrens," someone said.

"No," another person answered, "don't you see that helicopter? I'll bet it's coming to take them away."

It was 11:30 when the helicopter landed on the roof of the Central Committee building. Adriana watched it take off after several minutes, but she couldn't tell if the Ceauşescus had managed to escape.

A murmur carried through the crowd that the defense minister had just committed suicide. Others said, "No, the Securitate killed him. In his office."

As the crowd tried to figure out what was happening, Timo cried out, "Look!"

Many of the Securitate officers were running away from the crowd.

Shots still rang out, but it appeared they only came from the army, aimed toward the Securitate. The people were no longer being fired on.

Adriana spotted Captain Zugravescu turn from the terrace and flee. What a coward. The bully who hated her family was running for his life, showing his true colors.

Adriana took a deep breath. She looked around.

Blood ran freely over the cobblestones. Bodies and bloodied clothing were strewn about. The *piața* was littered with torn portraits of Nicolae and Elena and wadded-up manifestos.

Adriana heard new chants rise. *The people have won! We have the victory! We are free!*

Even with the gruesome scene before her, even with the knowledge that Simona had given her life and that Corina was fighting

287

for hers, Adriana's overwhelming sensation was one of joy. Overcome with emotion, she cried into Timo's chest as he and Marcu embraced her in a group hug.

The people had won.

Against all odds, they had won.

After some time—Adriana had no idea how long—she left Timo and Marcu and walked back toward the history building. Students and teachers were pouring out the doors, cheering. Gabi ran toward Adriana. One look at Gabi's face, filled with shock and wonder, Adriana started to weep. The two girls grabbed each other, crying and laughing at the same time, as they jumped in place.

"I can hardly believe it," Gabi said.

"Come look for yourself," Adriana said, leading her friend outside. The two girls walked slowly down familiar streets into an unfamiliar world.

The sounds of guns were intermittent now. People cheered and shouted that the revolution was over. The people had won! The army had turned and the Ceaușescus had fled.

At the edge of Palace Square, Gabi and Adriana stopped walking and stared at each other, eyes and mouths open wide. Gabi held onto Adriana and hugged her like she'd never been hugged before.

Relief, disbelief, joy, and exhaustion flooded over Adriana. So many emotions all at once, banging against each other.

She saw people crying tears of happiness mixed with tears of grief. Some prayed with a loud voice, thanking God for saving Romania. Others kissed the flag, kissed each other, grabbed strangers and kissed them.

A lone voice yelled, "It's not over yet. The Ceaușescus may return. You're celebrating too soon."

The crowd ignored the voice.

Students clamored on board the army tanks and military transport trucks, crowded together on the tops, hanging onto the sides.

They waved the tri-color flag with the round hole in the center. Someone draped a garland of flowers around the muzzle of a tank's automatic rifle. They drove slowly, through the square, cheering as they went, met by people on the ground also waving the three colors, the flag that symbolized their courage. The flag that declared their freedom.

Car horns honked as they joined the parade. People leaned out of the windows of cars and trams that crawled along the packed streets of Bucharest, yelling, "We've won!" and "The people have the victory!"

Yesterday Adriana had heard screams of pain and panic here. Today it was shouts of jubilation. Victory!

The girls hugged once more, then Gabi returned to triage, but Adriana hurried home.

CHAPTER FORTY-FIVE

TV NEWS

WHEN ADRIANA WALKED IN through her door, Mama and Bunica rushed to her and hugged her and kissed her as though she'd just returned from the dead.

"We heard the shouts from the street," Mama said. "They say we're free!"

"We are," Adriana said, exhausted and numb. "We won."

Adriana squeezed between them on the sofa. They were mesmerized by the news on TV. Bunica held her hand while Adriana laid her head on her mother's shoulder.

The newscasters still read their state-controlled scripts. They reported that thousands of people had come to Palace Square to listen to Ceaușescu. A few hooligans had infiltrated the crowd of loyal comrades to create diversion attempts and they had messed with the live broadcast of Ceaușescu's speech. In a monotone voice, one of the reporters read that the perpetrators would be captured and punished.

While they recited their lines like robots, a ragtag group of people appeared on the air. The mob stormed in behind the news desk, waving a tri-color Romanian flag, the colors of courage, with a circle crudely cut out of the middle.

Adriana looked at Bunica with wide eyes. They couldn't help but notice the handsome man, taller than the others, standing in the back row. Uncle Mihai was part of the group.

Several of the group made a "V" sign with their fingers, for victory. One of them pumped his fist in the air and shouted, "We have control! The army has turned! The people have now taken control of Romanian televis—"

At that moment, the broadcast went dead.

The television screen was black for several minutes. Then, live images from the *piața* flashed onto the screen. Mama and Bunica saw what Adriana couldn't stop seeing in her mind: bodies lying on the streets. They watched in amazement to see the Romanian army tanks still firing on the Securitate.

As the grainy video was broadcast, one of the men who'd stormed into the television station picked up a microphone. He said that the Securitate had been defeated within a few hours of the army turning.

Romania was now officially free!

As tired as Adriana was, she couldn't tear herself away from the screen. Mama made some soup and Adriana devoured it sitting on the sofa. Then she finally went to her bed to lie down.

The first thing Adriana did when she woke up early that evening was call Gabi. She was glad her friend was finally home.

"Gabi, tell me what you know about Corina." She held her breath to wait for the answer.

"She's alive, Adri. She made it through the surgery."

Adriana slowly released her breath.

"They patched her leg. It'll be a long road to healing," Gabi said.

"Her father and Alex are with her now. Dr. Tomeci is helping her father make arrangements to take her to Budapest when she's stable. He says they have better hospitals."

"What a relief."

"Corina's tougher than she looks," Gabi said. "Adri, they didn't have any anesthetics stronger than aspirin."

Adriana let that sink in a moment.

"Oh, and Adri, maybe I shouldn't repeat this, but ... when I was there, Corina's father was talking to Alex. Her father apologized. He said he made her break up with Alex, something about Alex being dangerous because he was part of the Resistance and Corina being a target because her mother was Hungarian." Gabi paused. "Alex said he didn't care that she was Hungarian. All that mattered was that she was alive."

Adriana let those words settle. She had no more doubts that her friend Alex loved Corina.

When Adriana hung up the phone, she walked into the living room and saw Aunt Violeta had joined Mama and Bunica on the sofa, all eyes glued to the newly-named Free Romanian Television station. Pictures of joyful crowds parading through the city were being broadcast. Random gunfire could still be heard in the background, but the newscaster said the country was now under the control of the people at all its strategic points. The revolution had spread to other cities besides Timişoara and Bucharest. People in Cluj, Braşov, Arad, Iaşi, and Sibiu had also joined the fight.

The atmosphere was jubilant, marred for some by reports of fresh sporadic bloodshed. Tens of thousands celebrated in the city squares, undeterred by intermittent machine gun fire. Church bells rang triumphantly in the background.

The newscaster reported that some of the heaviest fighting took place at the television station and the surrounding areas. They showed footage of buildings across the street from the station, pocked with bullet holes or even burned down. The cameras panned inside the station, revealing floors covered with broken glass. He said the country had been fed a steady diet of lies for many years, and it was the new station's responsibility to provide vital information and to tell the truth.

Then Mihai approached the news desk and whispered to the newscaster.

Violeta gasped. "Look!"

Mihai picked up the microphone. "I will now report to you the timeline we have pieced together for this historic day, 22 December 1989." He waved a stack of papers in his hand. "At about noon, the Ceaușescus fled to the roof of the Central Committee building. Eyewitnesses claimed they looked like they were about to faint. Four Securitate officers climbed into the waiting helicopter with them."

Mihai cleared his throat. "Their personal pilot, Lt. Col Malutan, was ordered to fly to Snagov, and then on to Titu. Near Titu, the helicopter dipped up and down as though it was having engine trouble. We have received a report from Malutan. He says he knew the people had control of the country and he claims he did this on purpose. Ceaușescu made him land immediately. Malutan landed the helicopter in an open field."

Mihai turned to the next page. "The Securitate officers ran to the nearest road and flagged down passing cars. The first was a Dacia driven by a local doctor who claimed to have engine trouble. They stopped the second car, driven by a bicycle repairman, and demanded he take them to Târgoviște. The driver, who chooses to remain anonymous, said he could hide them at an agricultural technical institute outside of town. When they arrived there, the director of the institute, who'd heard about the revolution, guided the Ceaușescus into a room. Then he locked the door and called the local police. About 3:30 in the afternoon, the police showed up and arrested the Ceaușescus. They transported them to the military compound in Târgoviște."

Mihai looked directly into the camera. "From Bucharest to Snagov, to a field near Titu, and on to Târgoviște. The Ceaușescus had quite a tour of Romania today. Nicolae and Elena Ceaușescu will be held in Târgoviște until their trial, which they were promised would be speedy."

Adriana looked at her family in disbelief. She started to laugh uncontrollably, a combination of emotion mixed with exhaustion. She couldn't stop. Soon her laughter turned into sobbing.

CHAPTER FORTY-SIX

CHRISTMAS CAROL

Sunday, 24 December

ADRIANA SLEPT MOST OF the day after the revolution ended.

When she awoke the following day, the clock showed it was only 1:00 in the morning. Her internal clock was off kilter after missing so much sleep.

Adriana tiptoed through the quiet apartment. She needed to be sure everyone was there and alright. As she crept down the hallway, she listened to Bunica's soft snore coming from Mama's room and saw Mama asleep on the sofa.

Adriana returned to her room and reached for her latest novel. It felt like ages since the last time she'd read, before all the chaos began. Maybe *A Christmas Carol* would distract her from the horror she'd witnessed the last few days.

She started reading where she left off. The Ghost of Christmas Present visits Scrooge next. He reveals the immense needs at that time in England, visible everywhere the ghost and Scrooge turn.

Adriana held her finger on that page and closed her book. So many glaring needs in Romania today. Having enough food to eat. Being free from fear. Being able to make decisions about your own life. Being able to trust other people again. The needs in Romania hadn't magically disappeared overnight just because the people had been victorious.

She shivered, but she read on. The last, and scariest, of the spirits visits Scrooge, the Ghost of Christmas Yet to Come. Scrooge sees terrible visions of the future. He begs the spirit to tell him if he has a chance to alter the course set before him. He cries, *"Why show me this if I am past all hope!"*

Adriana thought about the path Romania had been on. They'd just won the revolution. They had altered their own course. Change *was* possible. For Romania as it had been with Scrooge.

Scrooge wakes up on Christmas morning, a new person with a new resolve. He'd learned his lesson and his life was transformed.

Tomorrow would be Christmas for Romania. A new Romania with a new optimism. Adriana felt certain that, with lots of work, her country could become a better one.

As the first rays of light began to appear in the sky, she padded into the kitchen to start the coffee. Then she slipped outside to buy bread.

A light snow had dusted the streets. Much of the life of the city had screeched to a halt during the fighting, but she smiled when she rounded the corner and saw the *pâine* store open as usual. A line of people—cheerful people who greeted each other—snaked down the sidewalk. Already, the city felt friendlier than it had been.

When Adriana returned to her flat, with a loaf of bread sticking out of her *punga*, she immediately realized another thing had changed: Mrs. Petrescu didn't stick her head out of her door as she stomped up the steps.

Mama and Bunica sat at the kitchen table with their coffee cups.

"There you are, draga!" her mother exclaimed. "I was getting worried."

Adriana bent down to greet them both with a kiss. "I'm sorry."

Mama stood to slice the bread Adriana pulled out of the *punga*.

"Violeta's coming over soon so we can make plans," Mama said.

"For what?"

"Christmas," Bunica said with a smile. "Today's Christmas Eve."

Adriana had only celebrated Christmas once, in secret at Bunica's mountain village. She thought about the novel she'd just finished. Christmas dawned on a new day in Scrooge's life, and this was a new day in theirs.

"Yesterday, while you were sleeping, we got the word that my factory, and all the factories, will shut down so we can celebrate Christmas," Mama said. "This has never happened before. Not in my lifetime, anyway."

At that moment, Aunt Violeta walked in.

"I thought you'd still be sleeping," she said, kissing Adriana in greeting.

"I figured twenty-four hours was long enough for my nap." Adriana laughed.

"Sit, you two," Mama said. "Let me pour you both some coffee and we'll get started with our plans."

"First, I have an announcement from Mihai," Violeta said. She took a breath. "Zugravescu was captured!"

Mama grabbed Adriana and hugged her.

"What happened?" Adriana asked.

"I don't know the details, except that when he was taken into custody, he 'cried like a little girl.' That's a direct quote from Mihai. Zugravescu will never be a threat to our family again."

Adriana felt a huge burden release from her shoulders, one that she didn't realize she was still holding.

As they all took a moment to process the news, Adriana noticed her mother's eyes well up. She reached over and squeezed Mama's hand.

"Well then," Mama said, her voice thick with emotion, "let's get to the plans."

"One thing I insist on," Bunica said. "Going to church together. We must start our new life, as free people in a free country, on the right foot. The people in Opera Square in Timișoara recited the Lord's Prayer together."

"What's that, Bunica?" Adriana asked.

"Our Father, who art in heaven, hallowed be Thy name—"

"That's what you and Tati ... the night he died."

Bunica smiled and nodded.

"I've heard of a Baptist church tucked away on Strada Popa Rusu, in a nondescript building," Violeta said. "They're one of the few churches that remained open all these years. The pastor never bowed to pressure, although he faced lots of it, even being thrown in prison a couple times. Each Sunday, spies in the congregation would report the names of people who attended the service. Many of the people mysteriously vanished or lost their jobs—"

"That's in the past now," Mama said softly.

"Do we want to watch the news tomorrow? Mihai says that Nicolae and Elena's trial will be on Christmas Day," Violeta said.

"No!" Bunica said. "Our day should be about Christmas. And only Christmas."

"Agreed." Mama nodded. "Let's make a list of who to invite for supper."

"Mihai and I want to host it," Violeta said.

Mama jotted down names in her notebook. "Family first. The five of us, plus Timotei. Should we invite Mihai's cousin?"

"Absolutely," Violeta said. "Her name's Ofelia. I can ask her."

"Now we have seven. Who else?" Mama asked.

"Who do we know who's alone? Let's invite anyone who doesn't have family nearby," Bunica said. "We all need each other more than ever now."

"Gabi will be with her family, and Alex with his mother. Corina's father is trying to get her transferred to Budapest." Adriana bit her lip. "I can ask my teacher, Professor Filip. Her family's far away in Moldova."

"Good," Mama said. "That's eight."

"How about our neighbors? Add Mrs. Petrescu and Mrs. Stoica to the list." Violeta smiled. "Now we're up to ten. And just think. It used to be illegal to have more than eight in one apartment at a time."

"How will we get enough food for that many?" Mama asked.

"We can ask everyone to bring something," Violeta said. "Don't worry. It'll work out. I just know it."

Monday, 25 December

On Christmas morning, Adriana and her family walked to church while soft snow floated to the ground. The city looked pure and quiet and brand new. Snow covered the blood and bullet holes.

It looked like the whole city's population had turned out to walk to a church service. The last few days, many had been saying that God was the one who set them free. People who'd never visited a church in their life went this morning. They stuffed inside the church on Popa Rusu, many standing in the aisles and spilling out the open doors. Adriana and her family squeezed onto a bench inside. Some stood outside to listen to whatever they could hear.

Pastor Elie rose and opened the Bible. He read, with a loud voice.

And there were shepherds living out in the fields nearby, keeping watch over their flocks at night. An angel of the Lord appeared to them, and the glory of the Lord shone around them, and they were terrified. But the angel said to them, "Do not be afraid. I bring you good news that will cause great joy for all the people. Today in the town of David a Savior has been born to you; he is the Messiah, the Lord. This will be a sign to you: You will find a baby wrapped in cloths and lying in a manger."

The words landed in a deep place in Adriana's heart. This was her first Christmas after she'd decided to believe. She promised herself to tell Bunica before the day was finished and to tell Gabi soon, but right now, she wanted to hold the words inside and mull them over.

People broke into song. They sang carols that the older ones had memorized, without any instruments to accompany the voices. Bunica whispered that when she was a child, everyone knew the words. Adriana thought it was the most beautiful sound she'd ever heard.

When the service finished, everyone greeted each other with peace, saying, "*Pace!*" After years of oppression and a bloody revolution, it was good to be wished peace.

They walked back through the silent streets and arrived at Aunt Violeta's to prepare for the feast. Mihai had to take care of some business at the television station before the meal, but since he had wrangled a ham for dinner, he was excused. Mama boiled some potatoes from the ones she'd kept cold in a bag outside their window. Bunica added to the meal with her homemade *cozanac*, traditional sweet Christmas bread. They were counting on the others to embellish the dinner.

They had no gifts and no decorations. Bunica said just being together and celebrating their first Christmas in freedom was all the present she'd ever need.

Everyone had accepted their invitations, except for Mrs. Stoica. She'd slammed the door on Violeta.

Mrs. Petrescu arrived first, bearing a plate of *sarmale*. "I came ready to help," she said. "It's the least I can do."

"You can help Ramona and Adriana set the table," Aunt Violeta said, as she took the *sarmale*. "We've got the food under control for now."

While Mama covered the coffee table with a clean cloth, Adriana and Mrs. Petrescu counted out stools and chairs and carted them into the living room.

"I feel like I should explain myself," Mrs. Petrescu said, speaking to Adriana. "My little sister Iulia … the Securitate said they'd give me enough money to take care of her if I did what I did. I knew it was wrong, but I did it anyway."

"Please," Mama said. "It's not necessary, Luminiţa."

Adriana set the plates down. She looked at Mrs. Petrescu. "It's over now."

The next person to enter was Timo, carrying two loaves of bread in his arms. Marcu walked in behind him.

"I hope it's okay," Timo said. "Marcu had no place—"

"Of course it's okay," Violeta said. "*Bine ai venit*, Marcu!"

Marcu smiled. Adriana noticed the two young men were more subdued than normal.

Professor Filip arrived next. With her hair pulled up in a pony-tail, she looked younger and more vulnerable than usual. "Thank you for your kind invitation, Mrs. Nicu," she said to Mama. "I would've been all alone otherwise."

"We need family today, Elisabeta," Mama said. "And please, call me Ramona."

Professor Filip handed over her offering of carrots and parsnips. "It's all I could find," Professor Filip said. "The *piaţa* is nearly empty."

"It's perfect," Violeta said, and took the bowl from her hands.

"Come sit by me," Mama said to Professor Filip. "You must be exhausted. Adriana told me …"

Tears collected in Professor Filip's eyes. "The things I've seen—" She cleared her throat.

Mama hugged her. "We'll try to put those images out of our minds for today."

Ofelia arrived next. As always, she glided in like royalty, on a cloud of Chanel no. 5. She carried a fancy cake made with liqueur. How she found the ingredients was anyone's guess.

The last to arrive was Uncle Mihai. He burst through the door.

"You have to see this," he said. "Turn the TV on."

"Not today. I'm sorry." Bunica stood up. "No more blood on Christmas, please. Can you just tell us, Mihai?"

"The trial was held today. It lasted about two hours. Both Nicolae and Elena Ceaușescu were sentenced to death." Mihai cleared his throat. "Immediately after the trial, they were executed by a firing squad."

Bunica sat down.

Everyone stared dumbly at Mihai. Nobody spoke.

After a few moments, Mihai continued. "I doubt we'll ever know the exact numbers, but I've heard estimates that well over 1,000 martyrs died in the revolution."

Adriana inhaled a deep breath and heard others do the same, sobered by the news.

Aunt Violeta waited a beat and then cleared her throat. "Well, I think it's time for us to eat. Let's take our seats so we can enjoy our meal."

The food was a hodgepodge and so were the people gathered. They couldn't all fit around the coffee table, so some sat on chairs scattered around the room and balanced plates on their laps.

Once they were all seated, Bunica stood. "I think it's only fitting to offer thanks on this Christmas day. Please take the hand of the person next to you and bow your head."

Everyone took their neighbors' hands in theirs.

Adriana held onto Professor Filip on one side and Bunica on the other.

Bunica prayed: "Heavenly Father, we come to you with grateful hearts today. Thank you for family and friends. Thank you for freedom." She paused and let that word sink in. "Thank you for delivering us. Thank you for this food." She started to sit down, then added, "And thank you that you sent your son to come live among us all those Christmases ago. Amen."

Several echoed her *Amen.*

Quiet conversation ensued. Adriana expected to feel like celebrating, like she had on the day they won, like what she'd witnessed out on the streets, with people cheering and hanging onto the sides of trucks and tanks. But today, Adriana felt numb and exhausted, and it appeared that everyone else did too. The victory they'd won had come at such a great cost.

Just a few weeks ago, the people seated at her aunt's table had been informers, spies, resistance couriers, dissidents, and people just trying to follow the rules and stay out of trouble. Now they were a gathering of friends and family. People who needed to be together today.

After the meal, Violeta and Mama cut Ofelia's cake. Adriana helped serve it to everyone, along with cups of coffee.

As they ate dessert, Timo spoke up. "On the way over here, Marcu and I were talking about … well, what everyone's talking about: freedom. How we all wanted freedom, but there are lots of different reasons why."

"Isn't it enough just to want to be free?" Violeta asked.

"Of course," Timo said. "But our friend Serghei, his whole life— the reason he got up every morning—was about doing whatever he could to overthrow the evil regime." His voice broke. "And he did."

"I have an idea. How about we each say what we hope for most?" Mihai said. "I can start us off. I hope for freedom of speech, to be able to publicly criticize our leaders without fear, like they do in other countries. And to hear news of the outside world."

"Me too," Timo said. "That's what I want."

"I want to live my life without people watching and listening all the time," Violeta said. "And to be able to leave and travel to other countries."

"I think most Romanians simply want a better life. Basic things like water anytime we want it, electricity, heat. Food in the stores," said Mama.

"Da," Marcu said. "I agree."

"To be able to choose what I'll study and what I'll become," Adriana said.

"I hope my sister Iulia will be cared for properly," Mrs. Petrescu said.

"Freedom to worship," Bunica said. "That's what I've longed for. And today, it came true." She dabbed at her eyes with her napkin.

"Simona wanted that too," Marcu chimed in.

"The monarchy," Ofelia said. "I want them to come back to their rightful home."

Adriana saw Mihai smile at his cousin.

"I want it all," Professor Filip said quietly. "Everything you all said." Professor Filip had barely spoken all afternoon.

They finished their cake and sipped their coffee in comfortable quiet.

Professor Filip was the first to excuse herself.

"Thank you," Mama said to her as she kissed her goodbye. "Thank you for caring for my daughter and inspiring her. She's been fortunate to have you this year."

As soon as she left, Timo and Marcu followed suit.

Mrs. Petrescu left next. She thanked them with tears in her eyes, and then grabbed Mama's hands. "Ramona, thank you for inviting me."

After Mrs. Petrescu had left, Ofelia was the last guest remaining.

Mihai turned to his cousin. "Do you know if the royals ever received your message?"

"I don't know," Ofelia said. "But certainly, they've heard what's happened here. Switzerland has freedom of the press." She smiled. "They must be ecstatic."

"Would you like to see the earrings?"

"Now?" she said.

"I think today's the perfect day, don't you?" he said.

Violeta, Mama, and Bunica had already started gathering dishes from the table.

"Follow me," Mihai said to Ofelia. Then he turned to face Adriana. "You come too."

Adriana curtsied to him. "Thank you, Your Highness."

Mihai swatted at her and smothered a laugh.

He opened the blue wardrobe doors and then the doors to the secret room. Ofelia's eyes grew wide as she followed him inside.

"I always knew it was here, but I've never seen this room for myself."

Mihai slid the rug back, exposing the square in the floor. He pried the tile up and pulled out the wooden box decorated with pearls. "Close your eyes, Ofelia, and when you open them, you'll see the royal earrings that belonged to our ancestor, Princess Maria Hohenzollern." He lifted the lid and held the box in front of Ofelia. "You may open your eyes now."

Clearly, Ofelia wasn't prepared for the brilliance of what was inside. She caught her breath.

The waning rays of the winter sun caught the glow of the emeralds at just the right angle. Bright green beams reflected on one wall and bounced onto the opposite one.

"If you think this is beautiful, you should see the necklace," Adriana said. "It's safe in my grandmother's wardrobe. Anytime you want it ..."

"I'll let you know," Ofelia said.

"You should try them on," Adriana said to Ofelia.

Ofelia held the earrings against her ears and walked to the mirror on the bedroom wall to look. She looked regal, but then she always carried herself like a princess.

"I promised you I'd take good care of them. Now they're yours," Mihai said.

Ofelia caressed the earrings. "No. They're safer here. I don't know what I'd do with them in my flat. You keep them until the day our relatives return." She smiled. "They will come back someday; I just know it."

She handed the earrings back to Mihai, who secured them in the box under the tile, covering it with the rug.

The trio walked back into the living room. Bunica and Violeta were seated on the sofa with Mama snuggled in the wingback chair, everyone quiet and satisfied.

"And now, I must take my leave," Ofelia said. "Thank you all for a lovely day I will never forget." Then Mihai walked her out the door.

Adriana squeezed in between her aunt and her grandmother.

"Aunt Violeta, do you remember the first time you showed me the secret in your wardrobe? That first novel you gave me to read?"

"Of course I do. It was the one about Narnia," Violeta said.

"Just now, inside the room, I was remembering that story. When the White Witch cursed Narnia. She turned it into a place that was always winter, never Christmas," Adriana said. "I thought that was a perfect description of Romania."

Violeta nodded.

Adriana smiled at her family. "The curse is broken. Today is Christmas, and we are finally free."

EPILOGUE

A NEW STORY

Fifteen Years Later, December 2004
Cluj, Romania

ADRIANA SAT ON A bench in Cluj and gazed at the statue of King Matthias Corvinus—a Hungarian king—behind the large Gothic-style Catholic church.

Since moving to London, Adriana didn't get the chance to visit her home country often. She closed her eyes and thought about the whirlwind of the last few days.

Yesterday, she and Gabi had driven to Timișoara, the place it all started, for the fifteenth anniversary of the revolution. It had been wonderful to visit Timotei—who'd just been elected mayor—his gorgeous wife, and his parents. Adriana always knew Timo would stay true to his vision to help Romania grow from its past mistakes.

In two days, she and Gabi—the perfect liaison—would go home to Bucharest. Already, they'd had a lot of time to catch up in the car. They would be best friends always.

Adriana smiled to think of how perfectly suited Gabi was for her nursing career, and how as a nurse, she'd fallen in love with and married med student Beni Barbu. They had four children now. Gabi laughed and said that's why she'd volunteered to drive Adri around the country, to get a break from the kids.

After the revolution, Gabi's parents quit their janitorial jobs and her father became the pastor of a large congregation, housed in one of the many church buildings that had once sat vacant under the thumb of Communism. Mr. and Mrs. Martinescu promised to come to Adriana's event in Bucharest.

She'd get to see everyone there. Bunica, still active but moving a little slower these days, had moved from Armonia to live with Mama in Adriana's old bedroom. From their phone calls and letters, it sounded like she, Mama, and Aunt Violeta were doing fine. Aunt Violeta had bought her own boutique, and Mama worked there with her. Uncle Mihai kept an ongoing correspondence with his royal relatives, who still lived in Switzerland. When King Mihai was finally allowed to enter Romania—the Easter of 1992—Uncle Mihai and Ofelia had their first private meeting with him.

Professor Filip—Elisabeta—would also be at the event. She'd continued teaching and excelled as a professor, but she stopped saying no to love. Her friendship with Dr. Luca Tomeci had grown, and they got married soon after the revolution.

Not surprisingly, Alex had been the only one of their crew to continue to study engineering. He was now one of the country's foremost engineers, in addition to being a professor of engineering. Adriana had always known he could do it. The first thing he did as a professional engineer was to make sure the truth came out about his father being set up.

And then there was Corina. It was touch and go for a while, but she'd survived. She endured several surgeries in Budapest, Hungary and long months of rehab to put her leg back together.

Adriana thought about how much had changed in these fifteen years. All the problems in Romania didn't instantly get fixed after the revolution, and it took a while for democracy to take hold, but freedom did come, bringing new issues along with it.

Adriana got what she'd wanted all along. She'd been free to choose what to study at the University of Bucharest, and she had picked literature, later moving to London for a master's degree. One summer break, she returned to Romania and went to her grandmother's cottage in the mountains to write. The novel that came of that time, well, it was her proudest accomplishment. And the fact that she'd achieved this pinnacle alone—as a single career woman—made it even sweeter.

She smiled to herself. London had been good for her, in more ways than the degree. She'd made lots of friends in her church there, including—

"Adri!" She heard Gabi call her name. "You ready? Everything's set up."

"Sure," Adriana said. She turned and looked at Gabi. At thirty-two, Gabi was a grown woman and mother, but Adriana still saw the energetic girl that would bound up to her in the park on Sundays.

They walked to the bookstore down the street and entered the conference room from the back. A podium with a microphone stood on the small platform in the front. A table in the rear held stacks of Adriana's books, waiting to be signed. The room was starting to fill up with people.

Adriana saw the back of a woman with glossy dark hair seated in the second row. When she turned her head, Adriana squealed like she did as a teenager. "Corina!"

Corina rose to embrace her friends, leaning on her cane. Her limp was less noticeable each time Adriana saw her.

The three women hugged each other, a group hug, laughing and crying and talking excitedly. Adriana didn't pay attention when another person entered their row, until she felt someone tap her on the shoulder. She turned. It was Alex!

She let go of her girlfriends and hugged Alex's neck.

Alex's love for Corina had grown during her time of rehab. After just two years at the university, Alex traveled to Budapest and proposed to her. Corina said, "*Yes!*" and now here they were, two lovely children later, living in Cluj.

"Sorry I'm late," Alex said. "I ran straight home from class and got the kids situated with our neighbor first."

"You're right on time," Adriana said.

"When do we get to meet this guy you write about in your letters?" Alex asked. "I need to give my approval."

Adriana felt her cheeks grow warm. "You'll meet him soon, and I know you'll like him." Adriana smiled. She couldn't help but smile when she thought of Nigel. "It's getting serious, Alex. Nigel is the one ... I'm certain of it. He'll be in Bucharest when we get there. He's coming to meet the family. I think he has a question for Uncle Mihai."

"Really?" Corina's face lit up. "You mean ..."

Adriana nodded.

Alex hugged her again. "Good for you. Corina and I are so happy."

By now, most of the seats were full. The bookstore owner approached Adriana. "Are you ready to start?"

Adriana cleared her throat. "Yes, I am."

Corina squeezed her hand, and Gabi hugged her again.

Alex beamed. "We'll be rooting for you!"

"You three always have," Adriana said.

She walked to the podium with her book in her hand.

"I'm thrilled to be back in Romania," Adriana spoke into the microphone. "I've heard that teenagers today don't understand what their parents' lives were like in the 1980s. Some even say it wasn't all that bad. Before my generation grows old and forgets, I wanted to record what life was like, but not in a dry textbook. I wanted to do it through story. The characters in my novel are fictitious, but they're based in reality, and they're composites of real people." She smiled at her friends. "And the time, the place, the oppression, the history ... that's all real." She took a deep breath. "And now, shall I begin?"

The crowd clapped.

Her teacher's voice droned on. Something about trains. How you can figure the degree of freedom—the rotation—from the car's position on the track.

Freedom? Hmmph. *She snickered. Her degree of freedom was a big fat zero.*

AUTHOR'S NOTE

WHILE MY FICTITIOUS CHARACTERS' involvement in the events of the revolution are naturally made up, they are based on testimony told to me from several eyewitnesses of those events. I heard from these eyewitnesses when I moved to Romania in 1990, shortly after the historic events transpired, and still have their recorded testimonies on cassette tapes in my possession. In the years since then, I have read a host of reports, conducted many more interviews, and watched much documentary footage. Some details I learned seem to be contradictory, but I chalk that up to multiple viewpoints. If any historical details are incorrect in this novel, I take full responsibility for that.

A documentary entitled *Winds of Freedom*, narrated by David Hartman of *Good Morning, America* fame, records homemade video of the crowd in Timişoara's Opera Square. The crowd chants *Exista Dumnezeu!* (God exists!) and then Pastor Petru Dugulescu leads them in reciting The Lord's Prayer.

A couple weeks after the revolution, while I was still living in the States, a friend played me a cassette tape from an underground church in Timişoara. I'll never forget hearing the people talk of praying around the clock with their blackout shades drawn. They said they became weary of prayer the day the news broke in the West. I like to think the prayer baton was passed that day.

My language teacher in Bucharest spoke of the revolution with our class. She said that while the shooting ensued, she and other professors did triage in the History Department building. She broke down in tears when she told us of students dying in her arms.

Within the first year after the revolution, a guy with a Dacia—a friend of a friend, whose name I've long since forgotten—gave my friends and me an unofficial tour of the revolution sites. He drove us all over the city of Bucharest. We stopped at the buildings pocked with bullet holes in Palace Square, past the TV station, and to Heroes' Cemetery.

Palace Square has long been renamed Revolution Square, and reminders of the revolution still stand after thirty-five years. In April 2024, my husband and I took an official "Real Tour of Communism" in Bucharest. The bullet holes had finally been repaired and a few monuments to the revolution now exist in the square.

Our tour guide, Mihai, showed us a photo I had never seen before. In it, rows of revolutionaries stand unarmed, facing down rows of army tanks lined up on Boulevard Nicolae Balcescu, near University Square. Our guide claimed the photo was taken minutes before the first shots were fired, killing thirteen young people. The heroes who fell there were considered the first victims of the revolution in Bucharest. We saw memorials to those thirteen brave souls at the spot where they died, in front of the exhibition hall *Sala Dalles* (Dalles Room).

Heroes' Cemetery is filled with white marble tombstones marking the final resting places of about 300 martyrs of the revolution in Bucharest. Many more lost their lives, but estimates as to the total vary wildly. I have walked through Heroes' Cemetery a few times since 1990, each time reading and copying the messages engraved on the headstones, looking at the photos of the young people killed, and feeling a somber heaviness that contrasts sharply with the gleaming white of the headstones. Much of what happened to individual protestors in this novel is based on these heroes' final words inscribed as their epitaphs.

The victims in Heroes' Cemetery were all killed during a span of three days in December 1989; moreover, the birth years on the headstones show they were all born within a few years of each other. These heroes were all cut down in their youth. The graves are arranged according to fields of study in the university: mathematics here, languages there. The majority of those buried in Heroes' Cemetery were college students.

The anthem *Trei Culori* was replaced by *Desteapta-te, Romane* (Wake Up, Romanian!) in 1990. While I made it up that Adriana and Claudia were the ones who painted *Piața Tiananmen II* and the lyrics to *Deșteapta-te Romane* on the outside wall of the Architecture Department building, someone did. When I visited Bucharest in 2024, I saw that the faded words *Piața Tiananmen II* still remain, after thirty-five years. Sadly, the lyrics to *Deșteapta-te Romane* are no longer visible.

The term gaslighting is currently used in the context of personal relationships with an imbalance of power. The dominant partner contradicts and corrects the other's statements and memories until they doubt their own intuition. The practice of gaslighting in my book is even more sinister, carried out as an official means of torture by a group. The East German Stasi perfected the practice of *zersetzung* as a method to manipulate people psychologically over time. The result—the person questioning both reality and their own sanity—was so successful that secret police all over Eastern Europe adopted it, including the Romanian Securitate.

While this book is a work of fiction, the historical events depicted are real. For anyone who thinks Communism is not so bad after all, it is. It was in Romania.

ACKNOWLEDGMENTS

THIS NOVEL IS THE fulfillment of a dream conceived several years ago, the culmination of a series I've long carried in my heart. In many ways, writing is lonely work, but it is not done in a vacuum. I will always be grateful to the people who blessed my life by helping me during the creation of this work, and to God for placing them in my life.

To Rylie Fine, my editor, thank you for making my stories better. You understand and love my characters almost as much as I do. What a privilege and honor to have had you with me from the beginning. We've been on a five-year journey, starting with signing the contract for the first novel in the series and ending with publishing this third and final one. I mean it when I say I could not have done this without your skillful editing. I am blessed.

To Megan McCullough, my cover designer, thank you for creating another beautiful cover design for me which perfectly conveys the essence of the story. I love the uniformity of having all three covers in the series designed by your artistic hand.

To Donna McFarland, my formatter, I'm grateful for your eagerness to tackle another project with me. You are always willing to answer my endless questions from your vast supply of knowledge. Thank you.

To my YA beta readers—Charlotte Elhenicky, Jenna Garrison, and Aolani DiMartino—thank you. You three grew up with this series. You've read every one of the books, and you've given such wise input. I love seeing the young women you're becoming.

To my adult beta readers—Wendy Kohman, my friend who lived in Romania during the time I did; Marian Sims, who lived in Romania during the revolution; my husband Steve, always my first reader; and my brother Kurt Richardson, who's always had my back. Thank you, my friends *și dragele mele*.

To my community of like-minded women writers, Redbud Writers Guild, what a gift you are to me. Your encouragement, knowledge, and support have been a lifeline for me. Thank you all. Cheryl Bostrom, your input came just at the perfect time. I'm grateful.

To my husband Steve, my biggest fan. None of this would have been possible if you hadn't spurred me on to take up writing at an age when most people wouldn't consider a new career. I wonder if you had any idea what that would mean for you: having to take up the slack because your busy wife's mind is often in Adriana's world instead of our own. I love you for all that and so much more.

To the courageous souls who stood up in Romania in December 1989, thank you for inspiring me.

Lastly, to you, dear Reader. You are the reason I write. Your encouragement has fueled me on to the finish line. Thank you.

If you enjoy this book, please tell others. And please take a moment to rate and/or review it on Amazon and Goodreads. Thank you!

Made in the USA
Las Vegas, NV
08 November 2024